A Little Better Elsewhere

The University of Sydney Anthology

Foreword by Sarah Ayoub

University of Sydney

First published in 2026 by the University of Sydney.

Funded by the University of Sydney, Faculty of Arts and Social Sciences, School of Art, Communication and English.

Sydney University Press
Fisher Library F03, University of Sydney
NSW 2006 AUSTRALIA
Email: sup.info@sydney.edu.au
sydneyuniversitypress.com

A catalogue record for this book is available from the National Library of Australia

ISBN: 978-1-74210-587-1 (paperback)
ISBN: 978-1-74210-588-8 (epub)

Cover image: Alvaro Guerrero via Unsplash
Cover design: Olivia Russell and Liam Prendergast
Text layout: Hanna Holford and Urvi Agrawal

We acknowledge the traditional owners of the lands on which Sydney University Press is located, the Gadigal people of the Eora Nation. We respect the knowledge embedded forever within the Aboriginal Custodianship of Country.

Contents

Contents

Acknowledgements

A Little Better Elsewhere started with the concept of nostalgia. We must admit that as an editorial team, we were unsure the direction in which this would take our writers. Against the backdrop of genocide and political unrest, we were gifted stories that spoke of a deep pain for places and people who no longer existed. Lost to time, war, or the sad reality of growing up. We hope that these stories stay with you and remind you of things that should never be forgotten.

This anthology is the culmination of many authors and volunteers' incredible passion and commitment to both the art of writing and the joy of putting important voices out into the world.

We would like to firstly thank all our committed authors who were both featured or considered for this anthology. Without your words we would have nothing to share. Please keep writing. We would also like to thank each of our volunteers who spent many hours bringing this anthology to life. And to Agata Mrva-Montoya, your patience, dedication and immense willingness to share your knowledge and provide opportunities to your students means more than words can express. Thank you.

To Sarah Ayoub, for your thoughtful foreword and willingness to engage so meaningfully with this anthology. We admire your work and are proud to have your name on our collection.

We are also immensely grateful to the team at Sydney University Press for helping to bring this anthology to the physical world and to the University of Sydney as a place of learning and opportunity to formulate and express ideas in challenging and new ways. May every student have the chance to explore their passions and beliefs as we have had.

Lastly, we would like to thank our readers. This anthology was an opportunity for us to learn and grow both as writers, editors, marketers, social media managers and as publishers. Without you, we would not have had this chance.

Foreword

Sarah Ayoub

I shall begin in all honesty. I was asked to write this foreword by a student in my postgraduate narrative writing class in the second semester of 2025. It was a busier than usual semester: in addition to my usual teaching duties, I had taken up a casual research position at another university, and was working on my first junior fiction series, consulting on arts policy for a government group, and still freelancing as a features writer for a prominent news outlet.

I didn't need another thing to add to my to-do list, especially since it would be due in the first week of January when I would be wrangling the varying wants (never needs) of my three children in the heat of the NSW school holidays, no doubt wishing that my only time off work didn't coincide with the holidays of little people who think a problem worth bawling over is the local servo running out of their favourite ice-cream.

I wanted to say no. I wanted to say I was tired; that I was burnt out; that, as a sessional academic, I wasn't paid for anything that did not relate to the class I was giving and that they should ask a full-time staff member who had a salaried position to do it.

Obviously, I didn't say any of that. Which is of course, why I am addressing you here.

* * *

My reasons for wanting to say no, while legitimate, were part of a broader pattern of negativity that had begun to characterise my feelings about writing. Writing was something I had laboured over for a long time, but my passion for it had recently plateaued. I was unmotivated and cynical, and ambivalent about achievements others saw as successes.

Despite procuring a number of motivational books on being more productive as an artist, I was at a point where I rarely sat down to do *the work*, constantly taking on writing-adjacent gigs that saw me professionalise instead of create. I consulted, edited, workshopped, presented, board-directed and award-judged, but I didn't write.

Instead, I took any opportunity I could to wax indignant about the conditions of writers and creatives: precarious publishing contracts, abysmal reading rates, decreased funding opportunities and lowly advances, all compounded by the suffocating threat of artificial intelligence. I told my family I was thinking of pursuing a psychology degree because it felt "more stable". I gave a talk at the State Library of NSW, in the presence of government ministers and representatives from industry bodies, where I lamented that I was successful on paper but made no paper, and how that affected the way I saw my role as a writing teacher. I wanted my students to feel the magic and passion I once felt for story, I told the audience, but I also wanted them to know that in the real world, magic and passion could only take them so far.

I wanted to be honest, to tell them what I wished someone had told me: That this work can bleed you dry, and still get you nowhere.

***

But something happened when I opened this collection in the early days of 2026. A renewed sense of optimism, a shift in mindset. It could have been the new year and the hope it brought (or the hope that I clung on to), but it could also have been the words within.

I curled up in my armchair, the last of Christmas' fruit mince pies on a saucer next to me, and started at the beginning, with Raghad Hilles' title story, "A Little Better Elsewhere". I was captivated, and immediately saw my family in its pages. The grandmother whose love language was food, the overlapping discussions at the table, the insistence that whatever ingredient was better in the motherland.

I progressed through the collection, marvelling at the diversity of pieces and the skill of the writers who penned them. I keenly felt Rosanna Chim's reflections on her family's Hong Kong apartment in "When Did You Say You Were Leaving"; its nostalgia so visceral it prompted me to want to return to Hong Kong myself. I yearned for my own Lebanese village – and the history that unfurls from my own mother's lips in the process of rolling vine leaves – via Mona Elhassan's "Bougainvillaea". I nodded along to Lachlan Griffiths' poem "Developing Film", which reminds us of the many "places where memory cannot reach", and to Cherie Baird's "Free to a Good Home", which pondered the kind of love that leaves a space we know we can never fill.

I learnt about tithing in Jacob Lucas' "The White Salamander Tax" and appreciated the tenderness in Vanessa Yenson's "Doc Martin" and felt like an ancient millennial reading Joseph Parker Lucas' "Where to?", which was so iconically young and so iconically Sydney it would make a great lesson on voice and place.

I faced my own shortcomings as a mother to a neurodiverse child as I read through Alessio Maugeri's interrogation of an autism diagnosis that came too late in "Day One"; pondered "The Art of Gift Giving" (and how much the process really entails!) thanks to Urvi Agarwal; felt the ecstasy and agony of love, mismatch and heartbreak in Shania Daphne Andrea OBrien's "The First Bite", and was reminded to have faith thanks to Angela Fossi's "An Angel with Me".

There were many other pieces, too many to name here, all written with skill, perception and heart. Their writers had discerned and dissected the world, mulled it over, laid it out and remade it again. The works represented the tenacity, commitment to craft, and engagement with genre that comes with solid creative writing practice.

I cannot say I was surprised. I've been teaching at the University of Sydney for many years, and was once a wide-eyed girl from western Sydney braving a whole new world as a student here, so I've always known that this place attracts the biggest and brightest minds of the state, and indeed, the rest of the world. I was prepared to be wowed, but I was not prepared to be reminded of how writing is so much more than just "work".

Reading these pieces reminded me of what good writing can accomplish. How it can be something that heals, something that bonds, something that rallies, something that resists. I always knew that for writers from marginalised communities, like the culturally and linguistically diverse community I came from, writing was a form of what bell hooks described as "coming to voice".

These poems and stories wrote of love, homesickness, heritage, romance, partying, travelling, pondering, working, family, friends and so much more. They demonstrate the best of Sydney University's writing programs. In them, I saw the longing of my own heart: the longing to express, to share, to interrogate, to learn, to be in community. To arrange words and sentences and paragraphs this way and that, and make new meanings – both overt and covert – out of what is already there.

I loved perusing its pages, wowed by the talent in our subjects and the potential of its writers. I am certain that one day, we will see these very names on bookstore shelves and prize lists.

I hope that you too will find something you can relate to within its pages, because whether you're a writer or not, this collection is a reminder of what we can accomplish if we lean in to our vocations, and remember what joy it is to create.

It's also a lesson in saying yes to our here and now, just like I did, even when every instinct told me not to. For so long I had assumed things would have been better if I had done something a little differently, and failed to appreciate what it was that I was doing, even when it did not look the way I imagined it would.

We always think it's going to be a little better elsewhere. Thankfully, in the pages of this book, which traverses continents and time zones, elsewhere can be anywhere.

And I am all the better for reading it.

A Little Better Elsewhere

Raghad Hilles

We're having breakfast and my uncle praises the hummus in between bites. He says it's almost the same as the hummus back home. I resist the urge to ask what makes it different, seeing as it's made by the same hands here and there – but my not asking doesn't matter because my aunt is quick to agree with her husband. The chickpeas are weird here, she says, not the same we got back home.

My grandma reassures her it's good anyway. My uncle agrees, singing my aunt's praises again. My cousin passes by us in his work clothes. He avoids looking at anyone as he grabs a bottle of water from the fridge but my grandma and aunt call out to him regardless, insisting he eats before heading off to work.

Just some eggs, my aunt says, just a bite.

Let me make you a sandwich, falafel and hummus, eat it on the way. Here, I'll be quick, my grandma adds, already moving to reach for the bread. It's next to me, I pass it to her and add something to the conversation, just for the sake of it.

He's shaking his head, a fist to his mouth as he swallows the water, having taken too big of a gulp. He waves his other hand at them.

And so it begins. He insists he's okay not eating, he's not hungry and he's running late. He's kissing my aunt's head as he says this. My grandma insists that he take something, for the drive, if he's not hungry now. My uncle jokes he'd be out of here quicker if he let them cook him a meal from scratch rather than if he kept arguing with them. I hide my laugh behind my cup of tea. My cousin makes a show of tearing apart the bread and scooping up a reasonable amount of hummus. He's chewing on it as he simultaneously grabs a piece of falafel, waving it at us as though to say "look! I'm taking it with me!"

Habibti, he softly says to my grandma when she insists it's not enough. He doesn't add anything else to the endearment, leaves it at that. With a quick kiss to her head and a raised hand to the rest of us, he leaves. She sighs, shakes her head, mumbles something about our generation, her voice is laced with affection nonetheless.

"Once the war is over, I'm flying Ibn Omar down here and opening up a shop right in front of our house so we can get proper chickpeas," my aunt jokes, the conversation circling back to the hummus.

I smile. "Your siblings will riot if it's not in front of their homes."

My grandma laughs, my uncle mimics his brother-in-law – my maternal uncle – predicting what his reaction would be. None of us say it aloud, but we are all thinking it. How is Ibn Omar doing? Is he doing, at all? Or is he dead too?

To me, Ibn Omar is just a faceless name. I often hear about my trips to his shop when I visited Gaza for the first and last time. I don't remember it, having been too young at the time, but I've heard this story so many times an image has been conjured up.

My mum's brothers, teenagers at the time, used to take me every day to Ibn Omar's shop right across the street. With my shekel, I would buy more treats than anyone else ever could because Ibn Omar had a soft spot for me. My uncle would walk in with me on his shoulders and I would point out all the things I wanted. After each one I would ask Ibn Omar if my shekel was enough for it. He'd smile and nod, I'd ask if it's enough for one more thing, he'd say yes.

My grandma, upon hearing this from my uncle, told him to train me to pick out the essentials instead of the *haki faddi*, the empty talk – the useless things. She's laughing hard apparently, picturing me pointing at eggs and spices instead of lollies and chips.

As hard as I try to picture her laughing twenty years younger without the weight of loss and endless grief straining to be felt beyond their markings that appear in her sad eyes and the wrinkles on her face, I can only see her as she is today.

When she stops, she gives my uncle a pointed look. "You've been paying him the full amount, right?" It's not so much a question as it is a threat. He rolls his eyes, too old now – being fifteen – to be told how to act.

"Tab'an mama." Of course, mum.

And then, the state of Ibn Omar is no longer an unspoken question lingering between us. "Poor guy, his son was martyred, may Allah ease it on him and Mariam."

I almost question his age. He's too young to have a child, isn't he only seventeen? Then I realise he isn't. Sixteen years have passed since I met him. He's only seventeen in my loosely put together memories. I look down at my plate, empty besides crumbs of scrambled egg and olive pits. My uncle asks how my aunt knows this, saying he hasn't been hearing much about him lately. She tells him the mother of someone's cousin's neighbour ran into Mariam a week ago.

The same questions arise, lingering silently. Has anything been heard since then? Ibn Omar and his wife were alive a week ago, but are they still today? To this, no one has an answer. I get up, reach for the pot of tea and ask if anyone wants more. My grandma and uncle nod, and I pour the tea into their cups. My aunt had shaken her head no when I offered, but upon pouring her some anyway she immediately grabs the cup and starts sipping on it.

The tea back home is better too, something about the sage apparently. We fall back into conversations about what the day held for us, then about who else was martyred, then about a gathering an aunt had told my grandma to tell the rest of us about, then a funny story about the kids of that aunt at school, then the words of a politician, a throwaway comment about something else that was better back home, then a conversation about a ceasefire negotiation that we all say god-willing will actually be executed through, though I doubt any of us think it will, then about what today's meal will be at the gathering and when we will head out of the house. We're moving around as we speak, my uncle and I clearing the table, my grandma wrapping the leftovers and putting them in the fridge, placing the empty plates near the sink, and my aunt grabbing them to wash. I wipe the table down, grab the vase we had put aside while eating, and place it back in the centre. We speak over each other and the running water too.

Later that night, I sit with my cousins. We are laughing a little too hard about one thing or another, an aunt passes us by and someone forces her to sit with us, pulling her onto the couch amidst her protests that the dishes need to be done. I tell her not to worry about it, one of us will do it. She's about to say something else but is quickly sucked into our conversation. We're laughing harder than we ought to be, and she's laughing at us, shaking her head. She calls us idiots, says something about genetics. Her son and daughter both look at each other, and she tells him to shut up before he even says anything. He raises his hands up in the air, "didn't say anything mama," he grins, "you're the one assuming." I'm sitting on the floor next to her legs and so I rest my head on her knee, listening as she teases her kids. We're all scattered around, yet huddled together. My cousin holds my spread-out leg; she's absentmindedly tracing patterns as we speak. I've got a younger cousin on my lap; she's laughing too, despite not fully grasping what's going on. Truth be told, none of us are fully grasping it either. It's late and we're exhausted but refuse to go to bed.

I am told nights like this were common back home, but with the presence of my grandpa who couldn't sleep to silence. These are the noises that put him to rest, his kids and their kids bickering loudly throughout the house. They don't say it, but I know his presence alone made those nights better too, it is what made back home be *back home*. He's brought up because one of my cousins says amidst his laughter, "aaah ya sido, weenak la-tshofna hek?"

Oh grandpa, where are you to see us like this?

This calms us down, if just for a moment. No one speaks for a beat, the air hanging heavy with the unsaid. We're all smiling, though with a hint of sadness now. I ask a question about him, this great gentle man that everyone speaks so fondly of and yet who I've only met a handful of times. It's not the question I want to ask, but it's one that breaks the silence. My aunt tells the story of when my mum and her had gotten in a fight, she can't remember what it was over but makes a couple guesses – something stupid is the point. We all listen intently. "We were yelling when dad came home with Abu Joseph – they studied together in Egypt. His girls were always around; your mum was best friends with the younger one until they migrated out around thirty years ago …"

The original story never ends up being shared, the anecdote never made. I don't think anyone notices, or if they do no one points it out. Instead she speaks of so and so. My grandma, hearing us talk about my grandpa, walks into the living room. A cousin immediately gets up, tells her to take his place on the couch. She insists he sits back down, pointing to the kitchen and saying she wants to get water. I nudge my cousin off my lap and jump up. "Yallah, sit down, I'll get you water." My grandma obliges and as she takes the couch, another body makes it onto the floor. My little cousin follows me into the kitchen and whispers that she wants chocolate. I widen my eyes at her; she stares back with a manipulative pout that she knows I cannot resist. I make her promise to not tell her mum and she nods excitedly. I send her off with Teta's water and when she's back I wave the chocolate at her, giving it to her in exchange for a hug. I listen to my grandma speak as I pack away the dishes on the drying rack. "Our family and Abu Joseph's would always go to the beach on the weekend," she pauses to laugh. "Truth be told, all of Gaza went to the beach on the weekend. Anyway, we'd go with our picnic mats and food, your grandpa has this little radio that he'd always play music from, the beach always called for George Wassouf …"

She goes on, reminiscing with a certain kind of longing dripping from her words. We listen, laughing along when it would be warranted, and sighing along too. She's looking at me now, describing the beach, trying to draw a picture for me. I'm sitting back down near my aunt's legs and she's running her fingers through my hair.

"The ocean doesn't smell the same as it does back home," someone says, and the rest hum in agreement. A pause, a loaded silence. Then someone else adds, "Remember when Teta made Maklouba and brought it to the beach, the big pot and everything. Imagine if we tried doing that here!"

Laughter rolls through the room like the Gazan waves they often describe to me, the ones that smell and taste and sound different to the waves of any other sea in the world. My grandma is quick to her defences, speaking through her laughter: "Your grandpa was craving it!" As good a reason as any.

I listen silently to tales of a home I've never been to, streets I may never roam but have spent the past two decades hearing about, a sea that apparently smells like no other, food that can never be recreated even with the same ingredients and recipes that have once been passed through scribbled notes and now through WhatsApp groupchats, people who live only through the stories told about them. We go on like this for the rest of the night, sharing stories and teasing one another. We're scattered throughout the house, overlapping voices and laughs drift through the open doors. Music floats from someone's phone in the background, conversations about the mundane and the not so mundane fill the rooms, arguments over board games, the rolling of dice, shuffling of cards, the triumphant *Checkmates*, the sound of cupboards opening and shutting in search of snacks. We settle into a chaotic harmony.

We eventually get around to doing the dishes, only to fill up the sink with glasses and bowls that came after endless offerings of tea and snacks. A movie is playing on the television, but those who picked it out are now sleeping on the couch and those awake are speaking over it anyway. Occasionally, someone looks at my two little cousins running around and wonders how they're not tired yet. Let's go to bed, darling. They refuse, too scared to miss out on what else could be happening as they sleep, and even as everyone else drifts off one by one, they refuse so long as one of us is up – I don't blame them, we've all grown and continue to find ourselves doing it too, only falling asleep due to the long days we face before our nights together begin. Those awake nudge those asleep, whispering a soft "go inside, there's an empty bed" or a "take the mattress" or a "move to the couch", and blankets get passed around.

These evenings, no matter how recurring, never cease to bring us joy. And I wonder if I'll ever experience the better version of it, doing it all in a land that is mine, as opposed to constantly wishing we were exported back home – living out the same memories with the same people, just elsewhere.

Bana'murrai'yung (wet becoming cooler)

Chloe Isabelle Pryce

god, grant me sydney in the rain
bury me with the smell of strangers
smoking cigarettes beneath the moreton figs
wrap my paling body in the
traffic light strewn wetly across city road
give me the warm lush steam of the footpath
the breeze that whips too briskly for what I wear
through surry's concrete byways from the sea
pour down sheets of water, for the gutters
run them high and strong, and
hurl me gladly into the time of marrai'gang –
the long wet, the prayed-for change
show me the pelican on the canal, greeting the heron
take me, dripping and alone, along my way
tell me again that the world can be made new
turn the worms
and send them dancing into the bursting light

Everything and Nothing at All

Aishmita Kumar

Papa. When I think about you, I think about mangrove roots. It's less of a "thinking" now. Just like this is less of a "talking". I can only sense the roots, like a hand held up to your shoulder – close enough to feel their presence but never making contact. Like if I turned my head fast enough, I might catch a glimpse of them above the kitchen table: one singular, great trunk and thousands of roots, rising over each other like knotted waves, reaching across space. In nature, mangrove roots rise from the water, their roots arching as if gasping for breath. The only way to escape drowning is to reach upwards.

My mangrove roots glitter orange-gold. They are not solid, more a shadow. But the silhouette, the shape, is there. They don't ask permission to grow, just reach for what they can hold. They connect everyone in my family, twisting and looping and turning, but they start with you.

Everyone calls you Dādā now, but Papa is the name you chose. You hated how old Dādā sounded. In photographs you are slight but tall, glasses and a relaxed smile. But in the eye of my childhood, you are colossal.

Perth in January. The ground seemed to exhale, the hazy heat rising up from the tarmac, and stretching out across the earth. I was watching, my nerves like live wires, humming in the blistering air. They clung to the silence between Dādi and me. We drove past the Coles and Woolworths duplex, with its shiny glittering cars, until we reached a corner Asian mart. The store was no more than a large warehouse. On the glass doors, photos of thieves were printed out, faces pixelated and blurred, warnings printed in bold. The high ceiling was lined with industrial sized fans, and the air seemed to hang limply, the heat dampened for now. Dādi was half a foot shorter than me, even back then, and she walked with a strong limp. She had red hair that she dyed with henna, always fastened at the back of her head with a clip.

"Beta, pick from the back. The back fruit good, the one at the front old. They put it so people buy old one first."

Her nails were always painted maroon red, her small plump hands searching the fruit expertly. She left school at eight and was married off at fifteen.

Unlike Dādi, your English was perfect. You never slipped into Gujarati halfway through a story; words and sounds melting, slipping in mid-air. Sometimes I wonder why it's always you that's at the forefront of my mind, rather than her. How much I lost in the silences, the misunderstandings, the meaning that never quite reached.

When we returned home, you – having already covered the dining table with newspaper – showed me where to slice the chicken we bought, which parts to remove, the milky fat and the bright red innards. Your hands, covered in chicken slime, shone like black cracked leather, lined with veins like the branches of mango trees you used to climb as a child.

You grew up in poverty, I learned later, surviving on cheap fish from the markets in Fiji. You studied under streetlights, won scholarships to study in New Zealand, Australia and India. You finally came here, to Perth, built this big house for all your kids. But even then, the rooms were unliveable, piled high with mountains of clothes bought on sale, unused exotic diffusers, china teawares, still sealed and gathering dust. I remember you that way, head bent over the carcass, searching for bits of meat to salvage.

After dinner, we would gather on the sofa, and you would tell us your stories. Bits of history hung in the air, and I traced them out in the dim light, a glittering web linking us all beneath it. You told us about playing soccer barefoot with the other boys, and how sometimes it ended in a fistfight over a goal point. About being too afraid to go home after, because once your father saw your bruises, he would make new ones. About your mother washing your cuts outside, the cold bucket water making you yelp. You focused on the lights twinkling on a distant mountain. I imagine them, twinkling through the blur of tears, until they fill your vision.

"I loved my father very much," you said once, in your odd lilting accent. Was it Fijian? Indian? Kiwi? "He was a very nice man, until he drank alcohol. Then you'd want to stay away from him." You laughed.

Mangroves adapt to thrive where other trees wither, learning to ingest and filter salt, to live with what burns. It becomes a way of life for them, to grow around the toxicity, twisting and turning their gnarled roots to survive.

You told me that when your father died, you were a resident in medical school. You received the phone call while on break during a twelve-hour night shift. You stopped eating for months after that. Spoke to your father every night, begging him to come back. How did you carry the weight of what your father was, and what he wasn't? How did you hold the tenderness alongside the pain? How did you love the hand that struck you?

Some stories you never told, and I found out from my mother much later. Like the time they came to evict you and threw your furniture out onto the street – nothing more than a couple of milk crates. Your mother begged on hands and knees, removed the only gold she owned from her ears, so that you could stay.

Memory blurs with imagination, and I blend the parts I don't understand. The hazy silhouette of a scrawny boy, playing at the cowboy films he saw at the theatres, riding off into the distance on his two bare feet. The skin of your heels are pink, picking up dust behind you. Or maybe there is no dust, just wet earth. Maybe tarmac. I've never been to Suva.

Even now, your roots still grow. A chain of breath and memory, laced through the years. They weave tighter with age, gripping the earth. That's how mangroves survive: by latching on, by threading through, by becoming a net no flood can pull apart.

The last time you visited, I hugged you and felt the ridge of your spine against my skin. You were no taller than my shoulder. In the mornings I would hear your footsteps in the hallway, pacing back and forth. You muttered silently to yourself, nothing more than murmured gibberish, one second there, the next second somewhere else. One morning, you opened my door. Feigning sleep, I watched you through squinting eyes. Your hand was curled around the door handle. You stood with one foot over the threshold, one remaining in the hallway. Believing my ruse, you closed, then opened the door again, unsure whether to wake me. Maybe you needed help finding the tea, or the cotton buds to make your morning diya. Maybe you just wanted to make sure we were still here, that we hadn't all disappeared during the night.

This time you carried a case with you. It was blue, with little anchors all over it. You would panic when it wasn't within arm's reach. You tossed its contents onto the table. A collection of small white boxes, labelled "Temapezam, 10mg" and "Diapezam, 10mg" in blue typeface. The little white and yellow sachets gleamed in the cool morning light. The lines of your face were set with resigned complacency, as if maybe now that you were taking medication, they would understand you. My mother hummed with feigned nonchalance, the way she did whenever something unacceptable was mentioned.

This family of mine, our roots fracture. We ingest the salt, expel it, even as it corrodes our limbs, drawing the water out of us until it brims, until it overflows. Our consciousness is marked with its memory, something sharp-edged and biting, something we cannot name.

In the car, you were silent next to me, staring out the window, no trace of your stories or laughter. The sun began to set, the sky erupting in shades of peach and burgundy, turning the trees into indigo silhouettes. You began rocking in your seat, your seatbelt clicking with each movement. Your hands reached to undo the lock. I reached across and stilled them. "Manē ghabarā lāgē chē," you muttered. I didn't understand. Your hands clutched your case, began rummaging through its contents. Empty sachets littered the seat, fell into my lap. My hands felt dead and limp in my hands, my mind squirming. What happens when roots cannot filter any longer? When there is too much salt to bear?

Later, at home, you tried ordering Temazepam with an expired license. You called your old workmates from Perth. I had never heard you yell before. Your voice echoed across the hall, rising and desperate. The mangrove roots began to break, disintegrate, replaced by something brittle, leached of colour.

They had to force you to retire. Is that when you started taking the pills? Or had this been lurking all along, rolling beneath the surface? That ancient sadness, did I inherit it from you? I see you and see my mother: A twitch of the mouth, the pacing at night, the silence that swells. It was yours before. When did it become mine?

I remember the night I found you. How the moonlight bent backwards over your bed and then you, a blurry silhouette. You clawed against the window, hands outstretched, reaching for the latch. You lifted a spindly leg. Your hip buckled. "I just wanted to see," you murmured. I led you back to bed.

What had you been searching for? What was that one thing that you were standing on the periphery of? Perhaps the past, where I could not follow, out behind us like lights in the scrawny night. I think of you often – bare feet on dusty streets. You hang onto me when the air is heavy with words unspoken, when the rain pushes out the rot of the city, so that the smell of trash and sewage hovers in back-alley streets. When the world settles in, when it all fades out and I'm left in the crossfire, I think about you. I think about how you left me with everything and nothing at all.

In India, you carried my mother five kilometres to the nearest doctor in the dead of night. Did you whisper anything to her as you walked?

You turned twenty-one in a homestay in New Zealand, surrounded by friends. Did you think about your youngest sister then, who was left alone in India, too young to migrate to Fiji? Were you glad to leave Suva, its cheap fish and milk crates behind?

There was the time you broke my father's nose, just because he wasn't Gujarati. Did you ever regret what you did?

The shame, the pride, your silence around it? By the time I found out, it was too late to ask you.

And every year, without fail, you sent me your jars of homemade chilli pickles, packed tightly in newspaper and cling-wrap bags, stained yellow from where the oil leaked slightly through the lid. I would open them slowly, careful not to spill. But every time, the mustard oil would spill over the edge, cumin seeds clinging to the glass. That's what your love felt like to me. One moment it was neatly parcelled, pushed down, and the next, it was elusive and overflowing.

When I eventually left my room the next morning, you called me Pratiksha or Priya or Yoshna. I hugged you and felt the ridge of your spine under my skin. You asked me what tea I was drinking. You asked me to spell it out and then repeat it two more times. You sat for a moment, waiting for the information to click and snap into place, into knowing. Waiting, on the edge of the unknown, one foot over the threshold, another somewhere else. Instead, you lapsed into silence.

When Did You Say You Were Leaving

Rosanna Chim

It's said that Thatcher fell down the stairs of the Great Hall of the People because Deng Xiaoping had run so many circles around her during the September 1982 discussions on Hong Kong's future. As she emerged from closed conversations, the British Prime Minister missed her footing, tripped and fell. Graceless and undignified on all fours, kowtowing in bent submission before Mao Zedong's mausoleum. This terrible omen sent a message from China's epicentre of power, threatening the values of everyday Hong Kongers. To me, it marked Britain's hand in the slow unravel of Asia's once "most prized" and culturally rich cities. I look back to this moment in history when I consider the events of my own life, dwelling on its impact on my family.

* * *

I'm watching *Twilight of the Warriors: Walled In*, the latest film to restore Hong Kong's iconic kung fu culture since the collapse of its golden age. They created a little set for the movie, an exact replica of 1980's Hong Kong, showcasing the now demolished Kowloon Walled City. It's nice to see our city again, living on in little fictional scenes. The dirt-class Cantonese revives a part of me, and I notice Philip Ng looks just like my dad. Same monkey grin, wide jaw with a body of solid mass cut from muscle. I watch my dad in his mullet and eighties aviators fly across the screen to dish out the punches we had practiced in the living room together.

* * *

My car rolled off the bridge at Gosford, from the oppressive fog, rain, and winds. A doctor standing at the door tells me this. He discusses the state of my health but his shifting eagerness to remove himself from the room lets me know it's nothing serious. My attention drifts. I make an attempt in navigating a limp hand to the pulsing point of pain. Past the gummy squid texture of my eyes, up along my hairline, I prod at my forehead. There's a bandage covering the bulging swell of a wound under the press of my fingers. I pick at a corner, plotting to lift the sticky patch but a hand snatches me away from it.

* * *

In a hospital room, I'm not too sure when, I reached up to his neck with two fingers like how they do on TV.

He was still warm like on mornings before school, his mouth hanging open in a snooze. I'd crawl over the bed to wake him up, upset that mother had left me for work, and he would take me to Baker's Delight for a raspberry Danish.

But it had been hours since I'd last heard his wet laboured gasps, each a lungful of mucus. I still wonder how it could be that most people have never heard the exact sound of a person drowning upright in bed.

***

Standing over him, I trail across the sheets, down to his wrist and apply my two fingers there. I press hard, confusing my own pulse for his. I'm not doing this right. I've never felt for a pulse on anyone; what would I know about this? I'm no nurse. Where is the nurse? There's a nurse. She thinks he's dead because I can't answer her on whether I can find it. *Well, I can't find it because I've never done this, maybe you should.* I think she's made up her mind before she even tries. She gives him a quick one two and declares him dead. She says they'll take him down to the morgue and I'm worried he'll wake up trapped and weak in a cold fridge, after all I'm not sure I did it properly and the nurse was too quick.

After a few hours in the morgue, I finally come to terms that I've killed him.

***

When I finally see my forehead reflected on a mashed potato spoon at dinner service, a deep, red cut is stitched through my old scar. I ponder the meaning in revisiting the same fate. I ponder again, grasping at Cantonese words in my mind, but nothing attaches in the mystical way I hope for. Dad used to tell me that my prominent forehead was a prosperous mountain, brushing back little hairs to gently admire its curve.

"*Ngor geh malou-jey,*[1] only leaders have this type of forehead," he would say with a sure smile, in his best imitation of an uppity Chinese scholar. I'd wriggle free of his hold. His

---

1 Translation from Cantonese: "My little monkey."

tone was only proper when he spoke those words, not like his usual street boy Cantonese cusses.

I turn on the TV set hanging from the corner ceiling above my hospital bed to finish my movie. I let the familiarity of Phillip Ng's face breathe new lines of dialogue, hoping they stay with me in the quiet hours of the hospital room. I fall asleep to it, wanting to carry our story into tomorrow.

***

"Can
you
still
write
your
name
in
Chi-?"
"Of course she can."

***

A broadcaster on the telly is covering the removal of the Jumbo Floating Restaurant from Hong Kong's Aberdeen harbour town. I dig up an old article on my phone where Carrie Lam announces ambitious plans for its restoration. As I watch its delicate wooden form tow away from the harbour shore, it's obvious Lam's plans have been abandoned. The presenter speculates on the mystery company responsible for its relocation to an undisclosed location. ;*Are floating harbour restaurants even seaworthy?* Lam refuses to comment when questioned.

The news segment continues. It shows the brown papery face of a local fisherman, crumpling in stages of grief as he watches the six tiers of jade pagoda roof pull away from its home of fifty years, heading towards open waters. He pleads to the screen, to the government, to me, against its removal. That its cultural significance is much too important to him and his family, to those who depended on its draw of tourists, and to all Hong Kongers. His waving hands retract to brace himself as he heaves in tears, and his pleas become more and more inaudible.

The Jumbo Floating Restaurant has served the city as an iconic film set of many popular films including Jackie Chan's Rush Hour 2 and James Bond: The Man with the Golden Gun. It was once the bustling draw of tourists around the world who experienced unique Hong Kong culture, surrounded by the glow of sampans in the river, each their own little floating restaurant. Aberdeen harbour became so popular that two more floating restaurants were built to form The Jumbo Floating City. It dined the Queen of England herself.

The restaurant barge that was said to be in need of grave repairs, would be found shattered in wooden chunks along the coast of Vietnam the following morning.

***

When I wake the next day, the nurse takes away my phone. I watch her weave past boats of floating beds. A senior man lays motionless, gaunt, in a thin hospital gown sheet. His skin is so starved that any wrinkles have pulled taut against his skull. A cold reminder that chemo can cause a starved death; the medication is so powerful that the stomach lining blisters, unable to take to food for weeks.

"Asians never raisin! I'm still waiting to learn you people's secret!", a cheerful nurse exclaims as she pushes him down the hall. The old man doesn't respond. His glazed eyes aren't stirred by the movement around him.

The intermittent flickering light doesn't quite reach the end of the corridor, and both the man and his nurse are quickly enveloped into an unknown darkness out of view of my ward window.

I sink into my new book, letting my mind transform Monkey into a familiar form; Dad's now making *The Journey to the West*. The bodhisattva, Guanyin, tests him every few chapters and he collects demonic acolytes along the way with his monkey traits. He's always been charismatic, making new friends at every Fairwood cafe or local shop. The demons guarding each mountain ridge quickly show a friendlier side.

By the third chapter, he storms the underworld, tearing through the shadows of Hell to reach the Register of Life and Death. There, he scrawls rebellion into the very fabric of fate, striking out the date of death for all his little – defying mortality with a stroke of ink.

It's my first time reading it, but it's just like how he'd tell it to me before bed. One cloud somersault sends him across the world to visit Ao Guang, and I know when I wake up, he'll have made it back to our mountain monkey cave.

***

Dad, how did I only just learn that you fled to Hong Kong on foot at age nine to avoid famine? Why did no one teach me about the Cultural Revolution? The Great Leap Forward? But you still starved to death in the end. I watched.

***

I went to the Blue House today in Wan Chai, it's now a historical spot. Uncle S says you lived here when you were little. Forty people of several unrelated families in a tiny three by three room. One family of five to a single slab of bunkbed, skin to skin in the heat and humidity. He says everyone had lice. Sometimes a false ceiling was added to the bathroom to make room for another family. The rent was cheaper in the crammed horizontal void between ceilings to compensate for the smell.

***

In 2021, I quit my first real job out of university and flew back to Hong Kong after the death of my father. I stayed at a hotel. My family had put our 50 sqm Mong Kok apartment on the market during the city's unrest in 2020. I heard an aunt was tasked with clearing out all the furniture, photos and decades of vintage items. At times I'd let myself spiral, imagining her covering the colourful doors with white paint, but I always come to a sharp clarity that it's really Marie Kondo who I have to blame.

Every edge of the doorframe and door face was either a deep nineties shade of green, blue, yellow or red. Every door was labelled as a bus stop or train station, signposted Mong Kok, Mei Foo, Central or Sham Sui Po. I only found out after his death that my dad had let my brother and I choose these colours for our in-home bus route built from cardboard boxes and wheely chairs. Reflecting back – after my psychiatrist hints at autism – it all seems obvious now, but at that time, trains were just trains and buses were a double decker madness, best enjoyed on the front seats of the top deck. Seat belt safety check.

In 2020, the city lost more than just my dad and its cultural identity. We also lost my entire battery collection, six unmounted second-hand air conditioners, my brother Henry's twenty-year-old train-shaped coin tin, fifteen Doraemon plush toys from the same factory and a lifetime supply of Tempo tissue packs. Where some collections end, new ones begin.

During my trip, I captured the sounds of Hong Kong. Entire bus routes, each heave and fall of the exhaust as I drifted aimlessly without my usual fatherly guide. I struggled to remember the names of the favourite places we used to visit and hesitated at every stop. But the warm air comforted me and the Cantonese cusses of passing passengers reminded me of a simpler time. When I listen back to the audio, I'm testing whether my memories still hold the same emotions.

Bougainvillea

Mona Elhassan

Mama taught me how to make vine leaves. She used to stuff them with rice and mince and wrap them in the air and then stack them in between the fingers of her left hand. The spaces between her fingers would fill up with the stuffed vine leaves, like tiny soldiers in a line. She would carefully move them to a tray before starting a new batch. I've always had to wrap them on the cutting board to avoid making a mess of them, each one a different size and shape. Rice and mince in my lap. Recently, she started wrapping the vines on the cutting board too. It was, perhaps, the first sign of decline.

Lebanon, 1940–1958

Mama told me stories about her childhood. She was born in a village house on a hill with ceilings that touched the sky and a courtyard laced with a grape vine and bougainvillea. Sunlight danced in patterns. Her mother would comb her hair and teach her to pick and wrap the vine leaves. They ate meat once a month and wiped their bottoms with rocks. The women carried the clothes to the bottom of the valley to wash them along the banks of the river. They made a day out of it, with food, singing and dancing. In the summer, Mama and her siblings would drag a single mattress out onto the courtyard to sleep under a velvet sky sprinkled with stars. And although they bathed out of a bucket, they did it in the room where the furnace was, so it was never cold.

She was one of the first girls in the village to go to school in a big city. A single braid reaching the back of her knees bopped up and down as she eagerly hopped on the bus that took her there. As Mama learned letters and numbers and how to sew, the sun slung itself around the earth a few more times. The bougainvillea took on a weed-like quality, its bright pink blooms gradually overpowering the grape vine.

In 1948 Mama was ten years old. One day, big trucks parked in the school yard. Hundreds of families, women and children, seemed to spill out of it like water through a cracked dam. They slept in the school playground and gym. Their eyes bore into the students and burned with a hunger for all that they had left behind, all that had been taken away. Sometimes, Mama played with them at recess.

"Why are you here?"

"Another family moved into our house. But we still have the keys."

The children shrugged their shoulders when asked if they were going to live in the school forever. Mama wanted to know about their dads.

"Killed in the Nakba."

One morning, she arrived at school and the families were gone. She asked one of her teachers about their whereabouts. The teacher shrugged her shoulders. "One of those refugee camps."

Sydney, 1958–1989

Mama outgrew the bougainvillea, left the Mediterranean sun behind her, and came to Australia a bright-eyed bride with my father. They were told to find a better life, like it was something you could catch and trap in a jar. When their airplane landed, the passengers clapped their hands. A new world of recreating the old one ensued. Mama cut her hair and Baba planted a grape vine and an olive tree in the backyard.

"The sky is bluer in Sydney. But the stars are brighter back home."

Family dinners were feasts of grape vine, never ending tales of yearning that stitched their way into my psyche. Seeds of unbelonging sown into me. When I was a girl, I tied a rope to the olive tree and tried to swing back to the motherland. Turns out it is just a place I will sometimes visit but never really understand.

The hippie era brought new "freedoms" but we were always wogs. Back home, a war they called civil ravaged, and death was dished out in spades. Some of the kids from the refugee camps were all grown up and wanted to fight to return home, but don't we all wish it was that easy, that simple? The militiamen made the earth wretched and invited their friends across borders to share in the spoils. Men with guns threatened to attack our village so Mama's family ran away to the mountains and the bougainvillea died. She would yell "how are you" into the phone. Sometimes she wondered about the families from the school playground and what happened to them. Then the war ended although it was hard to determine who, and what, was won. New borders were drawn. Illegal settlements built. Uprisings crushed. Bombs detonated from far away found their way to their intended targets. The sun melted time away, melted glaciers, the earth heated up.

1989–2000

Yet we managed to carry on, unaffected by it all. I grew up and met all of life's milestones with the most dutiful of care. I was the first to get a university education in my family. I worked, made my own money, for a bit. And when the time came, I wore mama's wedding dress and made my own family.

2001–2022

Then the towers got hit and things changed. Fresh hell unleashed on our homelands while we tried to assimilate here. What is the difference between assimilating and disappearing into a crowd? Like desert cats, we walked with our bodies closer to the ground. We left no marks, but the eyes followed us, nevertheless, wherever we went. I would've whisked my family away to another planet if I could. Mostly we just got by, although I don't know if that is because it eased up or we got used to it.

2023–present

My daughter had a doctor carve her into the "perfect body". "For the wedding, everything has to be perfect." We spent hours pouring over the invitation lists. The seating arrangements were even harder to settle. The labour of keeping everyone happy.

Mama is a dot in a bed. When I look in the mirror, I see her face. "If Teyta goes, we have to call off the wedding."

Mama lives in my daughter's eyes. She got her perfect day. Back home, things change but some things manage to stay the same. Across the motherland's border, the Nakba continued. Bombs dropped into heaps of faceless, vanishing bodies. The children starved to death. Stray dogs got fat. It was easy though, to put those people out of our minds and carry on with our joy, unaffected by it all. We danced, we sang, we feasted.

After I saw my daughter off, I visited the motherland. I went to Mama's old house. My cousins had pulled out the weeds and had built a pool in the courtyard for their children. The interior of the home had been renovated entirely; I barely recognised it. Not because of the war, but because my cousin didn't particularly "enjoy that vintage style". I found myself alone, one afternoon, staring at the vitrine which they had perched against the wall in the fancy salon, where the old kitchen was. My cousin was in the new kitchen, brewing coffee. I could see there, among the antiques, a black and white picture of Mama in her school attire, her braid sitting over her right shoulder, face beaming. My reverie was interrupted by the sound of an explosion far away. My cousin found me, her face smiling, "it's far away, in the South. Don't worry." We drank the coffee and memories dominated our conversation. Two days before I left, I got a call from home, saying Mama had taken an unexpected turn. I scrambled with the hassle of ticket changes and the packing of my things and gifts for others. On the day of my departure, my cousin came over to say goodbye. I gifted her a potted baby bougainvillea and asked her to grow it next to the pool, where the old one used to be.

Lotus Bloom

Arani Ahmed

My light reflected, glimmered on the underside of mangroves. Muffled voices said I'm only passing through.

We stand in front of the open wardrobe. Stacks of saris before us, folded in unordered piles of cotton, silk, chiffon, georgette. There must be at least two hundred. They almost spill out. I run my hand along the edge of a deep blue cotton-silk sari in the middle of one of the stacks.

"You can use any of them," Ma says.

"No, you have to tell me which ones you don't wear anymore," I say, though we both know she no longer wears the bright ones.

She frowns. It's a lot of work to sort through them. It's easier if I'm the one who does the sorting and she agrees, or not, afterwards. She won't need to say it, I can tell from the silence.

Only now the breeze pushes me to stop, to feel a sweet rest. Watch, the swallows are playing.

I scan the other piles. I'm ready to make a kantha blanket with a patchwork of my mother's saris, my aunt's and my own, from "before."

Stacks wobble as I pull out the dark blue sari that caught my eye. Ma lays it on the bed, and I see it has a golden lotus block print on the body.

Ma says, "hmm." Then, she recites Tagore, "I knew not then that it was so near, that it was mine, and this perfect sweetness had blossomed in the depth of my own heart."

> That vague sweetness of foreign pine, lone mushroom, roots burrowing, sisters merged, a hanging silver cascade.

When I picked up kantha, Ma began to bring out items to show me. One at a time, weeks apart, as she thought of them. A tea cloth her mother embroidered, a purse she still uses that her sister cross-stitched, a small throw my father's mother made for me. She shows me each one, running her small hands over the embroidery, smiling as she tells me about their practice. Her own, and the women I've only met through what they left behind.

Ma unfolds the sari to show more of the gold trim. Matching colours and patterns begin to form in my mind. She sighs, and I wonder when she wore this last. I know that she'll let me choose it.

> Laughter rustles, flies to where I can't follow, blossoms in the deep river green.

Memory Lane

A Conversation between Two Selves, across Time, Headed Home

Zara Hussain

buckle in!
        wait, where are we headed again?
we're going home,
        oh yes – *home*
        and what is it this time?
dusty cracked plaster?
        or the sharp summer sky?
and what of each space you've occupied?
this bed that holds your shape,
these sleep-warmed sheets.
        what of the body – this tender bag of bones?
        a quiet bog for your soul to sink into.

hey, do you remember?
the halcyon days, golden and sweet
        and *heady*, like honey:
staring into the green
        eyes bleeding clover.
floating limbless in the wine-dark sea
        the tide's kiss and pull running
        warm fingers over your lips

come along,
past cobwebbed years
float through memory –
  cheap, unreliable time travel –
  a bird's-eye view of life.
can you fill in the details?
(try. try anyway.)
sixteen – a list of words on scrap paper
  golden whisper idyll autumn iridescent
  because
  words are just so pretty sometimes, aren't they?
fifteen – crisp Octobers, dappled with summer rain, snatches of poetry,
  spring herself when she woke at dawn
  would scarcely know that we were gone
twelve – racing the watercolour sunset home,
  orange and pink bleeding across the sky
nine – the sheer impossibility of *trees*
  the pulse and sway of the earth beneath you
four – milk teeth, bright eyes and awe,
  the wistful moon, rising over you
two – dimpled cupid's hands, hungry fists grabbing at the sky
  blue and bright and small enough to *bite.*
all this time,
life just rushing you by.

side-step, take a breath
understand: these words are placeholders
all of them,

none fit to paint the palimpsest
of years carved into your marrow

yet still, somehow, we're here.
we're *home.*
where warm light spills
into your empty cups,
with tenderness, kindness and luck.
a threshold swings open –
go gently, tread lightly,
come, be welcome.

Elderberry

Lakai Tungafasi

Mabu Island was the kind of place travel brochures didn't do justice. Palm trees leaned like banana leaves in a midday breeze. The beaches glimmered gold at sunset, and water lapped the shore like it had nowhere better to be. Even the mosquitoes were too relaxed to bite.

Owen was seventeen and had already beaten everyone on the island at *Sakana Kings*. Twice. Sometimes three times if they came back drunk enough and forgot how badly he'd thrashed them the first time. The game was half strategy, half bluff – like high card if the ocean had invented it. Fluid suits, bluff-heavy, and brutal in the final round. You played three rounds, built hands from a shifting set of suits and tried not to let your face give anything away. Owen could read a twitching eyebrow like it was a blinking neon sign. He hadn't lost in two years. And he knew what came next. More wins, more mangoes and nothing new.

He was simply the best.

He sat beneath a shade sail, cards fanned and grin smug. Across from him, Old Man Julo cursed under his breath and threw down his hand.

"Full crest. Coral. Beat that, you little sea rat."

Owen laid down three blue-backed cards. "Storm flush. Wild tide suit. That's mine." The small crowd groaned. Julo slumped back with a wheeze, muttering about the good old days. Owen grinned and scooped the bet into his bag – half a mango, six shell chips and a carved crab whistle.

"Next?" he called, eyeing the sun-baked regulars. Nobody moved. He shrugged. "Didn't think so."

Mabu was home. Sweet, sunny and slow. His mother, Mayra, ran the island's little café-slash-post-office-slash-everything. Her voice was soft, her hugs were always a little too long, and she hummed when she cooked – a tuneless, pleasant melody that wrapped around you like a blanket. Owen's little sister, Lila, had a gap between her front teeth and the unshakable belief that crabs could be trained like dogs.

Life was perfect. Too perfect.

That evening, Owen skipped stones into the tide while Lila officiated each one like it was in the Olympics, triumphantly tooting her new crab whistle.

"Five skips!" Lila shouted. "Bronze medal for Owen!"

Owen snorted. "Yeah? Wait 'til you see this next one."

The stone never hit the water. Instead, it struck something floating just offshore. It was a long, narrow box bumping against the reef. Owen waded out, fished it up and examined the markings upon it. It was dark, heavy wood bound with threads of silver kelp that shimmered in the fading light.

Lila watched with wide eyes. "Treasure?"

He popped it open. Inside was a single deck of cards bound in wet netting, and a curved brass needle. Nothing else. However, the moment his fingers brushed the cards, the needle flared white-hot and dove into his wrist.

"Ouch!" he screamed.

Lila gasped.

Owen yanked his arm back, already too late. Ink burst from the puncture, curling up his forearm in tight spirals, looping into impossible knots that shimmered and shifted under his skin like fish beneath the surface.

The cards in his other hand felt ... livelier. He shuffled them without thinking. The backs were ocean-dark, patterned with a fruit. A berry of some sort.

The ink didn't settle like normal tattoos. It burrowed – like it was etched rather than drawn. The longer he stared, the more permanent it felt. Images flickered across his mind. A bar underwater. Glowing chips. Various monsters seated around a few tables. A game much like *Sakana Kings*, but with sharper teeth and the scent of salt and ink in its bite.&

The tattoo pulsed again, once, like a heartbeat. A direction. Not just where to go, but why.

A real game.

Owen looked back at Mabu – the swaying palms, the sleepy café, his sister humming one of their mum's off-key tunes. For the first time, it all felt . . . still. He looked down at the shimmering tattoo, then at the stone still floating where the box had been.

"A challenge," he said with excitement coursing through his body.

He needed this.

He left at sunrise. No big speeches. No teary goodbyes. Just a canvas bag, some biscuits from Mayra, and the tattoo humming like a compass needle under his skin.

He hugged his mum, who kissed his forehead and said, "Don't chase storms you can't outswim, alright?"

Lila clung to his waist for longer than usual. "Will you bring me a crab?"

"Only if it plays cards," Owen said. "And wins."

The water was glassy that morning. His raft slipped away from Mabu like it was never meant to stay. From the water, he could still hear her humming – off-key, faint and perfect. His stomach twisted, unsure if it was from the sea or the leaving. He hadn't ever left the island before. Every ripple felt like crossing a boundary. He didn't look back.

He followed the pulse. The sky darkened somewhere past the reef. Stormless but overcast. The sea seemed to hush itself. The raft rocked more violently now, its wooden belly creaking as if the water beneath had grown impatient. Waves lapped higher, sloshing over the sides. Owen gripped the edge with both hands, knuckles white, heart drumming faster than the tide. He hadn't expected the ocean to feel so wide. And then – without warning – he was there.

The Deep End.

It rose like a shipwrecked cathedral from the ocean's belly. Just towers of perished wood and bone-white coral curling upwards into a silhouette that looked part beast. A tattered sign swung over a slanted doorframe. *The Deep End*. The 'P' was missing. Or had been chewed off.

Inside, the tavern was dim and swaying. Bioluminescent barnacles clung to the beams, casting a drowsy gleam. The smell was a mix of spiced rum, ink and wet rope. Behind the bar stood Captain Thatch, a mountain of a man with a grey beard that spilled to his chest like a curtain of smoke. One eye and no smile.

Next to him, bobbing in a half-barrel filled with brine and old playing cards, was Zadock. Bulging eyes. Gills. Fish skin flaking from his elbows.

"You the new bite?" Zadock croaked, swirling his cup. "Hope your wit's sharp, kid. The game's not picky about what it chews through."

Owen blinked. "Excuse me?"

Zadock grinned and turned to Thatch. "There, I greeted him. Toss me the bucket. I'm getting peckish over here." Thatch then took a small pail of chum and lobbed it to Zadock. It made a splash as it landed in the barrel and the chum was consumed quickly and grotesquely.

From the booth in the corner, a woman looked up. Maxine, who had red hair knotted with beads and bones, sipped from a chipped teacup and didn't blink at all.

"I saw you coming," she said. "Didn't expect you to be so ... *suntanned.*

Owen raised an eyebrow. "Well, I didn't expect the welcome committee to come in a barrel. Guess we're just full of surprises today."

"Barrel's optional," Zadock croaked with chum in his teeth. "For the ambience."

Maxine chuckled. "That's Zadock for ya. He might act like a child, but he's older than he looks."

"I *look* like a mouldy oyster," Zadock said. "That's called *charm* down here, sweetheart."

"As for myself, you can call me Maxine. And behind the bar? Thatch. We're the Dredge-Magnates of *The Deep End.* Welcome aboard!"

"I'm Owen."

Captain Thatch poured a drink. "You're here to play, then?"

Owen's tattoo pulsed. He hesitated, then nodded.

Thatch grabbed a set of keys from his coat. "Follow me. Let's see what pieces of yourself you're ready to lose."

The game room lay deeper below the surface of the tavern. Owen followed Thatch down a crusted staircase that creaked like it had secrets.

A round table sat at the centre of a hollow chamber, fluttering with soft blue light. Coral had overgrown the walls in spirals, and water trickled along the ceiling – though nothing ever dripped. It was like the ocean watched but didn't dare interrupt.

Six players were sat around the table. To Owen's left was an aristocratic anglerfish in a velvet waistcoat, with a monocle balanced over one bulbous eye. His voice, when he spoke, was like an old cello sinking in brine.

"New blood," he commented. "How *novel.*"

Beside him slouched a skeleton in rotted sailor garb, barnacles clinging to its skull. A tarnished, rusty cutlass was belted at its hip. It didn't talk, just grinned, its jaw slightly off-hinge.

Across from Owen sat a siren with eels for hair. Her skin shimmered purple and blue and her lips stitched into a smile that didn't reach her eyes. She winked at him, then exhaled a bubble in the shape of a heart.

Next, a sizeable porcelain bowl sat atop a cushion, holding only the head of a living shark. The bowl was cracked at the rim, and the shark hummed something vaguely operatic – almost enchanting.

The last seat belonged to a girl no older than nine. She was pale, damp and wore a shredded nightgown. She clutched a filthy teddy bear that looked like it had drowned and decomposed over many tides. Her eyes were enormous and hollow. She stared at Owen, astonished to finally see someone non-aquatic or rotten at the table.

Owen took the final seat.

Thatch placed a new deck in the middle of the table. It was thicker than the one Owen had found and hummed with that same low frequency. Maxine entered behind him and sat in the shadows, legs crossed, teacup steaming beside her.

"Welcome to the *Elderberry* table," she said.

"*Elderberry*?"

Zadock hollered from the doorway upstairs. "They call it that because it stains and sweetens."

"How do I play?" Owen asked, perplexed.

"It's just like *Sakana Kings*, except this game runs on memory. Ante up something true."

Owen frowned. "How do I do that?"

"Think of something," said the siren, stretching her long fingers. "Something small. Then *let it go*. The cards know."

Owen touched the top card of the deck. He thought of the mango stand by the pier. The one where Julo sometimes napped when no one was looking. The stand vanished from his mind like smoke in a breeze. A chip manifested itself in front of him. Light green. Sweet-scented. And shimmering.

The other players followed. The anglerfish placed a memory of the smell of silk sheets. The skeleton, a ship's name. The girl, a lullaby. The shark head gave up "the colour yellow." Somehow.

Cards were dealt – three per player. The suits shimmered like tides. Tide, Shell, Flame, Depth. Each had its own trick, Owen learned. Depth cards were neutral. Shells copied others. Flames burned a card in your hand. Unless it was a Tide card.

Owen played instinctively. Bluffing was second nature. His first round, he pulled a Shimmer Run – three shells. Enough to win. His chip flared brighter, then sank into the table.

"Not bad," muttered the anglerfish. "Beginner's luck."

The second round, Owen lost. Barely. He blinked and realised he could no longer remember one of the specific tunes his mother always hummed.

He sat back, chilled.

Maxine sipped her tea. "Careful. It starts with small things."

"But it builds," Zadock said from the doorway, swishing gently in his barrel. "Like rot."

Owen's tattoo flared. He pressed his hand to it.

And he kept playing.

At first, he told himself he was chasing the thrill – the sensation of a close match and the flicker of risk that made his heartbeat jump. But with each ante, it became less about winning, and more about feeling. *Elderberry* didn't just take; it gave. Not always kindly. Not always cleanly. Each loss left him raw, cracked open and changed. Sometimes for the better. Sometimes not. For a boy raised on salt breezes and soft mornings, it was the first time anything had ever burned.

For Owen, *Elderberry* offered something Mabu never could. The chance to become someone else. Someone whose past didn't trap him like driftwood in a tidepool. Someone bigger than the island that raised him. If it cost pieces of himself, so be it. He wasn't sure he liked who he'd been, anyway.

He played more rounds of *Elderberry* than he could count. The rules were always the same, but the stakes shifted with each turn. What began as playful trades – a sunny afternoon, a forgotten bruise, the taste of cold mango juice – grew darker, heavier and harder to let go of. He traded away the memory of a thunderstorm he once watched from under a woven blanket. The salty smell of Lila's hair after a swim. The warmth of swinging in a hammock after a big lunch. Gone.

In their place came fragments he never asked for. A skeleton's guilt, a siren's kiss, a modicum of borrowed envy. The memories he gained were never whole. They shimmered in the corners of his mind like a reflection in shards of broken glass. Real enough to sting, but impossible to hold. He stopped noticing when they changed him.

Before he knew it, four days had passed like nothing. The biscuits Mayra had made him were now stale. But *Elderberry* nourished him in stranger ways. And he was winning. Often. He had proved himself to be a worthy contender. The anglerfish watched him closely. The girl with the teddy bear shuffled her cards with a new kind of stillness. Even the skeleton looked slightly weary.

But Mabu ... Mabu was slipping.

He still remembered the island, but its edges blurred. The café still existed, but he wasn't sure what colour the awning was. He couldn't remember the name of the hill behind the mango grove, or whether the stars there were sharp or soft. Or how Lila's whistle sounded in her laugh – that breathless kind of joy, like surprise caught mid-giggle.

"I'm just making space," he muttered once, watching a chip shimmer before dissolving into the table. "I've got plenty left."

Maxine found him after that round. She sat beside him, her teacup steaming with something sweet-spiced and strangely sad. "You've stopped playing to win. Now you're playing to change."

Owen leaned back, suspicious. "What do you mean by that?"

Maxine's eyes brightened without humour. "It means you're learning what the others came here to forget."

Owen watched the skeleton twist a card between its fingers. "You mean grief?"

"I mean weight," she said. "Memory isn't just sweetness. Some memories grow teeth. *Elderberry* lets you choose what to carry and what to cut away. You don't always know what you're giving up until it's gone."

He frowned. "So that's it? Play until you forget the worst bits of you?"

"It's not about forgetting. It's about deciding who you'll be without them. The players who win the most aren't empty. They're refined. Like sea glass."

"Sea glass," Owen muttered, unimpressed. "So, all this is just some kind of therapy?"

Maxine shrugged. "The ones who lose themselves entirely become Dredge-Magnates. Like me. They're people who no longer need a past to hold shape."

"And people *want* that?"

"They crave it. There's a kind of hunger in *The Deep End*. A hunger for relief."

He thought of the anglerfish's eyes. The siren's sad grin. The girl with the teddy bear – so young, so ancient.

Maxine leaned in. "You've tasted their pain. But you've also tasted their freedom. The fragments you've taken. Grief, envy, wonder. They change you, don't they?"

He didn't answer. He didn't need to.

Maxine nodded. "You're close, anyway," she said.

He tilted his head. "To what?"

"To walking away changed. Properly. To ascending. To becoming a Dredge-Magnate. The others feel it too." The anglerfish gave him a slow, deliberate nod. The shark hummed something low and reverent.

"Your next round will be against me," Maxine said. "One final round. One final ante. If you win, you'll walk where others sink. You'll gain what they lost. You'll become a Dredge-Magnate. Unanchored. Unburdened. Limitless. If you lose ..." She smiled gently. "Well, the ocean will still take you home. Just not the home you remember."

"What do I ante?" Owen asked.

She didn't answer. He felt it before he named it. Deep in the ink that curled across his skin. A memory so large, so rich, it could only be wagered once.

Mabu.

Not a piece of it. Not a flavour. Not a detail. The entire shape of the place. The smell of sea salt on the cliffs. Lila's breathless laugh. His mother's hands. Everyone and everything that ever meant something to him. To wager it would mean losing it all. Not just forgetting it but knowing he had forgotten. He would never go back. And if he did, it would be nothing to him. Just another shore.

"Plenty have tried," said Zadock. Thatch had carried his barrel to the *Elderberry* table silently as they were talking. "Plenty have walked away with their tattoos throbbing and their hearts gutted."

Owen didn't reply.

Zadock continued, voice low. "Trade the whole island, and the sand still sticks between your toes. You just forget why it ever mattered to you."

The girl with the teddy bear leaned forwards and placed a card on the table. A lullaby drifted faintly from its face before fading. The skeleton tapped its bony fingers against its cutlass. The siren coiled her eels tighter.

"You don't have to play," Maxine said.

Owen looked at his cards. At his hands. At the ink that now stretched across his chest, neck, and ribs. Living lines that whispered not in words but in weight.

"I do," he said.

Maxine nodded.

He placed both hands on the table and closed his eyes. Mabu rose behind them. The whole island. Its sun, its salt, its stillness. The memory condensed into a chip unlike any he'd seen. Deep blue. Threaded with silver. It hovered for a moment, then settled. The table thrummed. The others watched in silence.

Maxine whispered, "Let it begin."

The cards dealt themselves. Suits shimmered. A Depth card swam to Owen's hand and changed shape three times before settling. Shells blinked like mirrors. Flame flickered at the edge of his vision. He played. Carefully.

He lost the first hand. A gasp moved through the room – silent but sure.

Owen blinked. He could no longer remember Lila's whistle, or the names she gave her favourite crabs. He couldn't remember how the sun felt on his skin when he was harvesting mangoes for his mother. He couldn't even remember his mother's name. He tried to clutch onto the memories, but they crumbled before him like ashes falling through his fingers.

He won the next round. The siren's card hissed as it vanished. The shark's opera faltered.

The final hand began. Owen stared at the cards. Then at the memory-chip of Mabu. Still glowing. Still waiting. The girl drew her teddy bear closer. Her lips moved, almost like she was praying – or remembering something she thought she'd lost.

His tattoo pulsed once.

He picked up the final card.

"Here goes nothing," Owen said.

The final card shimmered like dusk on water. His Shell mirrored the siren's Flame card, tipping the hand in Owen's favour. The anglerfish let out a low, appreciative rumble. The skeleton's grin faltered. Even the girl with the teddy bear blinked.

Owen's chip beaconed. The memory of Mabu flared once, then settled in front of him, intact. It remained – a radiant piece of himself, hard-won and now protected. The table accepted the ante but didn't consume it. It shimmered back into his chest like a relic returning home – a memory proven worthy.

The table exhaled. An intense catharsis rolled outwards. Not of sound but sensation – the pressure of a tide receding. The hush of finality.

Captain Thatch nodded from the shadows. "It is done."

Zadock's barrel sloshed as he leaned forwards. "You've won, boy. All of it."

Maxine stood and approached, her expression unreadable. "Congratulations. You held your ground. Most lose all that they love for a chance like this."

Owen stood, dazed. The ink across his body glowed silver now, steady and strong. He felt taller. Older. Emptier, yet full of something else.

Maxine stepped closer and produced a small velvet pouch. From it, she drew a silver cuff – filigreed, coral-threaded and faintly emitting a purple luminosity.

"This," she said, "is your seal of ascension. It marks you as a Dredge-Magnate."

Owen reached towards it instinctively but paused. "What does it do?"

Maxine's voice stayed level. "It completes the rite. Your tattoo will stabilise. The sea will know you."

She held the cuff just inches from his wrist.

Thatch's voice cut through the quiet. "And you'll never leave *The Deep End* again."

Owen blinked. "What?"

Maxine's tone softened. "The cuff binds you to this place. It anchors you. *The Deep End* becomes your whole world."

The realisation hit like a breaking wave.

"You never said."

"You never asked," she replied.

Owen pulled his hand back. "I'm not putting that on."

The tavern grew very still.

Maxine tilted her head. "You would turn down ascension? Unlimited power?"

"I came for the game," Owen said. "I didn't come here to be swallowed by it."

Captain Thatch stepped forwards. He held out a card. Blank. Gleaming. "If you refuse the cuff, you'll carry *Elderberry* only in memory – never in hand again."

Zadock croaked, "No cards. No bluffing. No chasing the thrill. You leave the game behind."

Owen stared at the card, then at the cuff still glowing in Maxine's hand. "That's the cost?"

"No card games," Thatch confirmed. "Not *Sakana Kings*. Not *Elderberry*. Not even *Snap*. *Elderberry* marks those who walk away. It remembers."

Owen's fingers twitched. He thought of the weight of a deck in his hand. The joy of outplaying someone who underestimated him. The game he'd spent his whole youth mastering.

He exhaled.

He didn't know what the island would feel like now. But it would be his. Even if the cards stayed silent. So, he took the card from Thatch. It turned to seafoam in his fingers and vanished. The ink across his skin dulled. It wasn't gone. But it settled, like embers choosing to rest instead of burn.

Maxine pressed something into his hand. A chip with a crab etched into it. It faintly shimmered in his hand. "A parting gift," she said.

Owen closed his fingers around it.

And the sea took him back home.

The island hadn't changed. But Owen had. The sky above Mabu was still that impossible blue. The mango trees still slouched in the heat. The wind still carried salt and laughter. He stepped off the raft barefoot, sand curling between his toes. It felt familiar. Quieter than he remembered. Like returning to a house you once lived in, only to find it smaller.

The café still stood at the centre of the village – paint chipped in the same places, and Mayra humming softly in the kitchen. He didn't knock. She saw him through the window, and the door was already open.

She said nothing at first. Just wrapped her arms around him and didn't let go.

"You're inkier," she whispered.

"You're off-key," he said.

She swatted him with a dish towel, and he laughed. It felt real.

Lila came running down the road moments later, a crab in each hand and a whistle around her neck. She barrelled into him, and for a second, Owen forgot how to breathe.

"Did you find one that plays cards?" she demanded.

"No. But I found something better." Owen knelt and placed the chip Maxine gave him into her hand. She looked satisfied, the chip glowing in her tiny, adorable palm.

Months passed. Tourists came and went, and Owen opened a small smoothie shop near the pier with the small fortune of shell chips he had made from *Sakana Kings*. He named it *The Deep Blend*. A chalkboard menu listed special flavours like *Anglerfruit Burst*, *Sirensip*, and *Zadock's Green Mystery* (which glowed slightly at night).

He taught the local kids how to play *Sakana Kings*. Not the new rules people were inventing. The original game. The one that required patience and intuition and bluffing better than anyone else at the table. Though, he never played himself. Not once. Sometimes, late at night, he'd stand behind the counter, his tattoo still faintly throbbing beneath his sleeve, and shuffle an empty hand of cards. Muscle memory. A flick. A fan. A cut. There were no cards, but the motion remained. And somehow, that was enough.

A boy came into the shop one afternoon, knees scuffed, cheeks sun-pink, a wide grin on his face.

"One mango smoothie," he said, "and a lesson in *Sakana Kings*, please." The boy placed three shell chips on the counter with a clack.

"You ever played before?" Owen asked, taking the chips.

"I play lots. My sister beats me too fast, though."

He poured the smoothie and slid it across to the boy. "Good. Losing's the best way to learn."

The boy took a long sip. "This is amazing."

"Secret's in the mangoes," Owen said. "But don't tell anyone."

The boy narrowed his eyes. "Is it true you used to be the best on the island? That's what Julo said."

"Depends who you ask," Owen said, his expression softening.

"I wanna be the best."

Owen chuckled softly, then leaned on the counter, looking out towards the shore. "Then start by enjoying the game – even when you lose. Especially then."

The boy nodded like it was gospel. "Deal. Thanks, mister!"

He dashed off, flip-flops slapping against the boards of the pier. Owen stayed behind the counter, the moment settling over him like the tide coming in. He watched the boy for a moment, the sunlight flickering on his face as he ran to the grove where his friends were waiting with a freshly shuffled deck. He'd heard that line before – from a younger voice, long ago. The smoothie machine hummed quietly behind him, and a salt-sweet breeze rolled through. He smiled to himself.

Some memories don't need holding.

They hold you – like a perfect hand, played once and never again.

Developing Film

Lachlan Griffiths

To print old photographs
is to wed alchemy to existence, moving carefully
into those places where memory cannot reach.

The scent of pine needles and saltwater stirring
insensate memories of fading days; we go again,
to print old photographs.

What answers lie in this shade?
It is the last redoubt of recollection; looking
into those places where memory cannot reach.

Fragments of childhood roused from the darkness
of mourning winter, resurrected as we go –
to print old photographs.

Come, you faces of dazed lotophagi, static prisoners
on that flashing eternity of film, held in vision,
into those places where memory cannot reach.

Fixity – or shall the withering of age
rob from me the capacities of youthful morning light?
To print old photographs, and then to venture
into those places where memory cannot reach.

The Flesh Age

Prue Foster

My body is an avalanche. It rolls down its own mountain
    slips into epochs. Folds out of its selves
        into the fill of its own crevasses. Full
            of the deserted.

Hollowed by the same force that filled it,
    hallowed by the desecration inflicted. Gone
        are the streams darkly trickling. Buried
            under ruins.

These homes immersed and absorbed
    by the faint scratching of dreams
        from behind bolted doors. The rises
            and falls

of last memory stones skipping; downhill
    speeding, up before leaving. Tremors
        trailing the momentum of misses
            and flails.

Come raise a pedestal, to sure up the next. Drill
    down to the sludge of mistakes and corrects,
        through the fine-bone shards of ornaments,
            ground up and spent.

Weather this worn shelter. It is parting
    itself, taking leaving for others as a long-practised
        art. Grab it close with abandon; its yielding
            and gross.

Late Summer, Balmain

Shania Daphne Andrea OBrien

We lived above a laundromat near trains that shook the street,
Where jasmine climbed the fences and the dusk was thick with heat.
The blinds were bent, the sink would drip, the windows wouldn't close –
But still our little house would glow like embers under snows.

You wore the sun like consequence, grey eyes too strange to name –
As if the harbour's silver curve had taught you how to flame.
We drank from chipped enamel mugs, ate peaches sweet and still,
Our laughter loud and loose and fast, our silences a thrill.

We ate our nectarines in halves, with juice along our wrists,
And lay on milk crates in the yard, with all we could have wished.
You swore you'd never leave the shore, and yet you watched the tide –
A man who smelled of pepper trees and always turned aside.

The others danced in linen shirts, with cherries on their tongues,
And passed around the cigarettes like hymns for staying young.
We shouted over supper, let the ceiling fans complain –
And love arrived in fragments then, like sunlight through the rain.

The stove was cursed, the roof would leak, the towels never dried –
But still we rose like altars with our longing set aside.
I see you now in strangers, in the way they light a smoke –
That glimpse of something holy we mistook for just a joke.

And when the heat breaks open now, and fruit begins to spoil,
I taste the summer's memory like honey in the soil.
You never said you'd stay for long – the ending felt that way.
You looked at me like Sydney does; all blue and far away.

Strange Memory Mechanisms

Jennifer Scarini

Strange, the value we hold in a memory. Not the delight or the pain of it, but the sheer magnitude of what it bares forth. The tapestry of all the intricate details that come together within a small snapshot of time can be complex. One reflection can expand like a universe in all directions, bringing back more than the original moment, and just like a dream, flip your mind through a flood of fragmented images within a microsecond. The variety and depth of what we recall, or the absence of certain details, tells its own story.

I'm not sure if curiosity ever killed any cats, but it certainly helps to build strong memories. My mind was once fresh and clear and my memories held tightly, no falsehoods among them, although neuroscientists would try to tell us otherwise. Some of the faces behind these memories, didn't make a great impression, but that is a field of study in itself. And for the faces that did, we should probably question why.

Memories of events tainted by emotion are probably easier to trap. They dance over your synapses and are stored in various parts of the brain. The destination depending greatly on the emotions attached and the types of memories. I've always delighted in my memories, and I feel lucky to be able to say that.

One such recollection, that sometimes catches me with an olfactory nudge, is the simple act of stepping over a puddle of water on the asphalt surface of a carpark off Smart Street, Fairfield New South Wales. An odd thing to recall so vividly, helped by the smell of the previous day's rain on a clear autumn morning. In my mind, the freshness of that moment is the pure definition of promise. Like I have already suggested, a memory doesn't just stand alone, it is all the things that come with it that delight me. These flashbacks, drawing me back to a simpler time, when I was free of life's worries and ignorant to its concerns.

It was a time when I was living life intensely, with new tasks, faces, chores and skills to master. Everything from that time is vibrant, particularly friendships.

Rain on a warm, tarred road is all I need to lure me back to the first few months of my very first "real" job. I worked in a bank, as many did in the "old days". There were plenty of jobs in banks back in 1982. Even for a 39-kilogram (dripping wet) sixteen-year-old. I am sure the newness of this job worked well to intensify and solidify some of my memories of that time, but this one is special for some reason. Like a vaccination, every time you are exposed to a virus you have been inoculated against, you get a little booster to help ward off the disease for a little longer. So too, fresh puddles on tarred surfaces stand to bolster and reinforce these particular memories for me.

I crossed Smart Street carpark on my way to the post office to drop off the branches mail – one of my daily duties, being assigned to the switchboard at the time. It wasn't just any kind of switch board, it was a PBX (private branch exchange) system, where you had a series of chords and plugs you had to plug in and pull out of assigned sockets, along with several switches, that needed to be flicked back and forth, to ensure the incoming calls ended up in the right place, to the right people. My trap of a memory could not recall how to operate the system today. It was not lost on me at the time, that such a system seemed somewhat of a novelty, if not archaic, in terms of the technology available, even then.

Different roles in the bank came along with various set tasks as part of the job description. Going for a daily walk to the post office was just one of them for the switchboard operator. Along with dealing with perpetual payments, manually processing transfers from an account at our branch to an account in another of the same bank. Other parts of the job meant collecting batches from tellers, these were transactions that needed to be electronically processed by another clerk to ensure they made it to the people's bank accounts. If you had time, you would also help process these. Not surprisingly the switchboard otherwise kept you pretty busy. Those were the days before bots and generic phone numbers, when you could call a branch directly and speak to a person who was keen to help you.

I was given one day of training for the switchboard role. The route taken to the post office – as firmly specified by a colleague not much older than I, was the Smart Street carpark. A space vaguely marked out by a mesh fence and a couple of gates. A plain unmarked plot with cars parked in it. The plot has since been replaced by a multistorey carpark and can no longer be strolled through. The memory all the more sweeter and richer, as it cannot be replicated. It's mine.

The stepping over a puddle, the reflected pattern of light, the fresh smell of tar and rain, and the relief and promise of autumn, is all that is required to bring forth these memories. I was feeling pretty clever, Miss-independent-working-girl, delivering the mail in a non-descript satchel to avoid someone noticing where I had come from and where I was going. Carrying a specified number of envelopes, carefully and lovingly banded in groups of twenty, along with the excess that didn't quite make a twenty. Clueless, but simultaneously aware that leaving the branch with this satchel on a regular route, at a regular time each day, might draw the wrong attention.

The post office itself was quite large, as far as post offices go today. Grey, off-white, stained by time and second-hand cigarette smoke, which was nonchalantly accepted in those days as something we should all put up with. A cattle run to the counter was the norm, but my memories of those that served me are strangely blank. Maybe there was just too much going on at the time, my poor brain could only capture a fraction of it. Maybe they were boring, or rude, or just generally unremarkable. Maybe our conversations were not rich or meaningful enough. Another lesson. Following handing over the mail to the postal worker, and collecting a receipt for the items presented, I had no place to go but right back to the branch, as I would not have dared deviate from the designated path, back tracking through the carpark.

This particular memory, as with all, is a vast interconnected web attached to other memories that lay part of this sensory experience. The satchel was not just full of envelopes, but those envelopes were filled with busy hands, working together to ensure the task was completed in time for the walk to the post office. There were always plenty of colleagues that offered help without being solicited. Going and helping others was something many of us did – it ensured the day went quicker if you were kept busy.

The conversations were rich and fluid, while filling envelopes and filing the duplicates of letters and statements, with people you no longer know, but wonder about every now and then. Declarations, confessions, revelations and advice revealed and remembered. There was Jan, who had recommended where to buy fancy zipper front uniforms so it would make life easier getting prepared for work of a morning. Advice about how many sick days you could get away with per month from Leanne – a girl I once spilled a very hot cup of tea over while theatrically telling my own story at morning tea. There was a detailed explanation from Mary, a teller, who would have been in her fifties or even sixties, outlining how she had had to leave work many years before because she was married and women were not permitted to work once married in the 1960s. Tony, who tried playing with my leg while telling me about his Cortina and not filling many envelopes – something as a child I tried to pretend didn't happen. Jackie, who just happened to share a birthday with me, who disclosed that I was being paid less than the dole. Nadra, who never said anything but smiled a lot as I nervously chattered about anything to avoid the uncomfortable silences. Shane, who just looked weird and recounted what we were doing rather than offering anything interesting to the conversation. Lisa recalling the day the technician turned up to fix the oil heater upstairs, returning downstairs, after a loud bang, with a blackened face and missing eyebrows. Along with many more conversations with Graziana, about what we might do when we got to enjoy being on the same lunchbreak again.

Being on the switchboard meant that I was on "third lunch" at 1:00 p.m. My tastes at sixteen were simple. On the corner of Smart Street and The Crescent was a small Vietnamese bakery run by Vinnie Vuong, the most delightful human you could come across. He had a big smile, bad teeth and a strong accent with very little knowledge of English. His bread was crusty and often still warm. I would buy one roll.

Vinnie must have thought I looked a bit malnourished, because he would often try to give me a few extras. Back towards the bank, in fact right next door, was a fruit shop, I'd buy a banana from them – never any extras offered by the person whose job it was to select the fruit for me. I'd slap the banana on the roll and eat that for lunch.

Some days, I would bypass the bakery and the fruit shop and just turn left when I walked out of the heavy doors of the branch. A few shops down was the newsagent and there I would buy a can of coke and a Mars bar, because it helped me work, rest and play. Mars bars are off the menu these days, but I enjoyed my fair share of them back in the day! I would continue on down The Crescent past Kmart and their carpark and do a whole loop back up Smart Street, past the delis, cake shops and my favourite, the fabric shops. Fabric that was cheap enough to delight me with the promise of very poorly made outfits – one I made to wear to my very first concert – Duran Duran at the Hordern Pavillion. Funnily enough, I also made Graziana the same outfit, but in brown, she declined to wear it for some reason. If I had chosen to loop back to the branch via Ware street, then I would be tempted by the record shop, an amazing shoe shop of very expensive Italian shoes, the strong smell of coffee wafting from the coffee traders, and a Bing Lee – the very first and original store that the original Bing worked in, I think he could have been 115 even then! As I made my way back onto The Crescent, Wynn's haberdashery store was just around the corner. It offered the most enticing goodies that delighted my eyes and my mind. Things I dreamed I would one day fill my home with, I never bought anything from Wynn's. My pay really was bad.

Eventually I'd make my way back to work through the heavy doors of the branch, past Mr Audova, the interpreter's office – who had around seven languages up his sleeve, over to the little door I could see my switchboard desk from. I had to knock on the door and wait for someone to let me back into the back office, so that I could resume my switchboard duties for the rest of the day, which was around two hours as banks closed at 3:00 p.m. back then.

The older I get, the more aware I become that these moments, which are conjured by a smell or flash of the familiar, that stand to reinforce the gift my life has been. That while not obscenely rich or famous, I am indeed wealthy as I have a body that is healthy and still serves me well, despite the Mars bars, and a brain that is full of similar memories of rich experiences that were lived intensely. Maybe that is where my wealth was always meant to lie.

Our memories really are a stitch in time – the more stitches the richer the tapestry we weave. I lament at what young people's memories will be like as they age. The time spent with their phones or in front of a computer.

Memories are lovely assets that can be held in one's mind, turned over and observed anew with all the faceted pieces reflected back to you in an instant.

Live intensely, so you can have vibrant memories. The capability to capture a moment in such vivid construction is indeed a gift. I encourage you, the reader, to notice those moments that gently offer you a glimpse into your past. That open a door to another time in your beautiful complex universe. For a memory good, bad, or ugly, is a gift from which your life is constructed. They are what we are made of. Smile at them and send them off until the next time you get to enjoy them.

The Whole of the Moon

Amalia Stone

It starts and ends with a full moon, everything that I'd thought I wanted. In the middle, there's me chasing the moon, and driving into a ditch. For the purpose of this story, the moon alone is unchanged. Everything else has moved on.

On the night in question, at a friend's party I was fancying myself in love, although it was nothing of the sort. In the nineties, that sort of thing happened to me a lot. Crushed grass under my head in the quadrangle, recovering from a two-hour lecture, chalk dust smell in my nose, blue pen on my fingers, I'd pencil out what I'd say to her. How I'd smile at him. Words that I'd imagine they would say, wholly mine, in situations that I would never allow to happen. Put it down to never having Barbie dolls with which to play; put it down to the New South Wales school history syllabus that focused more on the perceived benefits of an English colonial legacy than why treating other humans as objects was inherently wrong. Wherever it came from, it was on to me to know better.

On the night in question, a room full of sweaty not quite teenagers anymore, rubbing elbows and knees sitting on sticky carpet, I'd stared a second longer than I should have. I'd been caught looking by the object of my fancied affections, suddenly incredibly and overly real. Half-sick with excitement, half-sick with guilt, thinking of long-gone poet Sappho and the thrumming in her ears, when the light of their gaze moved on, I fled. Scuttled down the sad grey concrete steps to my car, the sound of The Smiths chased me out, Morrissey bemoaning his single life. The moon was bright over my shoulder; my shadow was long and narrow before me. The idea that the moon might be looking back at me was terrifying.

Well, I thought, I may have fled the party, but I'm no coward. I'll chase the moon right back. In my car, I drove. Down dark highways, lit windows in apartment buildings full of happy couples. Through suburbs full of red brick settled houses, illuminated numbers on their gates. All the way onto one of Sydney's headlands, surrounded by the dark bush, thick set on either side of the road, tall trees reaching up into the night sky, speckled with the arch of the Milky Way, dimmed by the presence of the great golden moon. It's no wonder that at the height of the hill, slowed so that I could peer up through the windshield, I failed to see what was right in front of me. I was moon-blind.

* * *

Earth's moon is the brightest astronomical object that can be seen by us in the night sky, at a stellar magnitude of –12.7 when full. Nothing to the Sun during the day, at –26.7. If you start your night looking at the moon, it's hard to see anything else in the night sky. The brightness kills your night vision. When you're a beginner, seduced by the dark maria, with their ridges and depressions, the craters that you long to touch, time seems infinite. You don't notice that the time you allot to the moon is time that you don't have to spend on planets and nebulae, comets and meteor showers, on matters, on people, closer at hand. That other people are real too. The night passes sooner than you might expect.

* * *

Khaki-coloured carpet, my legs criss-crossed, a glass of water is at my side. The object of my affection is several people away from me. Their partner is also several people away, in a different direction. I am triangulating, constantly, how close we are. A projector with oil drops stained with food dye is cushioning the light in the room, mediating the tobacco smoke. Surface tension and the bass are causing the oil drops to move, to intersect. The colours bleed one into another: blue meets yellow and makes green. Yellow meets red and makes orange. Brown is inevitable, but by the time of the night that brown arrives, no one will be caring about colours. While The Cure sing about a forest, I'm peacocking, talking about quantum theory, superposition of states, the way in which you can think of yourself as rigid, the way in which you can think of yourself as fluid. The side of my face flushes with heat, red and sweaty, with the imagined feeling of a hand. Depeche Mode moan. I'm having the same argument about whether people ever really change, with the same people with whom I always have the argument. We orbit the topic, as the carpet soaks up the spill of our drinks.

* * *

Apollo 11 was the first spacecraft to land on the lunar surface, Eagle module touching down on 21 July 1969. Six hours afterwards, Commander Neil Armstrong and then pilot Buzz Aldrin stood on the moon. Mike Collins continued to orbit in the command module, watching on; not everyone can get everything that they want. Of course, neither Armstrong nor Aldrin touched, in the true sense, the moon. Heavy gloves and thick boots interposed. Reportedly, if one were to touch samples of the regoliths taken from the moon, they would feel sharp. My hurts are all local. I've never had the privilege of being cut by something from out of the Earth's biosphere.

* * *

Earlier, before moon rise, we'd spun on a Hills Hoist with steel strands striping our hands. Stomachs tight with the speed of the down and the slow of the up. Silver wine bags shimmered in the light of passing cars. Red bricked apartment buildings rose behind us, flanking each other like cattle. Couples kissed. The smile on my face made my muscles ache, a headache to seed itself in my sinuses. Red pinpoint glows lit the night from the cigarettes friends were smoking. I watched, tracking the ways in which normal people behaved to one another when in love.

* * *

Astronomers track near-Earth objects obsessively, as well they might. If you're going to die in a cataclysmic collision, few are they who wouldn't want to see it coming. To use their last moments wisely, choose their final words with care. Earth has a number of co-orbiting objects, that come closer and further away in unstable orbits. Some of those objects will inevitably be caught in some other gravitational pull, or cycle into a different resonance. There are two known Earth trojans which find themselves in respective stable Lagrange equilibrium points with Earth and the Sun. It is possible to stay at a distance, a maintainable distance, and survive. But it takes care and calculation. The craters on the moon are testimony to the many celestial objects that have failed.

* * *

Earlier than that, we'd been at Manning café after a lecture. An ache had located itself under my chin in the soft spot at the base of my neck, as I looked at the way their hands were casually intertwined, like it meant nothing. Milky coffee had spilt on the table drowning my lecture notes, which had already reeked of artificial banana, the ester synthesised in that morning's lab. They'd shared their notes with me, neat blue handwriting, colour-coded headings, witty comments in green. During the day, you can only sometimes see the moon, at the right time of her cycle. I'd given the notes back, after I copied them in Fisher Library, my pages in black and white, theirs in colour. On my version, the green asides were invisible.

* * *

Looking back from the moon at Earth, it appears to glow with reflected sunlight, Earthshine. Just as the moon cycles in visibility from full moon, to half, and crescent and dark, so too does the Earth for the moon. Worse, as only one side of the moon is ever turned to us, the other side is always turned away, tidally locked. If you were to be on that side, you would never see the Earth at all.

* * *

Memory is a funny thing, and all I remember of that night is that I escaped the ditch. I don't remember exactly how, and this was before smart phones and social media, such that nothing records the evening. What is certain is that the moon was whole and untethered, large and yellow above the dark of the bush. What is certain is that after that event, I knew enough to see that I was wrong, and how I was wrong. The difference between the sun and the moon. It doesn't matter which path my wave took to get there, the electron of me is through one of the slits and recorded on the other side.

* * *

A triumphant version exists in my memory, where I chock the wheels of the car with nearby sticks. There's just enough for the wheels to dig in, and I reverse out, heart thumping. I drive up to the top of the hill, where I sit, I catch the moon, for a glowing gold victory moment. A silence fills me, engines still. Then I let it go. I leave it all: the moon; the party; the shame behind. I drive on home to my bed. I can take it from here, and I do.

* * *

Another where I fail, the sticks slip uselessly under my spinning wheels. I ring my parents from a nearby pay phone at 2 a.m. It's an uncomfortable feeling, for someone purportedly an adult, asking one's parents for a rescue. Time passes slowly. The moon shines down, the magic gone, as I wait. Finally, the yellow headlights of my parent's dark green station wagon blind me sitting on the edge of the road. My mother sniffs my breath, but I'm sober, just sad. We tie off my car to theirs, and the wagon pulls it out in less time than it took for me to drive it in. Untethered, my father guns the motor of the station wagon and drives far too fast away, leaving my mother with the unenviable job of asking the difficult questions. She takes my keys from me, and drives the sedan home, with me in the passenger seat. As she asks me what on earth I was thinking, our turn signal ticking as we turn from the main street into the side street that will take us home, a man in a trenchcoat flashes us, we the object of his warped desire. It's too dark to see. His face, his body, anything that he wants us to look at is obscured. This is a thing that has never happened to me before. It's not a thing that has happened to me since. When we've turned, my mother looks back at me. "What a night," she says. She laughs, a little startled thing.

* * *

The version that I like the most is one where I concede, wheels spun uselessly, my parents uncalled. The moon has lured me here, and in this ditch, I give her the victory. I watch her fat and swollen, through the windscreen. When that becomes insufficient, I open the door and step out. I lie on the roof of my car. I let her transit above me, from one side of Sydney to the other. She hovers at a perceived apogee, frozen in time. The chill of the car's metal sucks the heat from my body, until I give in, and crawl back into the back seat of my car. I'm not quite warm enough, but I sleep a little, cocooned in jackets, shopping bags, and a tarp that smells slightly of diesel. In the early hours of dawn, a man I don't know stops his car next to the ditch and knocks on the window. Between the two of us, my car in neutral, we're able to push her out. He doesn't ask for my name, or a phone number before he leaves. I drive to the main street, where I buy a hot coffee and a croissant with what is left of my cash. Rich butter taste in my mouth, grit in my eyes, the crumbs cascade down my front into the gutter like so many shooting stars. I don't know if this happened at all.

* * *

For the purposes of this story, the moon is still the moon, regardless of what happened that night. She continues her elliptical path about the Earth, coming closer and moving further away in turn. For the purposes of this story, it is only me who has changed.

Aubade

Lachlan Griffiths

The moon drops in slow wane outside my window.
There is only darkness here,
and night's last hour aches with cold
upon this new-mown grass.
Wristwatch-warnings of life's movement: one midnight
closer to
the unavoidable.

A seal broken by orange sunlight
making its careful parousia up from nightly death.
An awakening to reality; grasped at
in the hues of golden half-light
that break upon honey-stone walls.
Sights of beauty tinged forever
by the pallor at the back of the mind.

Gates open, trains run, and coffee pours
into early pots as the ink-black stain that swallows all colour;
that last flicker before the candle's snuffed.

Free to a Good Home

Cherie Baird

It's a kind of grief
when you've got all of this to feel
and nowhere to put it.
And it's a kind of love
when you can feel the space they had
and know you'll never fill it.

I could bundle up this heart,
slip it between two tattered vinyls
at a garage sale;
hide a tepid smile
of pained relief
when they point to that box
and I say it's free.
(They won't believe their luck!)
They'll think it's such a score
until they get more
than they bargained for.

What will they do
with this old antique?

So many holes; shrunken and bleak.
Hold it to the light –
now what do you see?

Can you see through me?

Can you feel this grief?
Do you want a piece?

Kala

Kuyili Karthik

Ship, 1980

As the record spun below deck, the ship engineer in his cramped cabin picked up his pen, which moments ago he'd filled with blue ink bought in Germany the other week. He held the Japanese gold-nibbed fountain pen to cream letter paper watermarked with a shipping merchant's logo. A record skip interrupted the running ink on Anirudh's page. It gave him an excuse to stop writing to Kala. Jimi Hendrix's voice faltered and caught its breath singing "Burning of the Midnight Lamp". Pulled from his terrible task of finding the words to write to Kala, Anirudh felt the midnight's loneliness seep into him. The page he mulled over was lit by the wavering flame of a single burning wick, lying next to it was Kala's picture. It stung Anirudh every time he pulled it out of his wallet. Soon after marrying Kala, Anirudh had steeled his heart, preparing to leave her in Madras while he accompanied the ship's voyage.

There's no point in sending these letters, Anirudh thought. It'll take a month or more, maybe five. He felt as pathetic with a pen to letter paper as he did signing the marriage certificate. On some nights in Madras lying next to her, he had felt a shameful inadequacy open inside him like a chasm. Soon after marrying Kala, he realised his heart was cold and unreachable, the inner sanctum of a temple built with the stony scaffolding of dreams and myth. Love was a fictionalised sentiment, a promise made to be broken, a hefty burden that Anirudh knew he could not bear. He had lost his way in a labyrinth of unions, of invasions and incursions, of bliss and emptiness, of disease and delusion. He had forgotten that between his skin and Kala's there was always an unbroachable gap. It was too late for the sunken man; he had surrendered his distant heart to his wife, who awaited his return from sea in their newly furnished flat. The maid came every so often, but apart from that Kala was alone.

Putting down his pen and rubbing his eyes, he opened his door into the tight corridors between the cabins. He climbed narrow metal ladders to the ship's cafeteria where black coffee, warm in the pitcher, swilled in ellipses with the ship's slow lurch. He pulled out a fragile-looking chair with spindly metal legs from a long table and cradled his coffee in his warming hands. A bitter ending in white porcelain awaited him. A few seats away, one of the sailors, an older German man, sat with coffee and a book with its cover folded back. A rough growth of silver beard peppered his cheeks which looked like white sails, hanging in deep folds at his mouth. At the edges of his eyes, crow's feet grew thick over greened skin, like veiny crumpled leaves.

His eyes twitchily blinking, the German began: "You've got ink on your hands, boy. Writing home? To your parents?"

"My parents are in this world no more. I have a wife in Madras."

"Ah. You've barely a hair on your face. But your people marry young."

Anirudh nodded. The coffee pulled him out of his fogginess and he surmounted the familiar hurdle of justifying one's predicament to a perfect stranger.

"We married just a month before the ship left from Madras – too young to leave her alone for so long."

The German shook into a sudden chesty laugh, as if a typhoon were stirring in his lungs. His face then turned grave, looking at Anirudh with the same scrutinising look of the stars above the ship deck.

"When you go back to her, you'll be older. You'll have seen the world spin past you on the ship. You will know the narrow canals and coasts, the ends of the Earth." As he said this his skeleton looked fragile under the harsh light.

He went on as Anirudh poured coffee for them both. "It's a lifetime without her. You can't live it with her. Can't share it, even in your letters."

The German pulled out some nondescript cigarettes he must have picked up on a recent stop, maybe the Netherlands. They dragged on them in silence. Anirudh's mouth turned to ash, bitter and burnt from the cigarettes and coffee. He looked at his fingers fringed with blueness and thought of that day they met, when she had looked into his ink-stained hands, making sense of his fate like a palm reader. "It's my parlour trick," she said, and Anirudh's palm caved to the gentle touch of her fingertip. She saw their futures winding together in the braided folds of his palm, in the rivers of ink joining in *sangammam.* She, the cartographer of his heart. She, the confluence of his fractured life.

Madras, 1978

Anirudh and Kala met on the side of a busy road. A flurry of saree skirts escaped from the metal bus door as girls disembarked. Their red *pottus* and black kajal ran with the sweat of the cloudy morning's blunt heat. The girls going to Bharatanatyam class wore twin plaits oiled into loops like rivers snaking into themselves. You heard their chatter first, their playful words and laughter jingling like the lively sibilance of anklets adorned with bells. Their eyes darted at each other like fish in a pond before resting on an unshaven, black-haired shopkeeper on the roadside in his blue metal shack. Anirudh was leaning on his glass counter of fountain pens and pyramids of ink bottles, studying the newspaper slightly blowing from a mechanical fan's breeze. Kala's eyes flitted away like they always did, doting on her hands and distant windows. They were always wide though, trained in the expressiveness of classical dance. For all her shyness, Kala betrayed her heart in the weighty dips of her eyelids, the tilt of her chin both resolute and delicate. Anirudh always stopped reading *The Times* when he arrived at the matrimonial ads: *Seeking fair Brahmin girl, tall, well-educated, artistically accomplished in Carnatic music or Bharatanatyam is preferred.* When he looked up from his paper, he caught Kala looking at him. Such beautiful eyes, Anirudh thought, held the compounded glow of every full moon in a cloudless sky since the dawn of time. When her eyes finally met his own dulled droops that morning, her love shone like a one-sided moonbeam.

After class, the denouement of the sun. Cool air brushed past Kala's skin, perspiring sweat, as she bounded down the darkened stairwell. She danced to the rhythm of the stairsteps, down and down and down. Each step was a suspension in air where she felt levity, pulled from the strings of her fate. She could taste love's exaltation as she swam from shadow to the dusk outside, sweetly leaking like ink into the clouds. Pleasure pulled her to the road, to the man behind the counter of pens. Kala was a pure movement towards Anirudh, a breaking wave on a beach at the tide's peak. She found Anirudh, an unmoving shadow under the corrugated metal shop ceiling. He looked up imperceptibly and Kala against the bleeding dusk filled his vision. The sun's last gasp was a pale, sheer veil of gold refracted in the film of drying sweat on Kala's skin. They murmured to each other in the exhausted tones that only the exertion of lovemaking could produce as the sun fell asleep.

From then on, they ate together in the dance school's sun-baked courtyard under a large, squat tree with branches that leaned down to the brown earth. Each week Anirudh would hand Kala letters penned in cursive with one of his fancy pens and eat the tiffin she'd bring him with the trust of a monk accepting alms from a perfect stranger. He felt *he* was the stranger, standing at a door which opened to a foreign world of homely comforts. She was a warm hearth which invited him inside. He accepted her generosity with trepidation, having lost his mother just three months ago. After eating they'd wash the pearls of rice sticking to fingers under the same tap, and the streams from their hands ran into the same drain that collected the rivulets in a dark pool.

Ship, 1980

Chords of light sang from a chink of sun in the matted grey sky, like golden sails unfolding heavily over the sea. It reminded Anirudh of walking three times around the bright firepit, the last of his wedding rites. The thick grey smoke had kept pluming from the hurtful heat of the orange fire, making him choke. After circling it, Anirudh faced Kala. She tied upon him a garland of flowers which bore on his neck like millstones. Knowing then that he would leave for the ship in a week, he felt like a condemned man sent to slaughter. He heard the priest's knell-like chanting again, turning over this memory with such rigour and guilt that all its fondness was eroded. In the ship's cabin surrounded by lapping water, he felt all his desires dissolve. Kala in Madras would always anchor him.

Ever since boarding the ship, he felt the peaceful abstinence of a desireless fasting artist overcome him. In their flat, in their wood-framed marital bed, he felt like a drowned man whose own heart had been the weight to sink him. However, in the ship's cabin, Anirudh felt the water's undulations as he slept instead of the rise and fall of Kala's chest. To her warmth, which he struggled to remember, he preferred the eternal flame of the coal engine, stoked into a pool of churning orange. Under the ship deck, amongst the machinery of physics and mathematics, he no longer felt this tug to the Earth's grave. He could keep the burning coals, held firm by steeled walls, alive forever, singeing him like a thousand suns. He came to prefer the windowless engine room to the cabins above with portholes. Beyond the portholes Anirudh saw sunlight play on the ocean's dimpled surface and die every evening. He hated to meet his muddied reflection in the porthole looking out at a black night. Kala was the dying sunlight – Anirudh feared he severed whatever held them together, cutting through the seas in paths that dispersed into foam as soon as they were forged. His heart shrivelled to a hardened point when he thought about leaving Kala. He'd left her a hundred times this way, anticipating a lifetime of leaving her. The sights his voyages bestowed on him were faint shadows of the life he'd set sail from, darkening his vision. The tide of Anirudh's life swept him away from Kala, but his mind was still bound in Madras' shallows, in misery. Anirudh never wrote back to Kala. He pictured her grasping the black grate of the windows with bangled arms, watching bicycles and fruit sellers go by, her eyes fixed to a resigned point, blinking, blinking out the minutes.

Madras, 1981

Kala greeted Anirudh with a tumbler of coffee. She leaned against the kitchen counter waiting for him to hold her. Anirudh looked into the coffee dregs. She was different on his return, heavier, softer, fragile. Her features were more blunted by the growing flesh heaping around her face. The house was hazy and thick with incense. The *pooja* cabinet of Hindu idols was stocked with metal incense holders, clay lamps, thread wicks and oil, and stacks of matchboxes. The idols were watchful even with the cabinet door shut, peeking through carved windows in the rosewood. Kala sceptically decorated the house with these typical wedding gifts, but her sudden devotion surprised her. If she listened to her prayers, she'd know she was searching for a tether that held her to Anirudh across the world. She led him to the sofa, disturbed that

Anirudh lingered in the doorway, reluctant to make himself comfortable.

"Anirudh, sit. Do you like the divan I picked?"

The softness of the cushions bothered him, they had the same unnerving texture as a pair of bare thighs resting together, but he nodded. Kala was scared to say it, but Anirudh suspected it when he stepped through the door and saw her.

"I'm pregnant."

Her big eyes swooped to the floor in that sorrowful way. Anirudh pulled her close for the first time in six months. The incense smoke was thick. It insinuated itself between the pleats in Kala's saree and lingered in her hair. Anirudh thought it must be fatal to the baby. He thought she had softened to his touch over time with the habit of a bird coming home to its nest. It was like sleeping in the same bed each night, the sheets grew softer but heavy with humid coastal air.

Anirudh found it hard to sleep after making love to Kala. The sheets had a dampness that clung to skin like groping clammy hands. Her nakedness frightened him. The warmth from her flesh seared the air like a burn. She was too soft, Anirudh thought as he veered into sleep. She was like a ripe and swollen fruit, glowing with vitality and the pulp of life but on the cusp of rotting. Ripe fruit reeks of death. One day Anirudh's caresses and kisses would give way to destruction. He tumbled into a nightmare where he'd kiss her and her flesh would fall apart, a gash he made would uncontrollably widen like a red rose blooming. He thrashed around in uneasy guilt, unable to sleep next to the heat of Kala's flesh. Our child would be like Kala, Anirudh thought, veering into sleep. It will be born soft and new and precious like the first light of the day. A light that flutters around the house and dies alone every night, unable to escape the white walls of the small apartment.

Kala put coffee in the filter the next morning, lit a lamp for the gods, and bathed herself. This was the routine she had cultivated in Anirudh's absence. To herself, she told stories in solitude, among soap and water, about the movements of nature and people, in the language of dance. She gestured to the delicate blossoming of lotus flowers with her hands, and her eyes would talk back, wide and black. Her fingers would splay like petals and wave like ribbons in the running water of the shower. Steam rose like ghosts from these wordless stories. A streak of blood then seeped soundlessly from her sex down her thighs among the splatter of water. It interrupted her story. When she saw it, the miscarriage was already diluted to a pale red. The prophecy that Anirudh dreamed last night had come true.

The days following the miscarriage were hell because Anirudh's face was frozen, unable to crack a smile. Kala felt an impenetrable coldness in his eyes after the event. A winter had descended upon them, the kind that paralyses Arctic oceans with a sluggishness that makes long sinister arcs roll across flat water. She had begun to discover, when he first left all those months ago, the wisdom of living as the world does, in seasons and moontides. To laugh with the birds and cicadas in summer, to ache in blues and greys like the barren trees and waters in winter. There was no other choice now but for her to shiver.

When he first left, in the summer, they had just opened the doors to their new flat in Madras. It was small, with some charm in the windows. The window in the small study looked onto neighbouring rooftops and their gardens, the view boxed in by the painted white frame and the whitewashed houses, a veil of blue sky over treetops. Planes flew by, right to left. In her childhood home in Madurai the planes also went right to left from her father's study. Pressed against that window, she would cast her daydreams and hopes up to the planes, like little hooks on fishing line, sending them far away into imagined landscapes. Sequestered in the capsule of her room, she watched them leave.

San Francisco, 1983

In San Francisco, the planes flew right to left, their noses piercing the sky. Anirudh determined he would study for his ship engineering qualification abroad after accompanying another ship's voyage from the Bay of Bengal to California. Kala knew Steinbeck's Cathy, how she hated California and the twins she carried in her womb. She knew she would not be like Cathy in at least one of those respects, so she agreed to live in San Francisco.

Kala brewed coffee every morning in the brass filter passed down through generations in her family. Before Kala left for California with Anirudh, her great-grandmother handed it to her with palms scored like crumpled paper with its infinite folds. As a child, Kala would run her fingers along her great-grandmother's arms, thinking that the wrinkled brown skin was like the thin furrowing milk layer that formed on undisturbed tumblers of hot coffee. The brass of the sturdy filter was scratched from the coarseness of her household blend of coffee beans and chicory. And yet, those flecks in the brass, her great-grandmother's wrinkles multiplying with age, the deep flavour of the chicory – it all paled in the face of the primordial redwoods.

They walked through the primeval forest of redwoods so often with necks crooked back in awe of the heights the trees scraped. Those giants were deaf to any mortal murmurings below. With roots that deep, their presence thrummed through the natural order of the West Coast. Enveloping them, the forest was like the mouth of a shady cave where the cool air was completely still and dense, a looming presence threatening to consume their little lives. All those human lives that began and ended in little splinters within the tree rings in the cross sections of the redwoods … the heavy breath of the trees and the chorus of all the fleeted lives before them was dizzying. It was easy in Madras underneath the short squat banyans, finding each other's eyes in the shade from the sun. But here, the immensity of the redwoods that shoot into the impenetrable heights of heaven, the shadows falling below like a black veil … *What were we who had strayed in here?* Kala thought.[1] The cold indifference of that unknowable mystery smacked them. She knew nothing held her to Anirudh in the vastness: they couldn't belong to each other. The feeling was palpable – Kala could reach into the emptiness between the trees and feel the thick cords of time and space pulling her and Anirudh in opposing directions.

In the car trundling through the woods, silence weaved a thick mesh between them. From the windows they saw light at the tops of the shorter trees. Moored to the shadow of her seat, Kala looked at Anirudh. With eyes fixed on the snaking road, he drove fast like they were running out of time. Kala felt every acceleration with a lurch in her stomach. It made her sick to be ignored and yet belted in, to be wheeled away like his valise. The car was second-hand, from a dealership that had waxed it impressively new. But Kala could feel a past settled deep in the car seats. She could smell it like the indelible cigarette smoke

---

1 Joseph Conrad, *Heart of Darkness* (Penguin Books 1995), 49.

Anirudh would exhale that would linger in his hair and behind his ears long after. The trees watched from their canopy as Kala dug her brittle nails deeper into the seats as if she were attempting to draw blood from skin. She feared if she didn't leave a scar in this foreign landscape, she'd wisp away like a sunset's brief clouds.

Through little tears in the wall of clouds, the sun shone over the leaden sea of the gulf extending from San Francisco Bay to the Farallon Islands. Past the redwoods, they walked along a sandy path to the cliffs on the sea. Anirudh charged into the glare of sun at the edge of the forest. Kala didn't understand why he never so much as glanced back at her.

"I want to walk with you," she pleaded.

Surprise stretched Anirudh's eyes at the edges. He took her hand firmly. Soon Kala felt it was worse, being dragged along, the skirt of her saree trailing behind. Anirudh still charged ahead, his eyes taking in an uninterrupted swathe of sea. Kala's eyes narrowed instead to the back of Anirudh's neck. She had to focus on his firm black hair to remind herself he was not yet out there on the water. Sweat from her palms made the friction between their hands wane. She felt Anirudh's skin slip from her as if a rip in the current were taking him back into the blue haze. She pulled him around.

"It's too short, Anirudh, to live this life waiting for you."

"I'm here. Apart from when I'm on the ship, I'm always with you."

"When I'm with you, I see you surrounded by the water. You're already gone."

"Kala, I have to do it ..."

"We're in such grief every moment we're together."

"I don't have a life without you, Kala, I don't."

"You do, you do it all without me, because you cannot share the world with me. Your world is too big."

"Everything *is* you, the world *is* you – the music over there, it sounds like you."

Brazil, 1985

Anirudh fled into the night, sheltering in his dark coat. The street was deserted, the sky clear of clouds, and he was warming up by briskly walking along the sides of houses and shops. He was alone and anonymous and trying to forget. Stepping further into the city, he loosened from Kala's orbit, feeling his guilt ebb away. He was leaving, leaving again, this time from San Francisco. The guilt was a force that drove him, with speed, with velocity, away from Kala.

The smell of coffee infiltrating the coastal air arrested him. A shop was grinding fresh coffee for the coming morning. Anirudh walked on, feeling knocked back into mornings of the past that smelled of Kala. The street swooped a little to the right and curved left, down a hill, like the parting in her hair. Lilting strums of a guitar floated down from a terrace above Anirudh. He stopped. Lighting a cigarette, Anirudh realised he was a ship moored to Madras.

He found a bar and was comforted by the sight of the sorely empty chairs outside being stacked away. Under the obliterating artificial white of the streetlamps, Anirudh felt transparent and naked again like he did in the bedroom with Kala. A cool breeze siphoned away the heat from his skin as he took off his coat and sat on a barstool inside. He spoke a few rusty, foreign words to the bartender. If only she knew, he thought, that the ship feels like a shell without her. I'm married to a cold damp sheet below deck. The feel of her skin slips from me the more I try to remember how it felt to hold her. A bare brown arm, lighter than Anirudh's, set down an opened bottle of beer on the bar. Coldness escaped in a grey wisp from the bottle neck. It said to him: you are a hollow glass bottle without a message, floating back to Kala. I am always in her current, Anirudh thought, washing back the taste of his cigarettes.

Madras, 1985

The splintered cane chairs curved low to the ground. The cradle of the chair dipped Kala close to the crumpled leaves beneath her in the garden. Ashoka trees shot up tall like temple spires in front of them. The dark green, waxy leaves rustled as the thin trunks swayed in the sea breeze. The women were looking at the sea through a gap in the trees, watching a corridor of water unfolding to the horizon. All she saw in the blue was Anirudh. To her right, in a chair of identical dark rattan and generous curve, her great-grandmother's small frame curled like a fallen leaf. Her thin hair was in a loose plait, the empty gaps between the white hair resembling her missing teeth. Like a silk saree taken out of a forgotten cupboard, her plait of white hair unfurled in the breeze. The scent of almond oil escaped from the limp strands, mixing with the aroma of fallen tamarind, ripe and sweet. Words fell loose from her great-grandmother's lips like leaves rustling in wind:

"Turn around, I'll oil your hair."

Kala turned away from the sea and her hair undid itself in the breeze. The stiff old fingers started by rubbing Kala's scalp; they didn't heed the pains of arthritis as they performed this familiar duty. Under the moving fingers, something seized at Kala's heart. She started sobbing, she couldn't see the sea anymore, and she knew she had lost him. Around Kala's shaking frame, the old, bangled arms wrapped around, tight and bony. Taking the soft length of her trailing saree, the old woman dried Kala's eyes. The fabric pooled in Kala's lap and collected a few more tears. The ripples of Kala's spine and ribs ebbed then became still when she stopped weeping, and her great-grandmother let go, leaving a faint tracery of gold bangles indented on Kala's waist.

"There was no one to oil your hair in America my darling girl, is that it?"

Doc Martin

Vanessa Yenson

Martin checked his tie in the mirror one more time. It was skinny and uneven and nothing like the Windsor knot his father had tried to teach him all those years ago. He could struggle with the order of the loops in the tie back then, with the threat of the strap around Dad's waist. What did they say – just like riding a bike? Well, he couldn't do that anymore either. Not that he'd been very good at it as a child. He just had less fear then; scrapes and bruises had been his daily uniform.

His eyes fell onto the navy blazer Sissy had laid on the bed. Mum used to do that for him when he went to school, too. She would place socks by his shoes, which had been Velcro so he didn't have to tie the bunny ears or chase the darn thing around the tree. Sissy never had trouble with shoelaces; he always heard her stomping around in her Doc Martens. He always wanted a pair, so he could be Martin in Doc Martens. Sissy had bought her own with the money she earned from her after-school job. Martin had spent hours sitting with tutors instead.

He ran his fingers along the lapel of the blazer. At least it wasn't grey, like his school uniform. This one had a pleasing sheen, without it being overly fancy. "Just enough for personality," is what Mum would have said. He couldn't remember buying the suit, but he remembered wearing it at

Sissy's first wedding. She had insisted that Martin be one of the groomsmen. Her fiancé Jock was a family friend, and so Martin was reluctantly added as number five. It had been a showy occasion, complete with doves and a horse-drawn carriage – after all, how many times does one get married? As it turned out, Sissy remarried two more times, and Martin never got to stand at the altar waiting for his bride to walk down the aisle. Sometimes life just dealt its cards unevenly. He had enjoyed that first wedding, when the bubbles in the champagne fizzed up his nose and made him giggle.

He swung his arms into the blazer and caught a glimpse of himself in the mirror. His head was full of thoughts of weddings and funerals, new life and endings, but in the brief moment before he recognised himself, he saw what everyone else saw: a vacant stare, slack mouth and slow, deliberate movements. And he hated his face and body for betraying him, for not reflecting how deeply he thought about things. He cared and felt the highs and lows more strongly than most, but he was always a step behind, laughing at a joke a tad too late, or being the joke and having to grin as if it didn't hurt.

Sissy understood. At least, she had cared when they were kids. She would stand up to the bullies in school, defending him from Dad who wanted to belt him for forgetting to take out the garbage and confiding in Mum about the playground squabbles. She had been his ally all the way up to high school, until boyfriends and friendship groups became more important. Martin didn't mind. She set a standard that most bullies didn't cross and Dad took him to Taekwondo long enough so he could fend for himself. He never progressed beyond blue tip, but his strength was enough to ward off most. The times when things did get out of hand, the other guy came out just as black and blue as Martin, so the teachers let things slide.

At her second wedding, Martin saw the shiner before the makeup artist arrived. Sissy had shushed him and told him Alistair hadn't meant it, that he was sorry and that it was nothing that a bit of foundation couldn't cover. Martin wasn't a groomsman that time, and Sissy apologised with phrases he had to look up afterwards: "minimalist aesthetic" and "financial responsibility". The wedding had still been over the top, but with fewer friends and a simpler wedding dress. Martin didn't drink the champagne that time. Instead, his attention was on Alistair, noticing that his smooth words didn't match his body language. Martin hovered around his parents after the ceremony, unsure how to tell them about Sissy's black eye. They had smiled and patted him on the hand, assuming he was emotional at Sissy's happiness. Sissy's grin had fooled everyone that day, everyone but Martin.

In front of the mirror, Martin stood a little taller, taking in his appearance for the first time in a long while. He didn't like looking at himself very much. With his receding hairline and glasses, he now looked more like Dad, but without the lines around a downturned mouth and the frown lines between his eyebrows. When he leaned in closer, he saw Mum's gentleness in his own eyes, and this pleased him. Unlike Martin, she had always been busy, with things on her mind, but he was proud to resemble her in any little way possible. He sucked in his stomach, remembering being Jock's groomsman at Sissy's first wedding nine years earlier, but when he breathed normally, he realised the suit still fit just fine; it had been a little too big all those years ago.

Jock would be there today. Martin hadn't seen him since the last funerals, when he still wanted to punch the living daylights out of him. When they split, Martin hadn't known what "having an affair" meant but it made Sissy upset, so that made him mad. Mum made both Dad and Martin wait in the shed when he came by, pleading for Sissy to take him back. In his mind, he could still hear the shouting and the begging. Sissy replied in tones so low that Martin couldn't hear what she said, but Jock left in tears. Dad punched a hole in the shed wall. Martin stood in the corner, rocking on his heels until the noise died down.

Sissy said that Jock's new wife would be there, and maybe their baby, and that Martin should not get upset. Bygones were bygones and there was a lot of water under the bridge. Martin felt his fingers twitch at the thought of seeing Jock again, remembering of the sound of Dad's fist bursting the wood panelling of the shed.

But Martin did like babies. He liked their simplicity – their emotions were easy to read – if they were happy, they smiled or laughed, if they were upset or hungry, they cried. And babies liked Martin, too. Mum and Sissy said he was a baby whisperer; he could soothe baby Jasper when Sissy had been at her wits end. When she stayed over while Alistair was away for business, they were all happy: Sissy got to sleep, Mum got to fuss and Martin got to hold Jasper. He loved marvelling at his tiny fingers and toes, staring into his big, dark blue eyes and speaking to him gently until he broke out into a gummy, dribbly smile. Dad spent most of the time in the shed, so Martin guessed he was happy, too.

Martin sat on the side of his bed, looking at the socks in his hands. Gone were his white sports socks from school; he couldn't help but chuckle because these socks matched his tie, and a six-year-old Jasper would approve. He slid them on and wriggled his toes, imagining his nephew giggling at them.

Mum would have smiled, had she been here; Dad would have frowned, but he wouldn't have said anything to keep the peace.

"Almost ready there, big fella?" Mo popped his head around the door, his deep brown eyes assessing Martin's preparation. "Do you need help with those?" He pointed to Martin's new shoes, still uncreased and smelling of leather.

"No, I should be okay," Martin said. "I learned how to tie them with Jasper."

Mohammed nodded, blinking rapidly. Martin could see an emotion flicker across Mo's face that made him worried he'd said the wrong thing, but then Mo coughed and gave him a weak smile. "Okay, well, we'll be ready to go in about five minutes. Give us a yell if you need help with anything."

Martin liked Mohammed. He liked the way he let Martin figure things out for himself. He understood that Martin just needed a bit more time, like an older model of computer that ran on an outdated operating system. He would get it eventually, and he would understand it more deeply than most expected. But Mo got him. Not for the first time, Martin was really, really glad that Sissy had married Mo.

None of them attended Sissy's third wedding. Although Martin was upset when she turned up with a new ring and a new surname, their parents had been furious. It hadn't helped that they were still angry that she'd left Alistair and their waterfront mansion but, over time, Sissy revealed the truth behind her seemingly perfect second marriage. Mum had sighed and clutched Sissy's hand when she saw the pictures of the bruises. Martin had learned what A.V.O. stood for and Dad had driven off, screeching tyres and burning rubber, only to return with shredded knuckles. Martin still wasn't sure who or what he had punched but he was aware that, even though it had been mended, the damage in the shed's wall was still visible.

Sissy's third wedding had been a civil service at the Town Hall on an ordinary Tuesday, with her best friend from high school and Mo's brother as witnesses. She wore an elegant green silk dress with her hair in soft waves around her face. In the photos, Martin thought she looked like an angel. Mo looked sharp in his black suit and matching green tie and Jasper was grinning in his new school uniform. He'd been extra excited at missing an afternoon of school.

As Martin slipped his feet into his new shoes, he thought of his parents' reaction to meeting Mo for the first time. They had stumbled over his name until he insisted they call him Mo. Both Alistair and Mo were charming, but Mo was sincere; it always felt as though Alistair was acting, as if he was playing dress ups for an invisible audience. It didn't take too long for Mum, Dad and Martin to understand why Sissy felt safe with Mo. He took genuine interest in each of them, taking extra care to ensure Jasper was loved and nurtured. And for that Martin loved him even more.

Martin could almost hear his nephew's sing-song voice reciting the instructions on how to tie your laces. Jasper mastered it on one of his last access visits with his dad and had been extra patient teaching Martin when he returned. Thinking of this lesson, Martin tugged at the laces, feeling the satisfying tension before passing the right lace over the left and pulling them again. How had he not got this as a child? It seemed so simple now.

Martin's vision started to blur and a teardrop fell onto his new Doc Marten. He brushed it off, afraid it would leave a mark and stared at his trembling hands, which seemed to shake more violently when he tried to steady them. He wasn't sure how long he crouched there, his body quivering and his face screwed up, mouthing silent screams. He could see stars behind his eyelids, as if the universe had stolen him from space and time, and he existed beyond the pain and the loss that sat as a big, empty hole within himself.

There was a hand on his shoulder, a calm, reassuring pressure. Sissy knelt in front him, as best she could with her swollen belly, and gently took the laces, tying them into double bows.

"Help me up, Marty." She held out her hand for support and he could tell she had been crying, too. "Let me look at you."

She brushed fictional dust from his shoulders and straightened his tie. They stared at each other in the mirror like they used to do as children, only this time the dress-up was for real. She looked terribly thin in black – even with the new baby in her belly – her collarbones stuck out and her cheeks were hollow.

"Mum and Dad would be very proud of you." Sissy's voice was almost a whisper. Martin knew their tears weren't for their parents, even though it had been almost two years since the accident and he still cried for them often.

These were new tears for a new loss.

"But do you think Jasper would have liked the tie? And the socks?" He lifted his pant leg so the cartoon blue heeler was visible in her childish joy.

"I think Jasper would say you're the best dressed person there."

White Will Drink the Wine

Shania Daphne Andrea OBrien

You wore your white shirt open wide, the sleeves a little rolled
Your hair damp from heat and light, your skin all flushed with gold.
You looked like something summer made – too lovely to be near –
And still I held the fruit too long, and let it draw you here.

The raspberries were split with heat, too fragile to embrace,
Its juice ran down my fingers as I reached to hold your face.
I meant to tease, to brush your hand, to offer something small –
Instead I stained your shoulder where the berry chose to fall.

It bloomed across the cotton like a secret I confessed –
A blush that said *I want too much*, and hid inside your chest.
You didn't pull away from me, or speak, or shift your line –
But love will spill, and hands will shake, and white will drink the wine.

I tried to speak, to lift the mark, to offer some retreat,
But still you stood with steady breath and kindness in your heat.
You let the berry darken there, a bloom you never pressed –
A mark that meant *You touched me*, and you wore it like a crest.

I think of that small moment now – how sweet the silence was,
How something ripe and ruinous became the thing we trust.
And even now, each breath of June recalls your shirt, your sign –
The red I left, the light you kept, the stain that made you mine.

Waiting for the Fall

Arani Ahmed

I step down onto the stones
        counting one   two
the stream runs over my feet   cool
                the water isn't deep here
                        I can see the red bed underneath

Sending the text is easy. Ask her out, but don't say so fully. Plausible deniability. You had planned to hang out anyway. And besides, the friendship is more important.

I've hiked an hour to be here
        I'm lucky to be alone
        sandstone rises up around me   the sky a
    circle above
        I can't hear the birds over the fall

She opens the door wide smiles. She's clearly just showered, wearing a nice shirt. Maybe it is a date? You've cooked and brought food over. It's delicious and you know you've impressed. You both can't stop chatting, stay up too late. After six hours, smoking on the balcony, you work up the courage to tell her you like her.

the waterfall is four meters high   thin
cascade
    the water rushes into the pool
I step tentatively   toes adjust to the cold
                          then my ankles
        my shins
I stop just below my knees   touch the surface with my
                    fingers

She laughs, and says she knows, this is obviously a date. You laugh, feel the embarrassment tighten your chest, why didn't anyone tell you. She says she's not straightforward like that. Right now,   you think that's cute.

it's hotter than I expected   and the walk longer
        my clothes itch   the need to be free of me
                                          my skin anticipates
silk

Should we do a tarot reading? She asks. This is officially the gayest date you've ever been on. The reading – about the two of you – shows says creativity, friendship, sensuality. Or was that fire? Sitting, knees touching, you agree that this is a good sign.

somewhere behind me   voices along the path
overhead   tufts of clouds are moving too fast
              too soon out of sight

She says she wants to take things slowly. In the same breath she asks you to stay. A discordant note of anxiety wavers in your throat. You've smoked too much.

All the lessons you've forgotten knock at your chest.

I wade further in rocks beneath my feet
calves numb forehead dotted with sweat
waiting for the plunge
waiting for the
shore
willing the body to move

Where To?

Joseph Parker Lucas

10:55 PM
225 Illawarra Rd,
Marrickville, NSW 2204, AU
↓
11:13 PM
133/1 Oxford St,
Darlinghurst, NSW 2010, AU

Victoria met him first, and now he's in the car with us. They met at the gym. Reformer Pilates, she tells me. He cuts hair for money and writes poetry for fun, and even though we haven't read it, we both assume it wouldn't be good. I wonder if she thinks that now, as she nods approvingly at his opinions. "Dylan," she says to him, "tell Jack what you said about the bars here." I hate that she values her new friend's opinions.

These are the two rules I've learnt from Dylan about going out in Sydney. One, you have to Uber everywhere. Two, it's important you compare it to Melbourne.

I notice the driver follows Cleveland Street to Anzac Parade and the girls' school. It's not the quickest way. "You should've turned left on South Dowling," I say. The driver apologises.

As we approach Taylor Square from the wrong road, Victoria places her hand on my knee. She wants the bag. I procure the tiny plastic sleeve from my shirt pocket and slide it over to her. She buries it in her bra.

These are the two rules I've learnt about going out in Sydney. One, I buy the bag. Two, Victoria tests it first for opioids.

"I'm cool for a bump?" Dylan asks me. It's the first question I've been asked all night.

"Can you transfer for the Uber first?"

11:21 PM
225 Illawarra Rd,
Marrickville, NSW 2204, AU
↓
11:30 PM
35 Erskineville Rd,
Erskineville, NSW 2043, AU

My friend Mikey tells me this story about a girl with a gun. She is nine when her parents take her to a range in Arizona. The father shoots first at a paper man hanging from a pole. He's a good shot. He's burnt a hole in the paper chest. The rangemaster is impressed and pats him on the back like a brother. The mother doesn't want to shoot a gun because she's Australian and doesn't believe in them. But she allows her daughter to hold one because Arizona laws allow it.

The girl can't stop jumping for the gun. She hops up and down and waves for the gun. She hits the Griddy for the gun. So, the rangemaster gives her the gun. But when she holds the gun, she slips and fires it, burning a hole in the rangemaster's chest – just as her daddy did with the paper one. If it weren't so tragic, everyone would've been impressed by her clean first shot.

"What happens next?" I ask Mikey. It's the worst story I've ever heard, but I don't want it to end. Mikey puts his hand on my thigh, close enough to my groin that my dick twitches. He's done it that close on purpose. "I'm not sure," he says, "but I'm seeing her tomorrow. I can ask then."

2:32 PM
225 Illawarra Rd,
Marrickville, NSW 2204, AU
↓
2:45 PM
6 Wilson St,
Newtown, NSW 2042, AU

There is a federal election, so there are corflutes on every street. A doorknocker with a nose ring asks if he can put one on the fence of my federation rental. He says it's got great visibility because I live on Illawarra Road.

"My apartment is in Waterloo. My door faces another door, so no one really sees it."

I think it's a joke, so I laugh.

He says he'll come back and install it if I put my name on his clipboard. It might not be him, he says, it could be another volunteer, but probably him. I think the nose ring is hot, so I say I'll be home on Friday.

I imagine him giving me a blowjob, or I give him one instead. I'll warn him that I might cry afterwards, but I'll make it quiet so as not to scare him off. I'll watch him attach the sign to my fence. I will make a pitcher of margaritas to reward him for his hard work. I'll stand in the doorway and watch him wipe his brow and thread the corflute onto the fence with zip ties.

I want him to give me his number, but that's not how it works. I give him my number and he writes it down in blue Bic. "I'll be in touch," he says.

On Friday, someone texts me they're out front. I am in an Uber and not home, so I don't reply. My driver sighs because two cars have hit each other a little further up the road. We're stuck for a while.

Outside the window, I see the doorknocker sitting at a cafe, eating a bagel with amorous intent. It's a shame. It must've been another volunteer who texted me.

5:37 PM
2 Great Buckingham St,
Redfern, NSW 2016, AU
↓
5:53 PM
671–675 George Street,
Haymarket, NSW 2000, AU

I'd rather go home first to change, but Victoria insists that I get a drink with her and Dylan in the city. I get in the Uber outside my office on Great Buckingham Street. I work on the second floor of a big warehouse block. I don't do much there. On Slack, I gossip with my favourite coworker about the others who sit on either side of me. I make five teas a day and tell my boss that I like her shoes or her new jacket or her earrings. I go crazy for the gold-plated feather ones that weigh down her lobes.

I confirm my name with the driver but don't say anything else. I put my AirPods in. The driver performs a U-turn, but as soon as he turns onto Elizabeth Street, there are cars backed up over three lanes. The ETA says four minutes, but I don't believe it. I text Victoria that I'll be there soon.

11:21 PM
225 Illawarra Rd,
Marrickville, NSW 2204, AU
↓
11:30 PM
35 Erskineville Rd,
Erskineville, NSW 2043, AU

The Imperial in Erskineville is heritage-listed now.

"I'm not even really sure what that means," I say to Mikey.

"It means we'll be here every Friday for the rest of our lives."

His hand is not on my groin but at my throat.

7:35 PM
60 Enmore Rd,
Newtown, NSW 2042, AU
↓
7:42 PM
266 Pitt Street,
Waterloo, NSW 2017, AU

"You're a creative person, aren't you? What sort of thing would you like to make?" Cat asks me in the Uber on the way to a magazine launch. Cat is a friend of Victoria's and has a fringe that covers one eye and nails painted with a chevron pattern. Victoria's ear pricks up; she's interested in my answer.

Drawing, writing, painting, 3D printing, papier mâché, DJing, ceramics, embalming (like painting a dead face). Stained glass, mosaics, graphic design (but only for club posters), producing music (but only for Soundcloud). Baking, frosting, sewing, crocheting. I only tell Cat some of this list.

"What do you do now?"

Victoria smirks. I can see it because I'm sitting diagonally to her in the car. Cat is being earnest, and so am I.

"Marketing."

They both laugh. When Cat points at me and laughs with her one eye and her nails, the chevron points like an arrow back at her. It becomes pointier and pointier. As if it's sharpening itself.

11:21 PM
225 Illawarra Rd,
Marrickville, NSW 2204, AU
↓
11:30 PM
35 Erskineville Rd,
Erskineville, NSW 2043, AU

My friend Mikey tells me this story about a girl with a gun. I tell him I've heard it before.

10:55 PM
77 William St,
Darlinghurst, NSW 2010, AU
↓
11:13 PM
6 Wilson St,
Newtown, NSW 2042, AU

Club 77 is like a dungeon. You walk in by walking down. The DJ spins on raised decks and pushes buttons like they're at a power plant. After a while, the men come in after they've already been elsewhere. Depending on the quality of the men, we decide whether to leave or stay. Someone walks around with a digital film camera. She wears a bikini and cargo shorts. The photos will be on Instagram in the morning. She's already photographed Victoria and Dylan. "What's this song again?" Victoria asks me, and it's always Gasolina by Daddy Yankee. I look down and notice the heel of her red plaid stiletto is in the cave of a man's open, screaming mouth. It's by accident. "Opioids in his ket?" she reasons after she slides the heel out and wipes the end of it with a tissue. We Uber to somewhere else.

8:45 AM
225 Illawarra Rd,
Marrickville, NSW 2204, AU
↓
9:10 AM
2 Great Buckingham St,
Redfern, NSW 2016, AU

The man with the corflute is in the car with me. It's an Uber Pool, so it's purely a coincidence. He's getting off at the University but wants to walk from the Rose on Cleveland Street. He might be an alcoholic. I imagine what we'd do together if we weren't in the car but in my bedroom. My fantasy has changed. He won't give me a blow job. I don't give him one either. He tells me about policies, power plants, housing, price gouging, tax fraud, the good-looking sons of the opposition leader, no eggs, Trump and then tariffs,

Superhuman AI, and Clover Moore. I debate the other side of his argument to make him feel important. We shout at each other because we can't meet in the middle. Afterwards, we shake each other's hand and say things we like about each other for five minutes. He's making me late for work.

8:32 PM
225 Illawarra Rd,
Marrickville, NSW 2204, AU
↓
8:40 PM
188 Church St,
Newtown, NSW 2042, AU

"I don't like you. Or it's more like I don't want to like you. Because I don't want to get hurt by liking you." That's what Mikey says to me. I guess I misinterpreted his hands. I ask the driver to pull over at the cemetery on Church Street. I want to pull out a gun. I want to try what the girl did. But I know I'd never be able to pull the trigger.

"Are you serious? Come on. Let's have fun tonight," this is what Mikey says when I decide to hop out of the Uber. His head is out the window like a dog. I want him to leave me alone.

"I don't like you, you're right. I hate you. I hate you. I hate you. I hate you," he says.

8:45 AM
225 Illawarra Rd,
Marrickville, NSW 2204, AU
↓
9:10 AM

2 Great Buckingham St,
Redfern, NSW 2016, AU

I cut myself while shaving, so I wear a pimple patch. I like pimple patches because people assume it's a pimple and not a mistake.

I tell Victoria I am Ubering to work again. She sends me a selfie of herself at her desk. I take a photo of my pimple patch.

10:15 PM
225 Illawarra Rd,
Marrickville, NSW 2204, AU
↓
10:40 PM
133/1 Oxford St,
Darlinghurst, NSW 2010, AU

Dylan shows up at mine for pres before we head out to meet Victoria at a bar in Surry Hills. She's stuck at work, so for now, it's just the two of us.

I cleaned the house top to bottom for Dylan. I washed and vacuumed. I wiped the tiny hairs from the rim of the bathtub. I told my roommate, who is always sleeping, to sleep in her room and not on the couch. I carried her limp body to her bed. I lit incense and moved furniture until it made sense. I took down art from the walls and painted new ones to replace them. I was still unsure about the colour.

When Dylan arrives, I am three glasses of wine deep. I give him a tour of the new house. I am unusually charismatic and charming with him. I brush his hair and make a fool of myself. He likes my new persona. He's surprised at how much he likes me and, for the first time, feels threatened.

He tells me about a hair cutting convention he attended at the ICC in Darling Harbour. He tells me all the big names were there. Hair celebrities and non-hair celebrities. Marcus McKinnon, Dahlia St George, Bapa, Lucinda LaBuBu, Orion Belt, Holger Hilt. I think he's made these names up. Havana Brown, he says next.

"Havana Brown?" I ask, surprised. "What was she like?"

He sighs happily and breathes into his wine glass. He's won the name game.

Later, in the Uber, I struggle to keep conversation with Dylan. I stare out the window and notice that the city is empty. There are no birds or bats in the open sky. Maybe there's a storm coming. I am already exhausted.

10:55 AM
2 Great Buckingham St,
Redfern, NSW 2016, AU
↓
10:58 AM
261–265 Chalmers St,
Redfern NSW 2016, AU

My boss encourages me to make fairy bread for the office because she's obsessed with it. Or maybe she knows I don't have much to do. I start by spreading butter to the edges of each slice of white bread, before faceplanting them into a bed of hundreds and thousands. I cut each one into triangles. My boss watches me while I do it, because she doesn't have much to do either. Sometimes I want to ask my boss, "What do we do here?" but I've been here for two years, so I should already know. Her earrings are slices of fairy bread today. I hate them, but I tell her that I love them. I work hard to make her a mountain of fairy bread.

When we run out of fairy bread, she forces me to Uber to Woolworths to make more, even though it's walking distance away. She gives me a list: more bread, butter, Nuttlex, hundreds and thousands, and coconut water for the office fridge. She tells me to expense it through Xero. It'll take two weeks for that money to come back. She doesn't know I won't have enough to get home.

11:20 PM
225 Illawarra Rd,
Marrickville, NSW 2204, AU
↓
11:33 PM
133/1 Oxford St,
Darlinghurst, NSW 2010, AU

Going back to university, studying something else, an internship overseas, working at a pub, leaving this city, not leaving this city, moving back in with my parents, freelance work. I tell Victoria I want to do something different with my life, so I can be something different. But I'm not sure what it is yet. I am open with her because Dylan isn't in the car with us.

Victoria looks at me with glassed eyes. I think she's about to cry, but I'm not sure why. She has a good job and enough money to live in an expensive city. There is no reason to cry. "To be honest," she says, "I feel sorry for you."

Victoria shakes out a Vyvanse pill from a bottle she keeps tucked in her bra and offers me one. She's refilled her prescription, so she doesn't mind. I take it and dry swallow. The driver looks at me through the rearview mirror. "I'm so drunk right now," Victoria confesses in my ear. And I offer the same confession back. We both laugh.

2:05 AM
225 Illawarra Rd,
Marrickville, NSW 2204, AU
↓
2:11 AM
3 Williams Parade,
Dulwich Hill, NSW 2203, AU

The man with the corflute is at my door, desperate. I am yet to text him back, and the messages won't stop. It is 2 a.m., and he's threatening to bash the door in. My federation rental is old, so I'm afraid the door might collapse. My roommate can't hear him because she is passed out on the couch again.

I walk up to the door and see his silhouette behind the glass. He knows I'm at the door because his silhouette can see mine. He texts me. Ping. Ping. Ping. Ping. Ping. Ping.

"Please, please, please."

"Let me put it up, please."

"Let me in, please."

"I've got everything I need."

"Just your permission."

"Please."

I look at the face of my phone but put it back in my pocket. He presses his face to the doorframe. I can almost feel the weight of him on it. He whispers:

"Would you do it if I gave you a blow job?"

I don't want a blow job from the corflute man. Instead, I order an Uber to get one from Mikey because he is awake and I hate him, but I don't.

In the car, I hear a strange noise coming from underneath. I think it's the man with the corflute gripping onto the undercarriage. He must have the sign in his mouth and the zip ties on his wrists because how else can he be holding on? I focus on his voice:

"Please. Please. Please. Please. Please. Please. Please. Please."

It rhymes with the sound of the indicator turning right at the lights.

I think I see the girl with the gun outside the window. She is walking up Sydenham Road, carrying an enhanced F88 Austeyr rifle. I hope she knows what she's doing with that.

3:45 AM
18 Lilian Fowler Place,
Marrickville, NSW 2204, AU
↓
3:50 AM
225 Illawarra Rd,
Marrickville, NSW 2204, AU

Sometimes people throw parties under a bridge in Marrickville. The police don't check there too often, so it's safe to dance. I used to think these parties began because lockout laws made it impossible to play music anywhere else this late. But that's not true. The bridge has seen parties for decades, long before coward punches ruined them for everyone.

I step over a man who may be dead. There is broken glass everywhere. You can't walk without stepping on glass. Everyone goes too hard under the bridge. The music is only okay. I don't like Hardstyle because it goes too fast, and there are no lyrics to sing along to. I don't know where my friends are.

I notice a girl and a guy fighting near the bridge. She looks scared and he looks scary, so I go to help. The girl is Victoria, and the guy is Dylan.

I imagine pushing Dylan into the dirt and messing up his hair because I know he takes good care of it. I pack broken Hahn Superdry bottles into it as well as twigs and leaves and mud. I bury him in the ground by the bridge and the music that he likes. It's not a bad grave because everybody is happy here.

I push Victoria into the Uber and tell Dylan to "**** *** *** ****** ******". Victoria will sleep next to me tonight.

"What happened?" I ask her in the car.

Victoria tells me that Dylan wanted to have a baby with her because he can't with a man. He doesn't want to foster or adopt because he would like to see what his kids will look like. He was pulling her into a bush by the bridge.

"That's not what happened," I say, and she laughs. I am relieved she is happy enough to tell me jokes.

"I am glad not all my friends are dickheads," she says before kissing me on the cheek.

12:45 PM
6 Wilson St,
Newtown, NSW 2042, AU
↓
1:13 PM
79 Fletcher St,
Tamarama, NSW 2026, AU

Victoria and I are going to a wedding in Tamarama. I'm in a suit and tie, and she's wearing a dress that used to belong to her mother. It's her boss's wedding, and I'm her plus one, playing boyfriend for the day. I think that's why she's holding my hand.

Tamarama is beautiful. Large cliff faces guard the rocks below. The sea is somewhere between pea green and Gatorade blue. I'm excited to see it.

Teenagers used to push gay men off these cliffs. Gilles Mattaini, Raymond Keam, Ross Warren, John Russell and Cyril Olsen. These are real names and not made-up ones. I am happy to celebrate the lives of people I don't know today and feel happy that I am still here. I am happy to look at the sky, the ocean, the beach. I am happy to look at my friend, who looks the most beautiful I've ever seen her.

In the car, she passes me a stick of gum.

"I'm ok for now," I say, and I've never said anything more true. I'm ok for now.

What the Lace Remembers

Ananya Thirumalai

Every night, after Alex has drifted into sleep with one hand on the cat's back – rising and falling like a lullaby I never learned to sing – and the other stretched across the bed like she's reaching for something she dreamed of before me, I light a stick of incense. She twitches once, exhales like the air's been holding her all along, and settles. I wait for that. For the room to go still. For the light to leave the walls. Then I strike the match.

Not for God. Not anymore. The gods I was taught to fear don't belong here – among rent receipts, wilting basil, takeout containers rinsed and stacked beside the sink. I don't light the incense for them. I light it for memory. For her. For you.

There are seven kinds, lined up in a cracked ceramic bowl on the windowsill. The bowl used to hold turmeric, and its inside is still stained with gold that won't wash out, no matter how long I soak it. The incense came from Harris Park, tucked behind the cash register at a Tamil grocer where the air smelled like split dal, milk powder, and something old – something that clung to the corners of the room like breath held too long. The boxes were sun-bleached and soft at the edges, like they'd been waiting to be remembered: sandalwood, rose, jasmine, camphor, vetiver, patchouli and Temple Dew – a name that sounds like devotion after it's passed through too many mouths.

Tonight, it's sandalwood. You always loved sandalwood. It made the prayers stick to your skin, didn't it? That sharp, sweet warmth that clung to your wrists long after the lamps had gone out. That smell that turned your body into offering.

The flame catches on the first try. It always does. The smoke doesn't rise – it unfurls, slow and deliberate, like silk being shaken loose. Like the way you used to walk across the verandah, ankles careful, steps barely there. I sit cross-legged at the foot of my bed, facing the mirror that's still draped in your veil. Ivory lace. Gold thread like veins. It smells faintly of dried jasmine, of old copper coins rubbed smooth between fingers, of mothballs and something I don't have a name for. When it moves – and it does, even with the windows shut – I swear I see your breath on the other side.

You wore this veil once, didn't you? Maybe not at a wedding. Maybe not at all. Maybe you only ever held it up to the light and wondered if it would suit you. Still, I can feel it in the threads – the weight of ritual, of sweat, of a thousand whispered names passed down and buried. You used to fold yourself into your mother's shadow like it was a skill, a trick you'd mastered. You knew how to braid silence with obedience. How to cry so quietly it didn't interrupt the afternoon.

I remember the room in Madras. Or – I think I do. The sunlight pooling like ghee on the stone floor, thick and slow. My – your – bare feet moving without sound. A bowl of kumkum with its edges crusted dry. A string of jasmine, its petals already browning. The click of bangles. The air thick with something sacred and heavy. Somewhere, someone was chanting. The lamps were already lit, flames held upright. A silver bowl. A girl kneeling. A woman's voice I've never heard again. I don't know if the memory is mine. But I miss it. I miss it like it once held my name in its mouth.

The mirror doesn't reflect me anymore, not properly – as if even it is unsure who I am, edges blurring like steam, like a dream, like water just before it breaks. Sometimes I think it's trying to remember me. Sometimes I think it's trying to remember you. Sometimes I wonder if it ever really knew the difference. I don't know who left first – me, or you.

There's a kind of homesickness that only shows up around you. It isn't for a place, or a childhood, or even for a language. It's for a version of myself who still knew how to kneel without shame. Who spoke her grandmother's prayers without having to explain them. Who never had to explain her own name, or correct it, or soften it. You, who stayed. You, who never touched another woman's hand. You, who are made entirely of the things I was too afraid to keep.

Things I said aloud to no one:
"I'm still here."
"Do you remember this?"
"I didn't mean to leave."
"I didn't mean to stay."
"Do you forgive me?"
"Do I?"
"I'm not sure who this body belongs to anymore."
"It's easier to burn things than to bury them."
"I think she loves me."
"I think I do too."
"I think I want to stay."

I reach for the letter I started days ago. The ink has smudged along the fold, bled into the paper like it was trying to escape the shape of the words. It still smells faintly of rosewater and ash. My hand shakes a little when I pick up the pen again.

But even as I write to you, I'm thinking of Alex.

Of the way she falls asleep with her mouth slightly open, her hair a mess against the pillow, her fingertips always brushing toward me, like some part of her still reaches even in sleep. Of the way she says my name when I leave the room for too long. Of how I flinch when she touches my wrist and it feels too close to ritual – too much like being chosen, too much like being seen.

We live a quiet life. The kind I used to think only other people were allowed. We argue about groceries, forget to do the laundry. Her shoes are always in the way. I find her notes in the fridge: "Last KitKat is yours, don't fight me." She makes tea for me even though she drinks coffee. She buys jasmine tea because I told her it reminded me of my grandmother. She doesn't know that sometimes I stare at the mug and can't bring myself to drink it.

I love her. That's the problem. It's not the sharp kind of love – the burning, teeth-baring kind I was warned about. It's soft. Undemanding. It asks nothing of me except that I let it exist. And I can't. Not fully. Every time she kisses me, I want to fold myself in half, like I'm taking up too much space. Every time she holds my face and says I'm good, I want to ask who told her that lie. When she says she's lucky to have me, I think of you. Of the girl I was supposed to be. The girl who stayed. Who never touched another woman's hand. Who was never asked to explain anything – because there was nothing to explain.

And then I remember the silence I gave up. The language I left behind. The prayers I dropped like coins on a temple floor and never picked back up. And I wonder if this is what guilt becomes when it has nowhere else to go. If this is what love does to me, who always believed it had to be earned in pain, then maybe that's why I can't stop waiting for it to hurt.

Maybe that's why it started. The slipping. The smoke. The veil. I keep telling myself I'm being haunted. But maybe I called it. Maybe I wanted a version of myself that could suffer for this – so I wouldn't have to admit I wanted it. Maybe I needed to prove I was still worthy of being punished.

I love her. I do.

But there's a part of me that only knows how to grieve that love. And I think she can smell it on me. Even when I light the incense. Even when I smile.

I press the nib to the page and begin, again.

To the girl I might have been,
I hope you still light the lamps at dusk.
I hope the smoke remembers me,

I've started writing to you the way I used to pray; quietly, cautiously, never fully convinced someone was listening.

You live inside the veil now, don't you? In the folds of lace that remember what I left behind, in the mirror's softened edges where I blur into you. You live where the sandalwood curls upward and smoke doesn't vanish. Sometimes, I imagine you're just slightly behind my reflection – to the left, waiting to be remembered. I wonder if you're happy.

Are your sarees starched and folded in neat stacks? Do you wear that one gold chain every day, the one your mother gave you after the first time she caught you crying and didn't ask why? Do you walk through temple courtyards with your head bowed and your breath held? Do you sleep beside a man you do not hate, settling for absence where desire should have been?

I think you do. I think you've made peace with the smallness of your world. And part of me – the part I never speak to aloud – envies you for it. Because you never had to explain yourself. Because no one ever asked you *why* you wore bangles or stopped. Because you didn't have to translate desire into safety, disguising it so no one would see it was for a woman. Because you never risked loving a girl who would call you brave just for existing.

And yet, I ache for you. I ache for the way you must press yourself flat against your mother tongue so it won't betray you. For the way you fold your softness inward. For the way your silence must smell like turmeric and apology.

I wonder – did it hurt less to fold your shame into your *pattu pavadai* than it does to wear mine out loud?

I write to you not to change you. Not to offer you escape. I write to remember you – so that your silence will not vanish, so that your girlhood is not wasted on obedience. I write because I carry you inside me like a prayer half-said and half-swallowed.

Maybe you dream of me too. Maybe in your sleep, you see a girl in a black skirt and smudged eyeliner, arms bare and ankles unbound, kissing another woman in the glow of a phone screen. Maybe you wake with the scent of incense and fear in your mouth.

I'm sorry. I didn't mean to haunt you. But I think we are both hauntings now – of each other.

Always,

The girl you almost were

I fold the letter with care, smoothing the creases like I'm tucking in something fragile – something that might wake if disturbed. The wax seal waits beside me, warm in my palm. Alex brought it home from a market stall, laughing when she handed it over. It's shaped like a rose, a little ridiculous, the kind of thing meant for fairy tales and fancy stationery. "For your witchy little letters," she said. I rolled my eyes but kept it anyway. It felt like love, the way she gave it to me.

I light the candle and let the wax melt, drip by slowly onto the paper. Then I press the seal into it, gently – too gently, maybe, like I'm afraid of marking it. The wax curls at the edges, a red bloom around the rose. It looks like a wound healing backwards. I let it cool. Then, without ceremony, I slide the letter beneath the veil. The mirror stares back – draped and silent – its surface dimmed by lace and time. It doesn't reflect me. It doesn't reflect anything clearly anymore. Just shimmer and shape, a suggestion of presence. Like it's trying to choose whose face it should remember tonight.

Later, when I fall asleep, the dreams come quickly, as if they've been waiting just past the threshold of consciousness. I dream of jasmines and monsoon. The air is thick with petrichor and prayer. A courtyard, slick with rain. Stones still warm from the afternoon heat. Anklets hit stone, chiming like a warning or a welcome. A slow turn of a head. You.

And for a moment – just a moment, so brief it could be imagined – I think you're dreaming of me too. Like we've met each other halfway, in the place where longing and memory brush against each other and forget which one they are.

Words I forgot and what they became:
amma – ache.

pavadai – shame stitched into silk.
veeram – a kind of bravery I never wore.
kanna – the sound of someone still believing I'm soft.
mangalsutra – the gold I never wanted.
madras – a place in my chest, not on a map.
sandalwood – breath lingers.
you – the shadows I still carry.

It started slowly. As most hauntings do. Intimate. Lingering in a way that felt like smoke in the lungs, impossible to hold and impossible to release.

One morning I brushed my teeth and gagged on the taste of ghee. Thick, greasy, clinging to the back of my throat like a swallowed secret. I hadn't eaten any. There was no ghee in the house. But my tongue remembered it – that cloying, heavy sweetness that sits in your molars like a blessing left too long in the mouth, heavy and unyielding, filling every corner of the tongue until there's no room to breathe. I spat into the sink until my gums bled.

Later, Alex stirred beside me in sleep. Her breath warm against my neck. She turned, barely conscious, and whispered, "Mom." Her voice was soft. Small. Not hers. Like it belonged to a child I hadn't met. I froze. My chest didn't rise. I didn't know what to say, so I said the only thing that came to mind: "I'm here." I didn't know who I meant it to.

After that, the veil stopped behaving. It no longer just fluttered when the windows were open. It moved even when everything else was still. It slid off the mirror one night without a sound and draped itself upon my desk chair like it was waiting to be noticed. I found it on the floor the next morning, damp and cold, oil blooming across the lace like sweat through cotton. My fingertips came away sticky. The whole room smelled like burnt camphor and something faintly metallic. It lingered for days. I scrubbed the walls. I still couldn't breathe right.

I asked Alex if she could smell it *too*. She hesitated – too long. Then she nodded, slowly. "Like . . . ruins," she said. "Like something ancient. Something watching." She didn't look at me when she said it. I didn't ask her again.

The dreams came back, sharper this time. No longer fragments. No longer quick flickers of scent and light. They returned with weight and shape, like memory masquerading as sleep.

I stood barefoot in the Madras house – not as a ghost, not as a visitor, but as a daughter returning to the place her family had built to hold her. The threshold didn't resist me. The wind wrapped itself around my waist like an embrace, as if it had been waiting for me to return. The lamps burned steady, already lit. And you were there.

You looked like me, but smaller. Lighter. Your body took up less space – as if it had learned not to be a burden. You held your shoulders like you expected to be struck. Your eyes had never learned defiance. You wore gold bangles, a thread of vermilion at your hairline, and a silence so polished it shone with emptiness, dazzling enough to hide everything buried beneath. You stared at me like I had split something sacred in half. Like I was the after.

I opened my mouth to speak. You shook your head, almost gently. But later, when I knelt by the brass lamp stand – my thighs burning, my palms pressed together in a shape I hadn't made in years – I whispered words I didn't understand. I felt them more than I heard them, pulled from somewhere old and half-forgotten. That's when I felt your breath behind me. Not your voice – just warmth curling down my spine.

"I heard your prayers once," you said. "You said them wrong. But I still listened."

I woke drenched in sweat. My mouth tasted like turmeric – raw and bitter, dry as powder. My wrists ached. When I looked down, I saw faint red marks circling the skin. Thin. Even. Like bangles had been there and disappeared.

Mirror says:
Your hands are older than they should be.
Your mouth remembers prayers your tongue won't say.
You sleep like you're bracing for an apology.
You carry another girl's shadow in your chest.
You kiss like you're afraid of being forgiven.
You light incense like you want it to hurt.
You look, and look, and look –
and still ask whose face it is.

Alex found me the next morning sitting by the window. The veil was crumpled in my lap, heavy with damp. The fabric sagged, yellow-stained, like something left too long in water. I must've been sitting there for hours. I didn't remember getting out of bed.

"This isn't healthy," she said. She knelt beside me, voice tight. Her hands hovered before they landed – on my knee, not quite steady. "You haven't been here lately. You sleep with your eyes open. You forget what day it is. You …" She swallowed. "You smell like someone else."

I didn't argue. What could I have said? That I was grieving a life I never lived? That I was waking into dreams I didn't know how to leave? That you were still inside me, dragging sandalwood through my lungs, threading my thoughts into knots shaped like temple bells?

I reached for her hand. She didn't pull away. But she didn't hold on either.

How to forget yourself without dying:

Breathe through the wrong name until it doesn't burn.

Learn silence the way your grandmother learned English – slowly, with shame.

Do not flinch when she kisses your wrist. Pretend it's holy.

Light the incense even when it makes your throat ache. Especially then.

Drink the tea. Swallow the memory.

Fold the veil, again and again, until the fabric forgets your scent.

Practise disappearing gently.

Let the girl in the mirror speak.

Don't answer.

After that, I no longer sought mirrors.

It wasn't a decision, exactly. I'd brush my teeth with the light off. Change clothes in the hallway. Let steam cover the bathroom glass and never wipe it away. The mirror had stopped showing me just my face – it showed every version of me that didn't make it. Every girl I might have been if I hadn't wanted another girl's hand in mine.

Alex noticed. Of course she did. She started speaking more softly, stepping more carefully around me, like I was something fragile or haunted, or both. Like she didn't want to startle whatever was living just beneath my skin.

We still shared the bed. We still ate dinner. But I stopped reaching for her. Not out of anger. Not even fear. Just ...

dislocation – the sense of lying beside her but never quite inside the moment. Every time she touched me, I felt like I was watching it happen from the other side of the glass. I'd nod when she'd speak, but the words didn't stay. I couldn't stop thinking about the girl I used to imagine I'd become – the one who was easier to love because she never asked to be understood.

Alex kissed my shoulder one night and I almost burst into tears. Not because I didn't want it. But because I did. Because it felt like desecration. Like something holy in me was being touched with unwashed hands. And I hated that. I hated that the shame was still inside me, even here, even now.

I started writing things down – scraps of Tamil I barely remembered, lines from bhajans I hadn't heard since childhood, names I didn't recognise. I found one in my coat pocket: *amma*. Written in my handwriting. Ink smears at the corners. I didn't remember writing it.

I thought I could carry both things. This love, and that grief. That if I just kept burning the incense and biting my tongue and being good, it would balance. But it doesn't. The body makes you choose.

And mine was starting to forget which world it belonged to.

On the seventh night of the haunting, I don't plan anything. I just wake up on the floor with the letter in one hand and the veil clutched in the other, everything smelling like sandalwood and sweat. My mouth tastes like metal. My hair sticks to the back of my neck. I don't remember lighting anything, but the air is thick – too warm, too loud, full of movement I can't trace.

There's a bowl of rosewater on the bedside table. I don't know when I poured it. I must've cried into it – my throat is sore, my eyes feel scraped out. The incense sticks are scattered across the bed like dropped matchsticks. Seven of them. I count twice. My hands shake when I touch them, like they're pulsing under the skin.

The veil is still damp. Still curling at the edges, like it's been breathing without me. I don't know how it got from the wardrobe to the floor. I don't remember touching it. But it's there, spreading itself across the tiles, lace glinting under the moonlight like something alive. Like it's about to move again.

Alex isn't home. I told her not to be. I think she knew I wouldn't ask twice. She's been watching me vanish for days.

The letter – somehow, I've written it. The ink has dried in messy lines, turmeric-stained and bleeding through. My name is on the bottom. I don't remember writing it, but it's mine. It feels final.

I sit down. Or maybe I collapse. I can't tell. The room spins slightly, or maybe it's the shadows that are moving. I mumble something – half-prayer, half-apology, all garbled. My voice doesn't sound like mine. Then the incense lights itself.

All of them. At once. I swear I didn't touch them, but they flare to life, a small, hissing chorus. The smoke lifts fast – too fast – like it's trying to get out. It coats the room, sweet and cloying and hot in the lungs. I choke. I cry. I laugh, maybe.

I press the letter into the veil; fold it like I've done it before. Like I'm following instructions I forgot I was given. The fabric clings to my fingers. The turmeric stains everything. My wrists, my knees, the tiles. The air is syrupy, full of jasmine and camphor and something darker underneath. I lean forward without meaning to. My lips brush the bundle. I don't know why. I don't know what I'm saying when the words come out. Something about memory. About not being taken. About staying. Then it burns. Fast.

The veil catches like it is waiting for permission. The smoke thickens, blooms into my mouth, my eyes, my ears. I think I scream. Or whisper. Or breathe for the first time in days. The flames flicker gold, then black, then nothing. And then – just as the last bit curls in on itself – I see her in the mirror. Not ghostly. Not sad. Just there. Real and still and watching, in that room I always half-remember; stone walls, brass lamp, a silence that presses like a palm between the shoulder blades. She nods once. Like we're done. Like she understands.

And just like that, she's gone.

I wake on the floor. Cold. Weightless. Like my body forgot how to hold itself together overnight. My mouth is dry. My limbs don't feel like mine yet. The tiles press hard against my spine, but I don't move.

After that, everything drops away. Not like a curtain falling. Not like a door closing. More like a bone slipping out of its socket – subtle, wrong but irreversible. My hands aren't hands anymore. They're something far away, twitching in a story I can't follow. My name feels unfamiliar in my mouth. Not ugly. Just ... someone else's. Something half-pronounced in a language I don't dream in anymore.

There is no room. No veil. No Alex. No smoke. Only texture – heat, breath, the hum of blood pulling itself along. Something is unravelling. Or maybe I'm being unspooled. It doesn't hurt, but it isn't painless either. I think of the cat. Of its fur rising and falling beneath Alex's palm. I think of a song my mother used to hum when she thought I was asleep. I think of the way you once folded jasmine petals into the pages of your schoolbooks and forgot them there until they turned brown and ghosted the margins.

Everything is layering on top of itself. Madras and the apartment and the temple and the window and the floor. I'm standing and sitting and lying down. I'm a girl and a ghost and a daughter and a shadow. The smoke is everywhere. It's inside me. It *is* me.

I think I start crying. Or maybe I'm just remembering what it felt like to be held. I don't know how long it lasts. There's no time here. Just breath and loss and the space between. The incense is long gone. Just a faint trail of ash smeared across the floor, like someone tried to draw a map and gave up halfway through. The air smells flat now emptied of incense and memory. Hollow, like after a storm when everything's still wet but too quiet.

Unsent messages, 2:43 a.m.
I miss you like a bruise.
Did you ever wish I had stayed?
I think I became someone you'd be ashamed of.
Alex laughed in her sleep tonight. I didn't.
I burned it. I burned everything.
You were never real, were you?
I think I'm ready to live in the body I chose.
Thank you for haunting me.
You can stop now.
I love her.
I love me.
(I'm learning to mean that.)

The veil is gone. Not scorched. Not torn. Not a single thread left behind. Just gone, like it slipped out of this world while I wasn't looking. Like maybe it was never real at all – just a fever dream I clutched too tightly. My hands still remember the shape of it. My skin still smells like jasmine and smoke.

The mirror doesn't shimmer anymore. It doesn't hold any secrets. It's just a mirror. Flat. Ordinary. When I look into it, I don't see her. I barely see myself. Just a girl on the floor with dried tears on her face and turmeric under her nails.

Just a girl, remembering another girl, who never got to choose. And wondering – maybe for the first time – if she does now.

The House of Me:

The front door smells like turmeric and hair oil.
The living room is full of shoes I've outgrown.
There's a window that only opens when she says my name.
The kitchen is messy.
The bedroom has a mirror I no longer flinch at.
The ceiling remembers every name I've ever whispered and never claimed.
The hallway hums in a language I'm relearning.
In the closet: one veil, folded. Dry. Sleeping.
On the floor: jasmine petals, crumbled.
On the bed: a girl who is no longer waiting to be seen.
And everywhere: smoke, not rising – but resting.

It's been weeks. Maybe more. I've stopped counting the days by which incense I've lit. There's no system anymore, no order. I still burn them – but not in a circle, not with purpose. I light them when I'm cooking lentils and the kitchen window fogs up. When I'm scrubbing the bathroom tiles. When the apartment feels too quiet, like it's holding its breath. The smoke still smells like memory – rose, vetiver, sandalwood – but it doesn't open any doorways now. It just lingers for a while, then disappears, like any other scent. Like any other ghost.

The mirror reflects me again. Not perfectly. Not every time. Sometimes I still catch a flicker, a blur at the edges. But mostly, it's just me now. My face, tired and uneven. My hair, always a little messier than I remember it being. Eyeliner smudged by sleep or time or both. But it's mine. My breath caught and then released. My name, spoken without flinching. My body, filled with a self I don't have to explain.

The veil never came back. I don't look for it. Not under the bed. Not in the back of the wardrobe. Not even in the mirror. Some things aren't meant to stay. Some things disappear not with violence, but with grace. With a quiet that feels like exhaling. A kind of peace that arrives so gently you only recognise it in hindsight, when nothing hurts quite as loudly anymore.

Alex comes home with rain on her shoulders and takeout under her arm. The paper bag is damp at the bottom, but she doesn't care. She kisses the side of my neck before she even takes off her shoes – fast, familiar, like a full stop in the ritual of arriving. We eat on the floor, backs against the couch, legs tangled. We argue about musicals. She says "Hairspray". I say "Hamilton". We both hum something out of tune and sing the wrong lyrics on purpose. She makes fun of my voice. I pretend to be offended. It feels like a kind of prayer.

I call my *amma* more often now. Just short ones. Updates. Recipes. The weather. Her voice sounds softer these days, or maybe I've just stopped bracing against it. She tells me about a cousin's wedding. I don't ask whose. I don't mention the dreams. But she calls me *kanna* again, slipping it in like it never left her mouth in the first place. Like maybe I never left at all.

Some nights, I still dream of Madras. The lamps, flickering. The courtyard wet with evening rain. The other girl – you – moving through it like a memory too stubborn to fade. But the dreams don't ache like they used to. They don't take anything. They just arrive. Quietly. You don't pull. You just watch. And sometimes, I lift my hand. Sometimes, you lift yours too.

Inventory of What I Am Now:
A chipped ceramic bowl on the windowsill.
A girlfriend who smells like roses and rain.
The ghost of a prayer I no longer need to finish.
A name I say without apology.
Bangles I wear because I want to, not because I must.
The memory of a veil.
The scent of sandalwood.
The smoke.
The smoke.
The smoke – and the girl who let it rise.

Gia

Yenfay Camp

Do you see me, still, in yesterday's palm,
Dipping leaves in gold, unravelling yarn;
In that vast of tall grass, untamed and unnamed,
Do you see me, still, as I moved without shame?

Singing sparrows since silenced, Summer's seduction spilt sour;
In waiting – I lurch – collapsing decades into hours,
Curved initials, soft bark, threading time against space,
Peeling sepia through gloss, my youth etched in your face.

You once breathed beside me, since before we arrived,
The right to my left, daisy crowned in wild skies;
Come Christmas, arms locked, twirling tulle, sparkling haze,
Was as it should be: weightless laughter, turquoise daze.

I heard about B – sorrow slung across waves,
I heard about your parents – empty hand, Midas' cage.
Meant to write, meant to call, meant to show at your door,
But I cowered, turned the key, synchronised innocence nevermore.

Now I pace, against wind, deforming memories through pride,
Rearranging constellations, hurling rocks at edged tide.
At which point did we sink, seamless flow to severed lines?
At which point did I break, your lifeline loosed, left behind?

Metastasised guilt, phantoms bearing your name,
Too weak to catch courage, too tough to tithe blame.
Staring bleak at the sun, but blind towards you.
My glass menagerie: wasted charms, vapid proof.

Vasbyt, bite the bullet, repattern the sands of time.
Paper dolls, crease refold, torn fingers now entwined;
Lurid lions, birds of prey, demons vulture the Savannah,
Lightless fires, moonless dusk, regret – a birthed hyena.

Part selfless, wholly selfish, Memory calls, rings twice:
Once kind in her diamonds,
Twice teethed to lodge knives;
As that's the trick with Memory, bejewelled or bemoaned;
She carves joy, then devoid, pulls ruins out of home.

Labyrinth thick, spiralled ink, I hesitate to turn
The hourglass – petrified – cracked from bridges long since burned,
Scattered ashes, I rewind, collecting dust for snow-globes;
Wherein we're a team, Nesquik castles, candied pearls.

Peering in, frosted glass, I funnel scenes through before;
Back when hope knew no limits, grief a figment kept to war:

Secrets traded true lilac, golden halo hanging vines,
Rhino rusted soft splodges, teddies' luminous lullabies.
At that, I snap back, dial tone drones unhooked,
As to even wink an eyelash, is to obfuscate our book.

But Gia, just know, come heaven or hell,
You need me – I'll be there, at the chime of a bell.
Though I watch you through pictures, when I once shared your
 dreams;
I remember our promises, carried past the grave to keep.

Despite oceans, through seasons, I'll keep blessing the stars,
Hoping true, that somehow, they'll refract off Mars,
So see me, won't you, preserved pure in yesterday's might;
As I see you, as you were, unfurling bright in tomorrow's light.

Muscle Memory

Ujjwal Nandan

Content Warning: This story contains themes of war, trauma, death, memory loss and psychological distress, which may be distressing to some readers. Please take care while reading.

I. The Horse's Mouth

In Picaso's *Guernica*, there is a horse with its mouth torn open – not in rage, not in fear, but in some paralytic purgatorial place between memory and scream. Its eyes are peeled wide with knowing. Its ribs protrude like church beams. And beneath it, scattered like offerings, are limbs that no longer belong to anyone.

No one in the painting looks at each other. Not the woman clutching her child. Not the lightbulb masquerading as a sun. Not the minotaur, or the broken swords, or the man on fire. It's as if they are all trapped in their own private catastrophes, unable to speak across the distance of grief.

When I was nine, I asked my grandfather what it meant.

He stared at it a long time.

Then said, "Some things don't happen all at once. They happen over and over."

II. Deployment: China

The wind cut through their coats with the cruelty of a deliberate thing.

Snow fell, not like feathers or lace, but like chalk – powdered bone – erasing the world from the top down.

They slept in shifts, their dreams iced over. A man next to him died in the night, face frozen in an expression so peaceful it was offensive.

He never remembered the dead man's name.

But he remembered the silence that came after.

III. Field Note: Vietnam

Humidity is like a punishment.
A silence too loud to trust.
Mud that pulls at the soles like hands trying to drag you under.
He watched a soldier write a love letter with fingers still trembling from a kill.
He watched ants dismantle a frog with more reverence than most men gave to each other.
He stopped writing his own letters.
He stopped looking in mirrors.

IV. Remembering

NOSTALGIA	PTSD
hold it gently, this memory still warm	hold it tight, this memory still sharp

from the sun-lit side of the mind
it smells like rain on hot stone,
feels like your mother's voice
calling you in for dinner.
you remember the tent,
the flashlight lighthouse,
the laughter – echoing.
and when it comes back
you smile,
say "I remember that day."
what a gift,
to carry the past
and still call it home.

from the blood-wet underbelly.
it smells like metal and matches,
feels like your own breath betraying you,
calling you out from cover.
you remember the gunmetal sky,
the flashlight flare,
the screaming – stuck.
and it always comes back,
you flinch,
say "it wasn't a day, it was years."
what a ghost,
to be carried by the past
and still call it … home?

V. The Tent Game

He used to build them with me – palaces made from pillows, blankets clipped with wooden pegs, a flashlight balanced on a shoebox like a lighthouse. He'd use army jargon in a silly voice.

"Private! Reinforce the eastern flank!"

We'd collapse together in a siege of laughter.

The last time I asked, he flinched.
Said, "What tent?"
Then, "Who are you?"

VI. The Napoleonic Symptom

The first soldiers diagnosed with nostalgia were shot.

Swiss physicians in the 1600s believed it was a disease of the blood – a swelling of the brain caused by cowbells and homesickness. Napoleon's men, weeping uncontrollably in strange countries, vomiting, shaking, sobbing for their mothers, were said to be contagious.

They were called weak. Undisciplined. Incurable.

Sometimes I wonder if my grandfather knew that.

Sometimes I think he agreed.

VII. Inventory of What the Body Remembers

(a partial list)

The weight of a child's head resting against the chest
The shape of a rifle even after the war ends
The choreography of grief: pour coffee, forget name, smile anyway
How to crawl without making a sound
Where the door is, even in the dark
The scream you didn't make
The scream someone else did
The scream still echoing

VIII. Sunday Afternoon, However Many Years Later

He asked me who I was.

I said his name.
Then, I said mine.
I said, "You used to call me soldier."

He smiled, but it was not for me – it was for someone long dead or long imagined, someone stitched into the seams of his fading mind. His hand reached out, slow and uncertain, and I took it.

Then he whispered, "Tell my mother I'm coming home."

I could feel my throat close around every unsaid thing – that she had been gone for forty years, that he was already home, that I was not the boy he remembered, nor the war he survived.

But I did not say any of it.
What good would that serve?

Instead, I held his hand a little tighter – anchoring him, or maybe myself – and listened to the soft, stuttering breath of the eucalypti outside the window, as if the trees were trying to remember how to speak.

And I realised, with a kind of reverence that nearly broke me,
that somewhere in his mind,

he was still a son,
still marching,
still twelve years old and terrified,
still carrying his whole life in a satchel too small for grief.

So, I nodded.
And I whispered,
"I'll tell her you're on your way."

IX. The Eucalypti

He planted them after the war – said they reminded him of the hills near Hue.
He said they grew fast. Fast enough to forget where they were planted.

When he died, I buried his uniform beneath one.
Now, when the wind moves through the leaves, it sounds like marching.

X. Muscle Memory

I see it again – the horse, the mouth, the scream trapped inside the paint.
Only now I understand:
it isn't remembering.

It isn't grieving.
It is stuck.

Mid-thought.
Mid-death.
Mid-love.

Just like him.

Just like all of us, maybe.

Because some things don't happen all at once.
They happen over and over.
They are remembered by the body.
Even when the mind is gone.

Squish

Sagar Nair

My mother axed down a baby palm tree and dragged it into the ocean. She said the tree was cursed and must be sacrificed to the water. I poked my fingers into crab holes and pressed conch shells to my ears while she hauled the tree out to sea. The waves slapped at her as though Mother Nature resisted the sacrifice.

A jellyfish stung her, and she screamed and ran to shore, the tentacles coiling around her arm. I peeled off the jellyfish, and before I could say anything, she ran back into the ocean to finish what she started. I felt like a lifeguard. I had an urge to squeeze the jellyfish.

After the ocean swallowed the palm tree, my mother snatched the jellyfish and flung it back into the water. The sting had tattooed earthworms onto her arm, giving her new veins.

"I'm vandalised," she said.

That night, she confessed that drowning the tree was a mistake and the sting was a punishment from God. I believed her.

* * *

I started having nightmares. In one nightmare, a palm tree used its roots to claw out of the earth and chase me. The roots became tentacles and strangled me. In another nightmare, a jellyfish took residence on my head. At first the jellyfish was helpful: it fed me, washed the dishes, buttoned up my clothes, brushed my teeth and flossed until my gums bled. I never had to use my hands. But at the beach, a lifeguard thought the jellyfish was eating me, and he beat my head with a tree branch. Even when the jellyfish was dead, he did not stop beating me. I wrote my dreams in a notebook, and when the pages filled, I wrote on the walls. I had a dream that I drank so much water I became a jellyfish.

One day, I woke to my mother stripping the plaster off my bedroom wall and eating it. She yelled at me for graffitiing the walls with my dreams. "You vandalised my home," she said, and I tried not to stare at the sting marks on her arm, still inflamed. After she chewed the wall plaster, she took a nap. The walls between our rooms were so thin I could hear her turn in her sleep, hear the mattress squish. Hear her breathe.

* * *

The next day we went to the grocery store. We shuffled through the aisles, and I sniffed the wheels of cheese. A man cradled a watermelon like a baby, and he mistook my mother for an employee and asked for a basket. She pointed to a basket display of tomatoes. We walked away.

I pictured the shelves falling on me and crushing my ribs. The ambulance would be called, and I'd have to be resuscitated. I'd need surgery. I kept asking if we could go home but she said no.

She shoplifted a magnifying glass, a pack of gum and a flyswat. The neighbourhood had a fly epidemic, and we sprayed pesticide until our lungs burned, the walls of our house a collage of flies squashed by our hands. A flyswat would help. But I feared the flyswat would become a tool of discipline and she would use it to beat me.

When we got home, she took the stolen items into the prayer room and dropped to her knees. I pressed my ear to the door. She asked for forgiveness for stealing and whispered a prayer. "Yes, yes," she kept saying.

She burst out of the prayer room and said God had commanded her to sacrifice another baby palm tree. Her hands were raised like she was reaching for God. I asked if she was sure, but she did not answer. She went outside, waved her axe like a magic wand, and asked the palm trees if they were cursed. "This time I won't make a mistake," she said. "I'll drown the right tree." But the trees wouldn't speak, so she squatted in the garden and sizzled ants with the shoplifted magnifying glass. She offered me the magnifying glass, but I refused because I habitually smashed glass and stepped on the shards with my tennis shoes, just to hear the crunch. The sound soothed me.

"An ant bit me yesterday," she said. "This is what they deserve." The ants hissed as she fried them. Fizzed like carbonation. In the distorted reflection of the magnifying glass, her head looked bulbous like a jellyfish. At sunset, she plugged the mouth of the anthill with a hose and flooded it with water. "Genesis," she said.

* * *

That night I woke up sweating. I entertained the idea that I was drenched in blood instead of sweat, that I'd been stabbed in my sleep. I invented a serial killer and imagined them crouched in my room, waiting for me to fall back asleep to finish the job.

The house was silent. I went to check if my mother was still breathing.

Water pooled from under her door. I burst in and smelled salt. Her body pumped out water and she sunk into the soaked mattress. Flies orbited her.

I poked her forehead to wake her, but my finger dented her skin. The dent filled with water and a fly dove in and drowned. I wanted to grab the shoplifted flyswat from the nightstand and smack the fly, but that would stamp a waffle pattern onto her skin. I'd done enough damage with the dent that looked like a third eye.

I went to the bathroom and filled a bucket with water and sloshed it over her body. She squirmed and stood on the mattress which ejected water like a kitchen sponge. She gagged and water squirted from her mouth. She rubbed her third eye. Her fingers were noodly, skin translucent like rice paper – her jellyfish sting glowed. "I'm the palm tree," she said, and ran out of the house. I followed.

She left a trail of water and her arms wiggled. The sun rose and watercoloured the clouds. The sky ambered.

We passed by the church where the priest throws spinach leaves at the congregation before blessings. We passed by the grocery store. I thought she was going to enter the moose meat shop but she kept running. I couldn't tell if she was shrinking or was just that far ahead. She jumped a guardrail and headed to the beach. I knew the path like I knew the Lord's Prayer.

She blurred into the distance and vanished.

When I reached the beach there was only a lifeguard. I asked him if he'd seen my mother. "No, but I saw a jellyfish using its tentacles as legs and running into the water," he said. "I must've been hallucinating." He rubbed his temples.

I threw a rock at the lifeguard and he went down. I didn't want anyone to stop me. I ran into the ocean and hunted for jellyfish. I squished them onto my skin and let them sting me. I hoped one of them was my mother.

The White Salamander Tax

Jacob Lucas

Kellyville, January 2008. The sun had gone full tyrant. My cousin, much older, commanded me to ride his bike to the top of the street and return back down, "no pedals allowed". I gulped. The chain was hefty and asked for muscle and devotion. Neither of which were stored in my puny calves, but I gave it regardless.

At the top of the street, I paused. My ears tuned to the sound of Charlie and Lola muffled in the house behind me. To the left, someone's baby let out a noise like a deflating lung. A suburban lullaby that hovered around me. I slowed my breath to swallow its rhythm. Allowed enough time for my heart to abseil down from my throat. As the butterflies rearranged furniture in my gut, I looked to no one in particular and nodded – and then released.

Down I went. I let the wind punch me in the face, let all control slip away. The bike rebelled, took a life of its own, pedals spinning, rubber growling. I understood for the first time what it meant to careen straight toward fear, like I was gathering debt.

Near the cul-de-sac, my hands remembered the brakes, but my body had other plans. I became the wind, stacking it on the asphalt. I stayed down there, long enough to feel bones ache in my palms. And then, I looked up.

A shape, rude and ginormous, bloated in the sky. A giant salamander, suspended in a heat haze, like a memory I didn't own. Lips pulled back in a way that could've been a smile, or a warning. It hung there, an impossible thing that didn't belong to me, but seemed to know exactly what had happened.

* * *

As a child who grew up in a Mormon family in Newcastle, we would often visit the Hills District. Specifically, to my aunt's house. There were more Mormons there, and therefore more religious activities. The reasoning was math-like:

> Higher Mormon Density = Increased Spiritual Opportunity.

This house resembled my parents' in a way. Same square footage. Same laminated floorboards with a stain no one admitted to. It sat in a kingdom of houses that were freestanding, brick-faced, all trying to look important. Kellyville, the suburb, curled like a sleeping python. Wide roads wind through as if laid by a child scribbling on a colouring-in book.

Driveways were confessionals for utes and people movers, vehicles named for what they carried rather than who they were. They sat parked with reverence, waiting for the sun to rise and permit their movement: deliver lumber. Shuttle small humans. Repeat.

Each house carried its own brand of intimacy. Entering these homes felt like I'd been there before. As if someone had copy-pasted their lives with only minor edits. A lot of them

Mormon, all of them familiar, all of them slightly off in the exact same way.

* * *

Inside my aunt's home, the walls bore witness. They were crowded with Latter-Day Saint art. Oil-paintings reprinted on satin paper, thick with halo light. Every major plot point was accounted for: boy in forest, angels trumpeting Christ's second coming, Jesus visiting the Americas with holes in his hands. Interior-designed in devotional maximalism.

One Sunday before church, my uncle lifted a frame off the wall and handed it to me, weighty with spiritual significance. "Hold this," he said. It was the Carlingford temple. A white spire scraped the sky. Stained glass flared through the belly of its centre chamber. At the very tip, the angel Moroni stood mid-blast, clad in gold, eternally bugling.

My uncle pointed at the temple and began a sermon of his own. About tithing, about how money helps construct buildings that would last until the millennium. "Ten percent of everything," he said, as though it was infinitesimal in contrast to God's divine plan.

Even as an eight-year-old, I understood the math of sacrifice. I didn't have much, but I had something, and they wanted a piece. He smiled. I nodded. We both looked at the painting. Although, looking back I'm sure I can see the glare of the salamander glowing through stained-glass.

* * *

Tithing is a core ritualistic practice in Mormonism. A transaction between its members and the intangible infrastructure of heaven. Members give ten percent of everything, birthday twenties, glass-bowl babysitting change, the first pay slip from Bakers' Delight. In return, they're promised blessings. Not financial ones, but spiritual dividends.

Mormons say the Lord multiplies. What is offered is returned tenfold. Maybe an easier time finding car keys. An extra scoop of mashed potatoes at potluck. Even the exact number of kids they prayed for. Maybe nothing happens at all.

Members are also told, vaguely, that tithing expands God's kingdom. Pays for carpentry and construction for new temples and meeting houses. Helps missionaries eat and rent. That it funds humanitarian aid, somewhere. The exact details aren't laid out, and most don't ask how exactly their payslip filters into these projects. Maybe they don't want to know.

Tithing becomes a self-cleaning doctrine, a spiritual loop-de-loop. Members give to grow their faith, and their faith grows because they give. It builds physical things like chapels and temples, but it also builds a willingness to keep believing. To keep offering. A scaffolding for the soul. Bit by bit, ten percent by ten percent. Receipts not included.

* * *

When I visit those streets now, tithing hums beneath everything like a low electric current. It governs choices with the soft tyranny of routine. The cars are not for flair but function, sliding doors that have a handle, boots that fit bulk toilet paper and prams. Front lawns shaved short and kept humble. No sculpture, no koi pond. Just grass. A welcome mat that knows its place, to be stepped on, daily, by muddy work boots, school shoes, polished black Sunday loafers. Practicality becomes theology.

However, as the Mormon population stretches out further west towards Penrith, Hebersham and Blacktown, the ten percent has real teeth. It speaks in hard choices: four-seater or six? Push mower or knee-high weeds? Lease or own? It's not spiritual theory; it's an Excel spreadsheet with eternal consequences.

Wives push strollers with cracked wheels down an uneven pavement, children dangling like grocery bags. Husbands zip up their hi-vis, lunch boxes packed with Aldi apples and fruit roll-ups. They're saints of the morning shift. And overhead, barely visible the salamander reappears. Peeking over the hills. Its skin shimmers as if doused in car oil. Its opalescent eyes blink once, twice, in sync with a mynah bird's call. It watches. It always watches. It knows what ten percent costs. And what it buys.

* * *

Tithing doesn't just stop at money. It worms into time and energy. The Mormon Church's net worth is estimated at roughly $450 billion, and by some accounts, the richest in the world. But somehow, mysteriously, none of that goes toward cleaning the chapels. That is up to its devoted members. This is called an "act of service".

I was about fifteen the first time I fully understood this aspect of tithing. It was after one of the tri-annual youth dances in Sydney. The soiree was a carefully engineered flirtation station, held under fluorescent lights and priestly supervision. At the end, the music stopped. The even cleaner versions of Taylor Swift narrowed to the yank of an audio jack, and it was time to clean.

Jelly-topped arrowroot biscuits died quick deaths in plastic bins. Modest girls crouched in knee-length taffeta, trading nae naes for knee bends. Vacuuming in a synchronised dance of crumbs and choreography. Boys spun their ties like lassos behind them and herded chairs into formation. Wives unleashed an arsenal of Chux, Ajax and mops, polishing vinyl like it had eternal consequences. Husbands were reborn as ship captains, barked orders, arranged carpools, optimised labour flow.

Tithing reared its second head. Not money, but motion. Not cash, but compliance. A different kind of offering to the same beast. Somewhere, the salamander swelled. Fed by crumbs and obedience. Gleaming under the switched-off fluorescent lights.

* * *

Although, tithing as a religious concept isn't a Mormon make. From street-view, the array of Sydney's faith network looks something like this: Catholicism dominates, broad and familiar, embedded into the pavement. It clusters most in Liverpool, Fairfield and the Inner West. Cathedrals and parishes planted firmly in the migrant sprawl. Further out west, Sydney begins to shimmer. Islam, Hinduism and Buddhism stretch out across Ashfield to Cabramatta like beads on a long thread. Incense, minarets, gold-plated Krishnas wedged between KFCs and Banh Mi bakeries.

Mormonism is a whisper by comparison. A decimal. Somewhere between 0.2 and 3 percent depending on who's asked whether it counts those who have long left. The undecided, or the long-distance faithful. However, what it lacks in size, it compensates for in systems. Tithing is not optional. Its doctrine disguised as direct debit. Other prosperity churches like Hillsong or Winners Chapel also ask for ten percent, but this is for those who can afford it. Mormons are more programmatic. They have their tithing systemised with receipts, meetings and their own church-assigned auditors.

Each year the tithing settlement arrives. Members sit across from their Bishop, a bit like a banker, and are asked if they've paid their full tithe. They must tell the truth because refusal has consequences. No temple. No spiritual access. No whispered blessings. The gates don't open for free. Tithing isn't for the rich, it's for everyone. It's a tax on belief. And somewhere, with its tail curled around the temple spires, the white salamander blinks satisfied.

* * *

In 1984, the faithful gave and gave. Over $15 million in tithing, tucked inside envelopes into collection bins, wired from bank accounts. Adjusted for inflation, that's $83 million in today's money. All funnelled toward one sacred monument, the Carlingford temple.

This marked the first of its kind in Australia. Members didn't have to travel to New Zealand any longer to participate in sacred ordinances like; baptisms for the dead, celestial marriages and endowment ceremonies. It became the holiest place in the country, maybe in the galaxy. The temple was painted in an obvious white. The kind of white that desperately insists upon itself. The kind of white that dares dust to try.

From then to now, members arrive like clockwork. Honda Odysseys lined up in precision. Dirt-caked Hiluxes fresh from the worksite. Devotees step out and shed the world. Car doors shut. White clothes emerge from garment bags, zipped and reverent. A transformation in the carpark.

Then, through the gleaming doors they go, into marble hallways and celestial rooms, into a palace designed under Heaven's instruction. The temple glows as the Mormon kingdom expands one tithe at a time.

* * *

The Sydney Australia Temple was announced in 1980, not in Australia, but in Salt Lake City. Its location in north-western Sydney was chosen for its convenience, its Mormon density, its proximity to obedient feet. Although, these feet almost doubled over.

By 1982, ground was broken and over 1,500 residents signed a petition opposing the build. Concerned that its dominance over the landscape will add to traffic congestion and assert unwanted religious prominence in the area. However, the local council approved it with only one dissenting vote, and so, the build went ahead.

The temple followed the standard Latter-Day Saint design. A standardisation that ensures a unanimous holy feeling across the globe, copy-paste architecture. Key features include white walls, a single spire, a stained-glass element. It's a functional divinity, a little Utah.

According to this standardisation, the spire must hold a human-sized gold statue of the angel Moroni on top, horn raised, eyes lifted to the heavens, proclaiming salvation to the suburbs. This statue is the church's signature branding. It separates Mormon temples from any other white building with nice landscaping.

However, in Sydney, things didn't go to plan. Council regulation didn't allow overt religious symbolism. The angel was deemed too prominent so when the temple opened in 1984, Moroni was absent and the spire stood naked.

Church leaders penned their disdain to council, members strategised in meetings and eventually the temple received its full glory in 1985. With the erection of Moroni, the Sydney Temple symbolised something bigger. How a financial system can successfully export theology. Beyond Utah, across seas. Above it all, the salamander gleamed, perched in a jewel-encrusted crown, counting coins in silence.

* * *

Although, it took a lot longer for Moroni to eventually trumpet his glory. Some 130 years. The Mormons arrived in Australia in the early 1850s, not long after the ink dried on the first published batch of the Book of Mormon in the United States. Missionaries, armed with testimonies and American accents, landed softly on colonial soil. One of the first was William Barratt, who stepped off a boat in Adelaide in 1840. He tried his luck, converting a few and then, as if the continent didn't stick, he returned to Zion.

The first attempt fizzled. Not for lack of zeal, but by design. Missionaries in those days weren't expected to root themselves in new land, grow local flocks and become part of communities they intended to convert. They were harvesters. The converted were expected to leave. To pack up their rucksacks, starry-eyed and migrate to Utah.

Australian emigration made this tricky. The newly colonised country needed bodies, not disappearances.

Farmland didn't harvest itself. Membership thinned, then vanished.

Then came World War II. A global shift. The Church launched its "Zion Is Where You Live" policy. Missionaries could now grow where they were planted. Converts no longer needed to uproot. A homegrown Mormonism could bloom. And it did. In Sydney, the 1960s brought the first full-time missionary force and an established congregation. Finally, the church dug in. The salamander, always watching, licked its lips. The soil here was fertile.

* * *

However, with expansion came scrutiny. The religion grew too big, too fast, and suddenly some wanted God's glorious riches. In the early 1980s, Mark Hoffman forged a letter. Not just any letter, a doctrinal time bomb. Supposedly penned by Martin Harris, one of the Church's earliest leaders, it revised the Mormon origin story.

The established story of the glowing angel Moroni delivering the golden plates (the Book of Mormon in its untranslated form) was replaced by a giant white salamander. A spectral amphibian. Big. Slippery. Smoking with magic and mystery. The letter detailed how it directed Joseph Smith where to dig for the plates. And dig he did.

The letter reeked of folk magic, divining rods and treasure maps. It pulled Mormonism out of the arms of Christianity and tossed it back into the dirt, something of the occult, something of the devil.

However, the forgery was convincing. Convincing enough for the Church to adopt it. Quietly. Nervously. Leaders folded it into doctrine like a receipt into a filing cabinet, hoping that it wouldn't crinkle too loudly. Hoffman made about $140,000 for the forgery. A small price, for rewriting prophecy. And so, the salamander, once spirit, once smoke, became cash. Folded bills, stacked in vaults. It blinked. It breathed. It smiled with paper teeth.

* * *

The letter didn't just rattle the faith of global congregations. It detonated them. Mormon historians scrambled, desks cluttered with loose timelines and broken testimonies. Local members blinked through Sunday meetings, suddenly unsure if their religion was heavenly or hexed. If the angel Moroni had been a myth, and salamander the truth, then what exactly had tithing been paying toward?

Meanwhile, Hoffman forged onward, literally. More documents. More artifacts. The church kept buying. Over $1 million worth in total. A desperate paper trail, stuffed with perspiration. Eventually, the fire crept closer, and when it threatened to expose him, Hoffman turned to mercury bombs. One detonated inside a car. Another in an office. Two dead. Salt Lake City hummed with sirens.

In the chaos Hoffman was caught. The forgeries exposed. But not without consequence. The Church began its slow rehabilitation. It plastered the cracks. Held emergency gatherings. Reissued narratives. Members returned to a house that had been rebuilt with matchsticks. But the doubt had already gone global. The foundation now hummed with suspicion. And tithing remained unshaken. The church needed its ten percent more than ever and the members desperately needed to believe.

* * *

Belief is the core motivator for tithing. It isn't an assertion of wealth but a cementation of faith. I recall when this was tested during my first job at the local cinema in high school. $300 a fortnight gave me enough to spend on a Boost Juice at Westfield, or a risky dash across the road at school to Subway during lunch. However, at home $300 was worth a lot more. A piecemeal for church profit. Split into one tenth, a cheque that was kissed upon with prayer.

$30 was a cure for guilt, it was a mark of religious devotion. And if $30 was somehow skipped over, my blessings would be skipped too. The Subway 6-inch rotting away, the Boost juice sourberry.

$30 at seventeen wouldn't devastate me financially but it would instil religious pressure. It would assuage spending with guilt. Financial comfort as something devilish. A $30 meeting with a church official, a tax that paid me out of religious damnation. A tax that was put towards another much larger tax.

* * *

I was sixteen the last time I entered the Sydney temple. I didn't know then that it would be my final visit, an exit interview. I was already slipping. Skipping tithing from my weekend shifts at the cinema. Getting second and third ear piercings. Developing early homosexual feelings that arrived like an unexpected door knock. All of this unauthorised. All of this enough to bar me from the holy halls. But not yet. Not that day.

That day I still held a valid temple recommend. I entered the salamander's palace one last time, shucking off my worldly clothes and stepping into a starch-white jumpsuit like it was a chrysalis. I stood beside my parents in a room cooled to a heavenly chill. We folded our arms and prayed in a low chorus, voices echoing across the marbled divinity.

Above us hung a chandelier like a galaxy. Thousands of cut-glass crystals suspended in total stillness, refracting a kaleidoscope of engineered reverence. Each crystal, a tithe. Each gem, a polished sacrifice. A trillion little gleams of complete obedience.

The temple glowed. Cornices dusted in God's preferred palette: velvet, gold, mahogany and diamonds. We prayed for safety. For him to be kind. The salamander looked down from the rafters and smiled. Draped in crystal, bored and hungry.

* * *

In Kellyville, my aunt's home does not resemble a palace. No grand columns. No chandelier quivering with light. No angelic jumpsuits or celestial carpeting. No one floats. No one glows. Instead, there are laminated floorboards. A microwave that hums. A bookshelf sagging slightly under the weight of well-used hymn books, "Praise to the Man" underlined three times in blue biro.

On the walls, a patchwork gallery. Jesus with perfectly combed hair and sad, radiant eyes. Joseph Smith looking off into a holy middle-distance. A framed photo of the Carlingford temple taken on an overcast day, the sky a smear of hopeful grey. Each item is a badge of loyalty. A quiet, decorative tithe.

Dinner is Kan Tong chicken in honey mustard. From the jar, a legacy dinner. We sit at the table, its surface wiped clean with Ajax and Chux. We say a prayer. Heads bowed, gratitude recited like a muscle reflex. Gratitude for the meal. For the prophet. For another day of modest spiritual compliance. Then we eat. There is no glowing chandelier, but there is a strap of light that filters through the blinds along the dining table. It flickers once, briefly. Maybe a wink. Maybe a well-timed ray. Maybe the salamander, just passing through.

* * *

Every now and again I think about the time I stacked it on the bike. Smack bang in the middle of the cul-de-sac. Knees scuffed, salamander hanging overhead. I think about the families in the houses who can't see its grin, unaware of its presence. Maybe, after sniffling back to my aunt's home the salamander travelled into someone else's. Creeping in the back door, ensuring the microwave heated baby formula to nipple temperature. The dryer cycle undisturbed to completion. Folding laundry, napkins, rocking fussy babies to sleep. Maybe members are comfortable in its indiscernible undulation. Providing enough food to stock the fridge, enough nappies to last the week. Enough to live.

Maybe the salamander only appears at the point of detonation. Materialising in front of those who clue onto its tricks. Those who rescind their coins. Maybe, it's at that point the salamander leaps out from its white castle to bear its full weight on them, suffocating their ungodly decision. Maybe I came to know the salamander because it knew that I would eventually leave the suburbs.

Pocket Worlds

Rory Blue

While restitching the pages of the books, she felt like Prospero. Well, Prospero, but slightly clumsier. Each page was little more than the width of a rose petal, rendering her hands – so often praised for their nimbleness and wit with a pen – gigantic and useless.

The turbulence on the train didn't help, but it was the only place she could focus for long periods of time, so what other choice did she have? Granted, she hadn't collated a manuscript in years – not since her sister had conceived of Lilliville, and she was bestowed the honour of first readership – and she'd always been useless at sewing. The thread kept falling from the needle's eye and into the shoe box. *Damn!* She blushed, as if her sister's characters were witnessing this. The unfolded tea sachets-turned-folio pages were hardly fit to be read by grown-ups.

She felt excluded from the game her nine-year-old sister had once devised, even though she had first invented it for them and now they had both grown up, and she was a real writer and her sister was dead.

* * *

At noon, the train stopped at a cottage-shaped station overlooking a waterfall. Her phone said she was in Valley Heights, thirty-three kilometres from the Blue Mountains. Ma had texted her before they'd lost wi-fi: "Pick up gravy for dinner on your way." Love-heart.

"Something to eat or drink for you, ma'am?" The young waitress in the doll's apron motioned to a selection of plastic-wrapped scones and fruit. She politely refused, then remembered she wasn't mid-air: the food on Earth actually had flavour.

"Actually, I'll have a blueberry muffin, thanks."

She picked the blueberries out of her muffin, transfixed by the water plunging through the rocks' contours. It was like watching the words erupt from the pages of a book: if she spent too long looking at it, she'd be sucked right out of the window and tumble in. She'd be carried back in time, and when she popped out into the cave on the other side, she would find herself a child in a tiny body whose impressions of the world refused the adult grids of space and time. *How terrifying it must have been to be a child*, she thought. To live in a world so alien, so utterly out of proportion with your own body. No wonder they had invented tools and books of their own size.

Her eyes tiptoed back towards the little book on her lap. Momentarily, the words flickered and were legible again. A moment later they were gone.

* * *

> Once a century in Lilliville, the people would ordain the next Blessed One. The Blessed One was chosen on behalf of the citizens by the Right Hand of Fate, who – at the stroke of midnight – would

plummet through the clouds and pluck out the poet whose mastery of words had touched the minds and souls of the people, and drop him onto the stage, into the throne beside the King.

Everyone in Lilliville wanted to be Blessed: by producing one masterwork, all your other words would be swathed in a rapt, shimmering light – even if all you'd written before was holy nonsense. Association with the name of a Blessed One alone was enough for any poem to be deemed virtuosic – even what you'd written as a child.

One day, a left hand emerged through the clouds instead of the right.

"It's a sign of bad luck," said the teacher, who used to belt her left-handed students.

"It's a sign of innovation," wrote *Lilliputian Daily*, who was patiently waiting for the Blessed One to be a woman. Their competitor, Thornwarts, feared the role was becoming too easy for the masses to obtain: they wanted Blessed Onemanship to be restricted to the upper classes, whose work was cultivated from years of study, and was not the outburst of some unkempt savage passion.

But the *Lilliputian Daily* was correct: for the first time in nine centuries, the Blessed One's first name was not William or James or Johann, but Julia.

Blessed be! The women rejoiced. All were astounded. Perplexed, the King of Lilliville promptly died.

* * *

She was getting the hang of it now. Two of the three once-dismembered books were now restored, tucked away safely in her breast pocket: *A Trial of Two Sisters, The Blessed One's Curse,* and *Schism of the Lilliputian Empire*. The more pages she rescued, the more Lilliville seemed to emerge before her as an actual, tangible place: the train window turned into a carousel theatre, passing a doll's house, a castle, and the church spires of gum trees. Half-asleep, the gum trees seemed to be falling onto the tracks in domino succession as they whizzed further and further behind her, dissolving into the horizon.

The question was never *why* her sister had destroyed the manuscripts. That enough was obvious: aged twelve, she had been struck by a particularly nasty case of adolescent shame, growing the urge to decimate any of her belongings which retained even the faintest aura of childishness. No, what amused her was this: with the same spirit of diligence that had led her sister to compose the manuscripts – spending hours sewing pages that detailed the lives of characters who shared precisely her ambitions, or were an obvious stand-in for how she felt about someone else – she later cleaved them along their editorial seams into meticulously segmented portions, leaving only the text itself perfectly preserved.

These segments were found in their grandmother's jewellery box, in the cupboard her sister was too afraid to enter, as if to bury them not only from others but from herself.

***

The valley mist enveloped her parents' house in a soundless haze. Pa sat next to the grandfather clock on the balcony, watching the clouds drift across the gulf. Only one of the Three Sisters was visible now; the eldest and the youngest had melted backwards, as if they'd been erased.

"When is your sister arriving?" Asked Pa, hopefully. He had dementia, the shock of which had never quite subsided for her. Locked away in the suitcase of his mind, sometimes, her sister was still alive. She wondered what age he remembered her as.

What she wanted to say was: "She is dead, she has been dead for three weeks now and tomorrow is the funeral."

But she didn't. Instead, she took out one of the tiny books, cupping it in her hand as if it were a cigarette threatening to burn the palm of her hand. They sat there wordlessly for an hour while Ma made dinner. By the time they went inside, the sun was setting in the west and there she saw the youngest of the Three Sisters glimmering faintly beside her next-of-kin in the diluted light, so that for a moment, it seemed as if she were alive again

Ma had made roast alpaca for dinner, like every Saturday. She was a born-and-bred traditionalist; in the shadow of her routines, time collapsed, making any one Saturday evening indistinguishable from the next. She also liked anything English.

"Look everyone," said Ma, swiping through her camera roll. For all her old-world scruples, her phone remained practically glued to her. "I've found a nice poem to read tomorrow."

"And where are they? I pray you tell."
She answered, "Seven are we;
And two of us at Conway dwell,
And two are gone to sea."

"She's not gone. She's just *far away.*"

Her daughter nodded without making a sound, knowing she wouldn't be able to withhold tears if she spoke. Pa had gone silent, staring at his plate as if dumbfounded. She tried to think of something to say to him – anything – but her mind was too full of Lilliville. Lilliville and her castles and snoring hills, Lilliville ruled by her sister and her. Even now, she couldn't tell them about it; the weight of their childhood pact seared her – this pact which now stretched between the lands of the living and the dead. It was the last place in the universe where her sister still existed. It was where Ma meant by *far away*, even if she didn't realise it.

She wasn't feeling talkative, and neither was Ma, but she felt guilty for letting her bandage the silence alone.

* * *

When she awoke the next morning in her childhood bed, she was reaching for the little books. After staying up late to finish the binding, she'd wrapped them in a muslin cloth and placed them carefully under her pillow. That way, while she was asleep, she would still remain close to them. But when she stretched for them, her hand passed straight through the cotton. Had the parents taken their books? Bewildered, she felt a jolt run through her body so abrupt that she woke up for real this time, patches of skin stone-cold from being tangled in the sheets too short for her woman's body.

The alarm clock blinked in crimson digits: 4:37 a.m.

She stumbled down the hallway towards her sister's room, passing the casket on the table in the living room. The lid was mahogany and looked far too heavy to ever be opened.

The sister's room was the same since she'd left for college. On the walls, there were posters of boy bands, whose members

– when asked for their names – she had not known. Patched up waywardly behind these, however, were what *really* interested her sister: the maps of empires and battles they had invented together. Some of these battles were inspired by the historical wars of Europe; others, by fights between them over borrowed clothes. There were lumps under the sheets at the head of the bed made by the plush toys her sister refused to discard but, as demanded by her age, had to be hidden from sight.

Nevertheless, she had wanted the maps to be there. Or more accurately: she had not wanted them taken down. She had also wanted – if only tacitly – for the words of the Lilliville Sagas to be preserved. Her room and the partially destroyed manuscripts were mere veils – battlegrounds where the war between her urge to preserve and her urge to conceal was still being fought, even now.

She thought of the casket which would be opened in a few hours, cradling her body, vacant as a doll's. Perhaps it was better if the lid stayed shut. She didn't want to deny the truth of the matter, like Ma was trying to; but then again, to accept it unconditionally – to experience Pa's shock as he remembered, as if for the first time over and over again – was unthinkable. She only wanted to preserve her, to leave her somewhere safe – for practicality's sake, if for no other reason.

She kneeled at the foot of the bed, where the valence was tucked under the mattress, forming two curtains. Under the bed, she unclasped the suitcase they had used as a makeshift theatre. An A4 page was still propped at the back – torn from *Shakespeare's Tales: the Complete Illustrated Works* – of Prospero's cell overlooking the shore.

NOW ALL MY CHARMS ARE O'ERTHROWN . . .

Peeling the pages open, one-by-one, she placed the three little books on the stage. Then, she seated two of the Matroyshka dolls before the books, their round gazes fixed on the words small enough for them only to read.

Here – inside the shut suitcase – she could be remembered and forgotten, the dolls replaying their stories all over again, for eternity. *What was* never had to cease to be.

Unlike the corpse, the evidence for Lilliville's existence would never decay.

The story didn't need an endpoint here. It could just go on and on and on.

Tree Rings

Annis Chan

they say we all carry them.
                    buried between my ribs, everywhere i go
                    there's little me – *four, five, six* years old –
somehow still breathing, gently
beneath the weight of my years.

the world never shrank, yet it was
infinitely larger in the bathroom
back when even the tips of
my toes couldn't bring me
to my face in the mirror.

                    seven writhes, tearing grins on
faces and wrapping paper on christmas mornings,
or when i stand
too close and catch a
zephyr of sweet violets (her favourite).

sometimes, now increasingly often,
                    eight and *nine* – when they go a little too quiet,
for a little too long – it goes
                    that *ten* and *eleven* forget
                    the tenderness of oblivion,

of sleeping on soft roots that once grew
organically –
weariless and wildly,
without influence and
without perturbation.

i then stir them awake
in a panic with a piece
of lemon candy. ’til today the acid
uncannily burns the sides of
our tongues and i almost shiver from their arousal.

to keep the scabs from
scarring, i will have to attempt
                    to make *twelve’s* frag m   e   nts and wounds
feel like yesterday – still bleeding –
the same way i have to breathe.

if i pray it silently and
earnestly enough, i’d just about
feel and touch the
warmth of my mother’s skin
through a rebirth; an illusion of a second seed.

like wine, memories once made
can only darken with age – and so to live is to cringe
every now and then at how
Time has soured what once was sweet, before
staring in pensive air at empty bottles – however cheap.

to live is to be wistful; to subtly wonder,
just as we ruminate on the ghosts of our lost leaves,
without them – ones through tens
who would i
                    whole and well at *twenty-one*
be?

(*The indented lines may be read as a parallel poem when read continuously on their own.*)

Coming Up for Air

Vanessa Yenson

Martin Place Station

When I was a child, I tinkered for hours on the piano, creating masterpieces of discordant noise, singing to an invisible audience, picturing their rapture and imagining their applause. When I started lessons, I was diligent – practising my scales and arpeggios and the Canon in C. I memorised the facts of the classical period, of the maestros who loomed large in that era and prepared for my preliminary grade exam.

I felt an electric nervousness skipping school and catching the train to the Conservatorium. Even today, the long, straight escalators at Martin Place that tower above me evoke the emotions of that day. I clutched Mum's hand, and although she patted mine, my anxiety remained. It was partly due to the impending exam, but the moving metal stairs didn't help. They scared me with their imposing height, their metallic teeth relentless in their repetitive cycle – like a big yawn closing at the top, parallel metal tines crushing together to disappear and circle once again. I thought of their unrelenting industry as I passed under the palm trees at the edges of the Royal Botanic Gardens, lofty fronds swaying in a carefree breeze against a brilliant cerulean sky.

When I descended later that day, I realised that the escalators also symbolised the inevitability of time – that no matter how nervous or confident I had been before, there would be an afterward – a time to reflect on how well I played or how badly I sang the third note above middle C.

As an adult, I want to hug that little girl; whisper for her to hold on to innocence a little longer.

Kings Cross Station

When I was an adolescent, I caught the train every day to high school. After the dazzling morning light shining through the windows in the brief expanse of open air after Martin Place – where we could spot the Brett Whitely Big Matchstick sculptures by the Art Gallery and the Westfield skyscraper towering over William Street – the train would plunge back into darkness. And we would emerge at Kings Cross Station with the fine coating of black dust on its name in triplicate on the tiled walls.

Kings Cross. Kings Cross. Kings Cross.

An unconscious reminder that we were leaving the gentile world of office workers, who had disembarked at previous stations in their suits and polished shoes, while we headed into the grungier, dirtier existence of the red-light district.

After a day of lessons, gossip, volleyball and music behind the majestic sandstone walls of our private school, the walk back down Victoria Street seemed to stretch, as if the trip home had lengthened in the seven hours of learning. Our ankles pitched and yawed navigating the uneven pavement, dodging the chewing gum, globules of shiny spit and abandoned syringes. Backpackers loomed in the periphery, sitting on steps, leaning on door frames, sometimes only visible by their bare feet hanging out of car windows, the cheapest of all accommodation. Men in suits sat in cafés, watching the stream of schoolgirls mark the time of their business discussions. I noted their cups of coffee and the languid, dancing smoke that trailed from their cigarettes. Oh, how we longed to sit in a café and watch the world go by!

The rumble of our approaching train meant scrambling down the escalators, our descent noisy with stomping Doc Martens and graceless with swaying backpacks filled with textbooks and folders. There was no time for fear or thoughts about crushing metal teeth, only missing our means of escape and needing to wait a ghastly seven minutes for the next one.

Time runs differently when you're young – with its impatience and inexperience – when your whole world is wrapped in the schedule for trains and lessons, mealtimes and activities.

Saturday is volleyball.

Sunday is dance.

Monday is piano.

Tuesday is tennis.

Wednesday is choir.

Thursday is ballet.

I know I loved all these pursuits and I wouldn't have had it any other way, but I also look back and wish I had paused; that I had relished the freedom of spending time on the activities that brought me joy. Because now, in my rearview mirror, they are indistinguishable and sometimes, often, forgotten.

Interloop, Wynyard Station

When I was at university, I went out at night. I traipsed into the city or the Cross, caught the train to North Sydney, or stayed local for two-dollar drinks and three-dollar cocktails. I would lose myself in the intoxication of the music and the strobe lights reflecting off disco balls in otherwise darkened nightclubs. The bass reverberated in my chest, its rhythm bewitching me to move, to express myself. I shut my eyes, smiling at the delight of being in the moment – dancing freed me from a world constrained by rules and shifts at work, assignments and exams.

University classes and twenty-first birthdays were sliced apart by a leukemia diagnosis. My studies were put on hold, and I attended all the parties that I could, though I missed many. Celebrating life became an obligation – masquerades and seventies themed parties, formal sit-down dinners and casual nights out on the town. Dancing away the horror of cancer seemed like the perfect antidote to the maddening decorum of hospitals and the debilitating effects of chemotherapy.

Above the shiny metal escalators leading to the York Street exit at Wynyard Station hangs an impressive sculpture of its decommissioned wooden predecessor, with the 244 original steps woven into a continuous loop. It is a mobius strip of wooden tines that mimic piano keys suspended in midair, a melody of the past serenading inattentive commuters rushing to their meetings and deadlines.

When I step back to examine it, or look up as it looms overhead, I can't help but marvel that something so ordinary could be so beautiful. The elegant curves belie its five tonnes of weight and fifty metres of tread. It looks effortless and ethereal, and I cannot comprehend the kilometre of welding that was required for its construction, for its birth. I imagine the hundreds of thousands of shoes that rode on the wooden steps, from the handmade ones of the Great Depression to the sensible shoes of World War II. As a young adult heading out for the night, I remember my wariness of getting my stilettos caught in the gaps, afraid I'd be trapped on the moving stairs, unable to escape.

But this fear never came true.

Perhaps it was just that I managed to free myself before the end.

Les Halles Station, Paris

Nineteen years after cancer treatment, I am in Paris, giving myself permission to breathe deeply and take the first steps in a new, creative direction. Memoir writing classes have started, with the afternoons free to explore the city. Even though I have been here before, I discover something novel each day.

Strolling through the Père Lachaise cemetery, paying homage to the graves of famous writers and singers.

Standing at one end of the curved walls of Monet's *Water Lilies* in the Musée de l'Orangerie, immersing myself in their beauty.

Sitting shoulder-to-shoulder on wooden benches, absorbing the live music of trumpets and bass at some quintessential jazz club.

Gathering the courage to read my work at an open mic night at Au Chat Noir with fellow memoir writers.

There's a heartbeat to the underground metro – brisk footsteps, averted gazes, bodies that duck and weave like water around each other. Quick glances at signs for station names and lines and exit gate numbers correlate with subtle but firm changes in direction, with hapless tourists treading water on the edges. There's a faint whiff of stale urine that mingles with musky perfume and the rhythmic sound of Romani jazz that permeates from an unseen corridor. The beat and the harmonies beckon in ebbs and flows, sound ricocheting off walls and thick fluffy coats, competing with conversations and laughter and station announcements.

If I were to stop in the middle and let humanity flow past, I would still feel as though I was moving. The labyrinth of tunnels and moving walkways, advertisement signs and glossy tiles are akin to organs of the body – a living, breathing leviathan of the city – and we, the commuters, like cells that traverse the blood vessels.

The gate opens to release me from the white-water rush, where the pace slows. Tourists sigh with relief and pull out their maps and their phones like shipwrecked castaways who can now orient themselves to their location.

Shafts of light descend, angled lines contrasting with the shadowy undercurrent. As the escalator climbs, the sun breaks through the clouds, and I feel as though I have come up for air.

His Light Guiding Me

Angela Fossi

Grandpa often sat on the green lounge,
watching old war movies.
His favourites were *The Dirty Dozen*
and *Sink the Bismarck!*
He shared war stories:
in one, a man pulled him up
from the trenches, saving him from death.
When he reached the top,
the man was gone.

Every holiday, we watched
my favourite movie, *The NeverEnding Story*.
Grandpa doted on me, placing the beta video
in the player, his brown eyes
filled with warmth, like his embrace.
Together, we entered Fantasia;
I was Bastian, Grandpa was Atreyu,
we were saving the land from dying,
flying on Falkor's back.

Grandpa prayed, morning and night,
on bended knee, at his bedside,
instilling a faith in me.
When I think life is too much to bear,
he appears in my mind's eye,
saying, "Have faith."

Grandpa was a keen photographer,
capturing the beauty in life:
moments in nature,
and the family he cherished.
After his mind gave way to Alzheimer's,
he slowly slipped away.

His Nikon camera was handed down
to me; I was inspired,
trying to capture moments in life
the way he did. I hold onto his camera,
the way I hold onto him.
Though his soul rose to be with the Lord,
he feels as close to me as breathing.
My memories of him are the wings,
connecting me to heaven.

Family Is the Thing of Dreamlikeness

Jensen Chou

I

Wafting from the engine of a crumpled car, a plume of black smoke swayed into the sky, the moonlight revealing the car's dented front, the debris of its bumpers oscillating in the wind.

A male driver jumped from a silver truck and ran to the car he had just crashed into. He tried to open the car door but it didn't budge. He grabbed a wrench from his vehicle and tried to pry it open, but it was still deadlocked.

The smoke spilling from the car turned thicker and thicker. The man coughed, covering his mouth with his hands, and retreated. He yelled, "Hi! I've called emergency services. Hang on, please! I'm so sorry!"

His words reverberated through the deserted place. He watched the smoke swallow the car. Heart pounding, body shivering with sweat. He felt cold. He approached the car again. He smacked and smacked and smacked its side window. "Hey. Don't sleep! Hey!" He searched for something, anything that could be helpful in this moment, but at midnight there was nothing to be found. He dared not call out again.

Beneath the broken windshield, the passenger and the driver, unconscious, had fallen into another existence.

* * *

Family is like a place I cannot inhabit
a concept I have never felt connected to
I have lived with my grandma
for as long as I can remember
When I was little
Grandma told me I would see my parents
once they were not busy
I kept waiting
But children are oblivious
I forgot to wait for them later on
I almost forgot them
Today, she brought them up again

"On the day of your birth, your mom experienced severe bleeding during childbirth. Dad ... died in a car accident on his way to the hospital." Grandma trembled, gripping Alton's hands. Her bony, callused hands felt warm, but they hurt him. She sat on the faded scarlet sofa, trying to maintain a straight posture, but she couldn't, no matter how hard she tried. After a few seconds, she said, "I want you to be well. That's why I tell you the truth. You have your whole –"

Alton pulled her hands away and escaped from this house that harboured most of his memories and dreams and fantasies.

He found himself circumnavigating a cinema, its façade an Egyptian-pyramid shape, with colourful neon lights radiating from its centre. This area was crowded with people, most of them in pairs; their shadows danced as the lights shifted. He entered the hall and loitered near the ticket booth, looking at the posters off and on. In the end he ordered an Uber and chose a beach as his destination. His Uber knight arrived a bit earlier than the expected time. Alton checked the car number and got in. "Hi mate." Alton pulled his hood up and put on sunglasses and earbuds.

"How's your day going, mate?"

"Good. How are you?"

"Good, I ..."

Their conversation did not continue. The driver turned down the volume of the rock music that was playing and changed it to soft music as he saw Alton fall silent.

Alton closed his eyes to prevent his tears from dropping down.

Buzz. Buzz. Buzz. Alton's phone roared in the pocket of his trousers. He dropped the call without checking. And a call came again. He jerked his phone from his trousers.

It's Grandma.

It's Grandma.

He muted it and slumped onto the seat and his tears fell on his trousers. He didn't hang up. He powered off his phone after the call finally ended.

Huh, does knowing about the death of my parents, who have never taken care of me for a second, really sting me?

The more he tried to find an answer, the more unsettled he felt. He wanted it to stop.

"Mate, when will we get there?" Alton asked.

"It should be about ten minutes, and we –"

A series of braking sounds interrupted the driver.

Behind them a truck was looming.

In an instant they were ten metres apart. One metre apart. Then less than a foot.

A deafening sound echoed, reverberated and dissipated. They lost consciousness.

* * *

Eyes unable to open, body paralysed, Alton felt he was lying in a dim place. Something reverberated from a distance. Knock. Knock. Knock. The sound became clearer over time and turned to a constellation of voices:

"You fucking communist!"

"Get out of my country!"

"Don't you want it, good boy?"

"It's our secret, don't tell anyone."

"Do as I say! You hear me?"

"Open the door!"

"No one will help you."

To anyone else they were all the same distorted drones, as if they came from a warped phonograph. But Alton recognised something in them – several faces appeared in his mind. More voices emerged, grew louder and louder, until in the end, they could no longer be heard as muffling and tinnitus filled his ears.

Maybe Alton had slept for some time.

A smell of spiciness flew to him.

He opened his eyes and found himself in a place where his years of absence had made it almost unfamiliar. He was in Grandma's house. He had not been there since he and Grandma had moved to Batania ten years ago. Nothing of this house had changed. At the centre of the kitchen sat a slightly chipped black walnut table enough to seat up to ten people, surrounded by scarlet chairs. Behind the table was a bluish three-tier cupboard engraved with chrysanthemums. It was old, covered in Alton's scratchings, but Grandma had never considered replacing it with a new one.

As he walked deeper into the kitchen, Alton found the source of the spiciness – the stone stove, from where some steam and the aroma were spreading. The smell stirred a memory of one dish – sweet and sour ribs. He swallowed his saliva and stepped to the stove; its cooking surface was covered with condensed steam, but the pot cover felt cold when Alton lifted it. He picked up a piece of ribs, mixed of fat and lean, with chopsticks found next to the cabinet. He blew on the ribs a couple of times to cool them and took his first bite with care.

?

He bit the rib again. Still, it was tasteless.

I forgot it's a dream.

Alton left the kitchen and found a woman sitting on the stone stairs of the backyard. He stopped behind her.

"*Mao*, come have a look." She turned around with a smile, her hands knitting something. "Choose a colour you like." Her voice was slightly different.

No one in this world would be more familiar to him than she was. But she looked so young. Tentatively, Alton said, "Grandma?"

"*Ai*, come choose one, come," the grandma urged.

Alton approached and found the grandma's face had become less wrinkly and gaunt. By her side sat a bamboo pannier in which were placed unopened wool balls in different colours. Alton did not look at them. He stared at this woman and kept calling her, "Grandma, grandma, grandma ..." His tears fell and wetted his collar.

"*Ai, ai, ai.* Are you alright? Has anything bad happened at school?" Grandma asked as she squatted beside Alton and held him in her arms to get a closer look at him.

"No, I … just miss you."

"We just saw each other this morning, *Mao*. You don't like schooling, or do you miss me that much?"

"I think I –"

"Yip, yip, yip." A series of barks from behind interrupted Alton and a golden retriever jumped onto him.

Alton was knocked over by this fluffy creature two times as big as him. The golden retriever licked Alton's cherubic face over and over.

"*Aiya*, Beibei, don't play on the stone floor *ya*! It's covered in dust."

The golden retriever untangled himself from Alton lethargically, his claws tapping Alton's chest, as he woofed.

Alton was still lying on the ground. "Grandma, what's his name?"

The dog gave Alton an unfriendly look.

"*Mao*, has the first day of school turned you into a little dummy? He is Beibei. You named him, remember?" Grandma lifted Alton from the floor and brushed the dust off his clothes. She placed the wool balls in front of him. "Choose a colour for your woollen slippers."

Alton pointed at the blue one.

"All right. The pink and black ones are reserved for your mom and dad now," Grandma said and strode to the living room.

Mom and Dad?

Hearing these distant names was reminiscent, nostalgic enough to stir his heartstrings. He felt something was forgotten. He was told that ...

I was told what?

They died. A voice flashed in Alton's mind.

Maybe seeing them, though in a dream, is good.

Alton stayed in the backyard, sitting in the bamboo armchair Grandma had brought for him. He waited for his parents, like he had for the past eighteen years. Though knowing this was not real, he still wanted to meet them.

* * *

In the moonlight, two people were approaching the stone stairs that adjoined the backyard, each carrying a gift box.

Alton sat on the chair, his head towards the entrance, his eyes unfocused. His feet were conjoined with his distorted shadows.

A man's voice dragged Alton from his memories. "Alton, Dad's coming!" He left the big box with the woman and ran to the child, his hands waving like windscreen wipers.

Alton looked at the source of the voice. The man approaching had a tall and slender figure; as he got closer his features became more identifiable. He was in a black suit, the same one he wore in the marriage photo taken with the woman behind him. He looked one hundred percent the same as in the picture.

He stopped in front of the child. "Who makes you cry? Tell Dad. Dad will beat their ass off!" He wiped Alton's tears with his hands.

The roughness of the man's hands made Alton flinch but he was still speechless. The man hugged the child and kissed his forehead. "Who did this? Tell me." He looked back at his wife. He whispered, "What's wrong with Alton?"

The woman dropped the boxes and offered her arms. "Maybe he's a little sleepy."

Alton was passed to her.

"My boy, who makes you unhappy?" The woman kissed Alton's hands, put him on her back, and cradled him as she sang,

The moon is bright, the wind is quiet,
The tree leaves hang over the window.
My little baby, do not cry.
My little baby, go to sleep quickly,
Sleep, dreaming sweet dreams.

"Mom, Dad," Alton called their names for the first time in his life. *Dad, Mom, I don't want to sleep. I dread not having the chance to see you again.*

"Mom, Dad."

"Dad, Mom ..." The more times he called his parents, the louder his voice became. In the end he was almost screaming. "Mom, Dad, I miss you!"

"I know, I know, sweetie," the woman said, her voice somewhat hypnotic.

The man pinched Alton's face. "Look what we bring for you!"

When Alton looked, the man blocked his view with his hand. "It's something you've wanted for a long time!"

But Dad, how can you know that?

The man lifted Alton onto his shoulders and held Alton's waist with his hands. On the way to the kitchen, noticing Alton's shivers, the man asked, "Do you feel cold?"

"I'm not feeling cold, Dad."

"Then why are you shivering? Those who lie will be punished."

* * *

In the dim yellow light, Grandma was by the white brick stove, preparing dinner. She chopped different kinds of vegetables into slices. The air in the kitchen was permeated with the pungency of chillies.

The couple entered the kitchen. "*Ma*, we're home. Alton says he feels a bit cold. Can you find a jacket for him?"

"*Ma*, I'll help you chop the vegetables."

"*Ai*, Shamyung, Morie, welcome home," Grandma said. "There are some Kyoho grapes in the fridge. Enjoy them while they're fresh." She wiped her hands with a cloth and went upstairs, but stopped beside Alton and asked, "What's wrong with *Mao*?"

"I asked him, but he's reluctant to say. Maybe it's something about school. I'll discuss it with his teachers tomorrow," Shamyung said.

"The first days will be hard, but don't be sad, *Mao*. If someone bullies you, you can do it to your dad," Grandma joked and stepped out of the kitchen.

A smile crept across Alton's face.

"It takes my whole life to make you spare a smile. How was your day at school? Was it hard?" Shamyung pinched Alton's cheeks.

I wish I could answer your questions, Dad. I wish I had any memories of this world.

"Dad, I miss you. I miss you and Mom."

"Alton, do you remember how many times you've said that today? I'm sorry. I will try to come home earlier tomorrow."

"Will you?" *Dad, can I still see you and Mom tomorrow?*

"Of course I will. When have I ever lied –"

"Promise me." *Promise me to see me again in my dream.*

"I will come home earlier tomorrow, Alton. I promise. Give me your hands. Let's sign *a contract.*"

Alton extended his hand and Shamyung covered Alton's palm with his. Their hands formed a lock of palms, their fingers intertwined.

"Pinky promise, a hundred years and no change. Whoever breaks it is a puppy!" Shamyung said, but got no response from Alton, only a burning gaze, his eyes filled with tears, like a dam on the verge of collapsing. He let out a heavy breath and kissed Alton's tears. "Crybaby, say your contract speech or it will be voided."

"Pinky promise, a hundred years and no change. Whoever breaks it is a puppy," Alton said, his voice trembling.

The moment felt almost sacred. The world seemed to pause for a second, as if their bond brought by the contract would last forever.

"Sealed! Whoop!" Shamyung screamed, and, in a low voice only audible to Alton, he asked, "Do you still not want to tell Dad what happened today? You –"

"Here you are." Grandma held a red woolly coat behind Alton, eyeing the length. After that she dressed Alton in the blink of an eye.

Alton recognised it immediately, the coat that Grandma had knitted for him. It was once his nightmare. Every time he wore that coat, he would receive numerous good comments from Grandma and her friends, but when he wore it at school, he only got teasing looks and snickers from his classmates, and he never wore it again. This time he didn't reject that coat like he had before. It had been a long time since someone dressed him like that.

* * *

For the first time Alton attended a dinner with his parents. He answered their questions as best he could, and in the end he could not even believe what he had said. He ate every bite of the food he was served, though it was tasteless to him. The more food he had, the more emptiness he felt.

The dinner was finally finished. Alton didn't feel a shred of fullness.

Morie was helping Grandma clean the room. "I know you will never stop smoking," she said to Shamyung.

"I haven't done it for a week." Shamyung sat up straight in the armchair.

"Really? Your jacket wouldn't say that."

"Darling, I promise I will quit it, but it takes time."

"You are very good at taking your time at doing everything, aren't you? It's not a bad thing, you know that very well."

"You must be tired. Let me do this for you." Shamyung jumped off the chair and held Morie's hands, attempting to take control of the mop she was holding.

Alton sat in a chair watching their banter sadly. It was warm and boisterous. Too foreign to him.

II

After dinner, the moon disappeared. A blue sun took its place, from where heat was spreading. In the light, several puppies were running after each other, and two of them started fighting.

A stern bark sounded. The fight stopped.

Alton turned around and found Beibei sitting beside him. Squatting, Alton petted him for a moment. Beibei's eyes blinked and blinked. He sniffed and licked Alton's hand.

"Are they your babies?" Alton sat behind Beibei and leant against the wall.

Beibei looked at the puppies proudly from afar, his tail swinging, tongue flicking in and out. He ran to the puppies and returned with them. The four had pure golden fur, though not as pure as their father's – all of them had a black spot on their noses. Two were looking over Alton with curiosity. Behind them were the two who had fought each other earlier. They avoided their father but approached Alton when sensing Beibei's gaze. They seemed to be nervous, the way they sat stiff as a stone.

With care, Alton stroked down from their heads to their necks. He felt like he would break their bones if he touched them any harder – their heads were only as big as his palm.

"Take a seat," a female voice sounded as a bamboo armchair was placed in front of him. Alton looked up and found a young lady in a bluish cheongsam looking at him. It took him seconds to realise she was Grandma. Her cheeks had become completely unwrinkled, her hair no longer grey, her frame not stooped. She looked so young. Horrifyingly. Never had Alton seen her so young in his life.

The puppies surrounded Grandma as she passed a glass to Alton. “I’ve made some watermelon juice. The hotpot must be too hot for you.”

“Thanks.” Alton gulped down the drink, wishing it could calm him a bit.

“Does it taste terrible?” Grandma took the empty glass from Alton’s hands.

“No.”

“You look like this.” Grandma’s lips pouted and eyebrows furrowed to imitate Alton’s expression. “Is there something you want to tell me, *Mao*?”

“No.” Alton changed his position to lean on the woman by his side. And he was hugged. Shamyung’s and Morie’s voices spread from the kitchen. From his point of view, Morie and Shamyung were arguing. “Grandma, are they quarrelling?”

“Who?”

“Mom and Dad.”

“Why are you asking that? Did you see something bad happen?”

“See.” Alton pointed at them.

Grandma smiled but didn’t turn around. “You almost got me. But they are still at work.” She tweaked Alton’s cheek.

Alton looked ahead again and found that Morie and Shamyung were no longer where they were. The kitchen was hollow, as if their arguing were his imagination.

Maybe it’s time to leave before something worse happens.

Yes.

?

Something pierced Alton’s heart and his throat tightened. A sense of being scrutinised washed over him.

“Grandma, did you hear anything?”

"I heard someone lying." She carried Alton into the living room.

Only you can hear me.
I can hear you as you can hear me.

It's just a dream.

Huh. Let me tell you something.
You were planning to kill yourself at the sea,
jumping from the cliff,
only to be drowned by your acrophobia.
What a cruel boy you are to yourself …

Alton's heart pounded. He almost forgot to breathe.

But her call dragged you back from death.
Am I wrong?

Who are you?

Calm down. I am you.

A pack of wool balls was placed in front of Alton. "Choose a colour you like," Grandma said.

It left him goosebumped. Hadn't he chosen the wool? Why? Why would Grandma … He chose the blue one as he had earlier, curious about what would happen.

"The pink and black ones are reserved for your mom and dad's slippers now!"

Who on earth are you?

I've told you. I am you,
to be more precise, your subconscious.

So this is your world.

You can say that, but we are conjoined.

What will happen next?

Something you've expected for a long time …
and …

And what?

And loops.

Of what?

You will know.

Will I see you every day?

No. I have to manage many dreams,
but I will try to reach you if you need me.

You said you're my subconscious.
Shouldn't you only manage my dreams,
are they that many?

You don't remember dreaming a lot.

The voice left as the sense of being watched disappeared.

"What are you staring at?" Grandma's hands swayed before Alton.

"Nothing … I've just found knitting is so sophisticated."

"Not very sophisticated. The key is patience, and … patience." Grandma grinned. "The more you practise, the fewer mistakes you make." She put down the yarn and got up from the sofa. "What would you like for dinner?"

"Anything. You always make my favourite dishes."

Grandma burst into a laugh. "Do you know you are so sweet today? I'll go check if we have ribs. If we do, I'll make sweet and sour ribs." She left the living room.

Alton rose from the sofa and stopped at the wall on which many photos were hung. Opposite it stood a brown wooden bookshelf filled with various books, three times Alton's height. Hanging in the centre of the wall was a black-and-white photo of two – the woman was in a cheongsam, sitting on an ornate, high-backed chair. She looked like Grandma, only younger – perhaps in her twenties; the man beside her shared some resemblance with Shamyung but looked rougher. He was in a Zhongshan suit.

Standing on tiptoes, Alton tried to remove the photo to have a closer look but stopped halfway. "That's the trouble with being a kid." He sighed and looked down and spotted another photo of Grandma, in which she looked more like she did this time. She was carrying a baby in the crook of her arm. Alton looked over these photos again and again. He wanted to remember every detail of them.

* * *

The half-closed door of the living room swayed back and forth, creaking in the wind.

Alton left the living room and found the sky had clouded over. A crescent shimmered overhead; at the horizon, a full moon lay hidden behind a veil of clouds. He leant on the wall, legs crossed, staring at the two moons.

"Yip, yip, yip." A puppy jumped onto Alton.

Alton took him in his arms. "Where is Bei –" His voice came to a stop when he noticed there was something different about this puppy – his fur was pure golden. "Do you know who I am?"

The puppy licked Alton's fingers.

"Alton, Dad's coming!" Shamyung screamed from a distance. His voice had once brought Alton warmth but now the warmth in it made him tremble.

Their meeting had at some point turned into a congregation of hauntings. It was hard to see the man's face in the moonlight. He carried a box with something swinging around in the wind. The woman didn't show up this time.

Managing to maintain a lively voice, Alton ran to Shamyung and said, "Dad! Where is Mom?"

Shamyung fell still for a moment. "Mom is not living with us now. We've been separated for a year. Don't you remember?"

"I … I dreamt about you and Mom last night."

"We can arrange a time to see her, if you want." He crouched down and placed a kiss on Alton's forehead.

"Sounds great! Is this gift for me?" Alton asked, his body shaking.

"It can't be for anyone else. You wanna open it now?"

"We can open it after dinner." Alton dodged the box, not even sparing it a glance, as if it were a box from hell.

"Do you mean lunch?" Shamyung smiled, held him closer, walked him to the kitchen, unaware of the twin moons in the sky.

Shamyung placed the gift on the table. "What's for breakfast?" he asked. And he turned around to realise Alton was no longer by his side. He looked at Alton who was standing outside the door. "What's wrong?"

"Nothing's wrong. I'm good."

Alton entered the kitchen. It had changed a lot – now all the wooden furniture was gone, replaced by high-tech equipment: an intelligent fridge, a microwave, and a dishwasher. Sunlight was cast through the new windows cut above the sink. Everything there appeared to be placed after calibration. He could not believe he had been there earlier.

"Where is Grandma?" Alton asked.

Shamyung touched Alton's forehead. "You're sure you're OK?" He crouched to look at Alton.

"What? Dad?"

"Don't you remember ..."

And there was sorrow in Shamyung's eyes.

Was Grandma ... dead?

"Dad, I dreamt about Grandma last night." Alton squinted a smile. He had lost count of how many times he had lied. He turned around to hide his tears, but a hand was in his way – Shamyung pinched his nose.

Shamyung exhaled a heavy breath. "Go to see your gift. It's in the living room."

Alton left the kitchen but didn't step into the living room. He wanted to stay but wanted to run away at the same time. Grandma. Dead. Mom. Disappeared. Things. Changed. What would happen next? He felt he had forgotten something very important. As he tried to remember it, drones of voices began to emanate from his head.

They were too faint for Alton to catch. He only heard someone mutter and mutter in his head. In the end it became clear.

Don't dig any deeper.
Don't dig any deeper.

A sense of being watched suffocated Alton. His vision was blurred, sweat dropping from his forehead. Some flowed into his eyes.

You wanna leave?
Open the gift and you shall leave.

The voice played in his head over and over. Things were floating in his sight, or he was floating. He felt himself light as a feather.

And a hand pressed on his forehead. "You don't look good, dude."

Alton lifted his head, finding Shamyung with a worried expression. The voice in Alton's head began to mix with Shamyung's voice. He could not distinguish if the voice was in his head or from Shamyung. So he responded to everything he heard.

It's time.

Don't miss the time.

Shamyung touched his own forehead and touched Alton's. "Doesn't feel like a fever. I'm taking you to hospital now."

"I'm not going anywhere."

Shamyung laughed. "Well. What's for dinner, boss?"

"Can you cook, Dad?"

"You've been babbling all day long. Have you not been eating the food I cooked since you were a chick?"

"Sweet and sour ribs. How's that?"

"Easier than breathing."

Shamyung set the table and looked at Alton expectantly. Hesitant, Alton looked at the dish off and on and finally managed to find a rib that could be called a mouthful. Their rough appearance – each one as wide as three fingers – had given him an ominous feeling. He blew on it to cool it down. He knew it would be tasteless. At least he thought he did. But it wasn't. Not enough to be called palatable. It tasted plain and real.

"How does it taste?"

"Not bad, but Gran –" Alton stopped as he remembered Grandma did not *exist* in this world. After a few seconds, he said, "It tastes quite good. Insipid but savoury."

"Sounds like a gourmet." Shamyung took a piece of rib, chopsticks in hand, and his expression darkened. "You are such a nice kid," he said. "I haven't made this dish before. Why did you want it?"

"I saw it on TV," Alton lied. He did not care about truth or lies anymore. He wanted to know this man more, knowing he might not have another chance to see him again.

"Dad, what's your favourite dish?"

"Mine? Mapo tofu."

"I thought it would be sweet and sour ribs."

"Why?"

"I had a dream. In that dream Grandma told me her signature dish was sweet and sour ribs."

"She would've loved you, if she were alive."

Yes. She loves me, Dad.

They talked about their hobbies, fears, and biggest regrets. The more questions Alton asked Shamyung, the more Alton trembled. He laughed with Shamyung, tears in his eyes. He felt like a journalist for asking so many questions.

They had entered the living room. In front of them was the blue gift box Shamyung had brought.

"Why won't you open it?" Shamyung asked, noticing Alton's gaze on the gift. "Do you want me to open it for you?"

A distant voice crossed over Alton's mind:

You wanna leave?

Open the gift, you shall leave.

Alton took a deep breath. "It was great to meet you, Dad."

Shamyung stared at Alton for a moment and he smiled. "You ... never mind."

Alton tiptoed to kiss Shamyung, who was sitting on the sofa. And his kiss was reciprocated. "Let's see what's in it!" His tears fell on his hands when he opened the box. Inside was a notebook. Alton stretched out his arm to pick it up, and when he took it – his world went blank.

He lost the sense of balance and gravity. He was flying and falling, his vision filled with white, blank, red, and blank.

Perfection

Clara Tan

She dipped her paintbrush into the water, dabbed it on a ragged piece of cloth and then lifted her arm to drag the brush against the traced outlines laid out before her on the canvas. Every brushstroke bore the weight of something she couldn't quite grasp – a sinking feeling that melted off the darkened tips of the brush as she blended the myriad hues together. This monotonous repetition continued, with the process of dabbing and blending thick acrylic paint spurring her on and on.

With every brushstroke, she felt closer to the visions of an alternate world – moments that she'd lived through but couldn't recall as sharply as before. Nonetheless, her memory unravelled itself as she depicted a time and space that clawed relentlessly at the edges of her perfectly polished shell of a life. It beckoned her to morph into a softer world.

London, 2000

Ma had always been a perfectionist. From being the golden child with conspicuous amounts of achievements in her home country's top schools, to being a young office worker that hustled through the wrath of office politics in Central London, Ma had it all. Even her flair for painting came from a place of dexterous intricacy, with not a single shade left unblended. But the beginning of the new millennium called for change. Shortly after New Years', Ma finally decided that her time living abroad with her husband had come to a close. Her flesh ached for more – she yearned for an extension of all the sharpened edges of who she already was. She was tired of being the perfect model of a young woman she forced herself to be. The rigidity of her nine-to-five office job only caved in on her and deepened this emptiness where she also desired to step past what was already familiar to her.

She made up her mind to have children, under the guise that starting a family would be an imperative in stepping away from her former identity. She and her husband would go back home and she would dedicate her life to raising children. Though uncertainty still loomed in her head and she knew this meant the loss of the glamourised life she had once acknowledged to be her greatest opportunity, she decided that devotion to being a family woman was more important than freedom. The socially modulated model of an idealised life rooted in the homogeneously cultivated norms of adulthood made her feel as though nothing truly belonged to her. She craved control. Perhaps birthing children that shared her blood would grant her a way back to her own innate self. At least, that was the hope she held onto as she bid goodbye to the land that had once brought her hope but not the identity she yearned to live for.

To have traded London's dense skies of gloom for an even heavier path of motherhood … was it worth it? The transition from spending her weekend nights watching musicals with her husband to changing diapers all week was a sharp one. Now aged sixty, despite having crossed the crux of motherhood, the what ifs that she assumed had faded into irrelevancy came bouncing back. What if they'd remained in London? What if they'd never had children?

Ma could still recall her life as a young mother with clarity. Those were the years when maternal love filled the crevices of her soul. The sound of her babies' laughter as they played together ignited a brightness amid the plights of motherhood. The annual Lunar New Year family reunions felt more complete than ever, with her children squabbling over *Bak Kwa* slices the same way she did with her sisters as a child.

Yet, with each pregnancy, her physical and mental health depleted increasingly. The blood and sweat of her motherhood seeped from her soul and dripped into the backdrops of her children's lives. Despite her supposed sense of contentment, there were days when regret flooded through her veins. Days when she was wistful for a life that no longer existed and disgruntled with what was no longer hers. By her fourth pregnancy, Ma succumbed to a new low. She quit her job. Her postpartum body felt like an empty vessel and her mind was devoid of zeal. At some point, her hands were blotched with eczema and her skin stung everyday. She stopped painting.

Her life had become what felt like a cluttered mess of decisions, but she told herself that she would continue to mould the children to standards of utmost perfection – or rather, that motherhood would be her only means of fulfilment, even if it were to be hindered by an undeniable regret. Day and night bled into one another, fizzling into the hazy background of her daily life that circulated around sending the children to school, cooking dinner for them and settling them to bed. Her eyelids grew heavy at approximately 11 p.m. every day and she often drifted off into a deep slumber of nothingness.

Every now and then she would retrieve a long-lost memory from the trenches of her hippocampus – like a lost file being recovered from its bin – and wrap her hands around its invisible membrane, trying to comprehend what she had left behind. She recalled the long train rides to the neighbouring European cities, where she and her husband munched on delectable sandwiches while lamenting about missing the local food from back home. Lunar New Year 1998, the first new year they spent away from family, sitting in a brightly lit Chinese restaurant that served authentic delights but lacked the warmth of familiarity. Despite the fact that they were miles away from home, Ma knew that those years had been a happy time, filled with the ecstasy of new experiences. But those flashes of memory were momentary. To her, remembering her past felt like a betrayal to her new goals – her children.

One night, Ma's husband found several old photo albums dating back to the 1990s. As the children crowded round the dining table, he began flipping through each page. Photographs of them as a couple depicted their honeymoon days in Europe and their working life in London. Her husband's descriptions of each photograph dragged on and on, and with every detail he extracted from his vivid memories, it dawned on her that she no longer remembered things the same way he did.

"You don't remember? *Les Misérables* 1999?" Her husband probed.

"Barely."

Ma tried poking at the corners of every lived moment, however she could, yet their outlines were barely traceable and only a soft gloom simmered beneath what she once knew to be endless possibilities. Her memories of their freedom existed in blurred snippets that hid beneath layers of desperation to seal her identity as a mother and wipe out anything that came before.

She and her husband never got along these days. Perhaps her inability to remember their vibrance further sent her along the spiral of resentment. She envied the fact that his memories of her were so full, while her memories had faded into a desolate abyss. Most of all, though, she detested that he could not fathom the pains of motherhood and that work bore the bulk of his worries. Yet another part of her understood that this was an integral part of her own decisions that she had to learn to accept. After all, her return back home was fuelled by a need for a fulfilment that transcended beyond her individual achievements. Here, love was hers to build. This sense of control was once all she wanted. What more could she ask for?

Nonetheless, in her empty attempt at remembrance lay the poignancy of a strange sentimentality. No matter how hard she tried to fill the void of the past, she found that it was not fixable. Remembering it only brought her pain.

In her bid to be the perfect mother lay a relentless resolution to prove to herself that her decision to have children followed a rightful life trajectory. Every time Ma sensed any flashes of past happiness, she drove them out by inflicting pain on the children. She knew she loved them but her love was tainted with a depression that had weaved its way into their shared blood. Any failure or disobedience on the children's part reflected her own self-imposed downfall and would trigger the deep wound of silent regret in her. There was an irony in this need for perfection, for deep down her violence stemmed from the fact that she saw her children as the ones who bore the embodiment of loss, of aging, of the fact that she could not grasp onto those glorious days that she had thrown away on her own accord.

As the children grew older and Ma's maternal responsibilities lessened, Ma sometimes mulled over how they might recall their childhood. She couldn't help but worry that their love for her was already tainted with doubts she herself had instigated with her actions. Would they remember her as a monster of a mother? A scourging presence whose mental episodes always ended with broken hangers and her eyes bloodshot with tears? Of course, she prayed they would also remember her love – maybe they'd see the side of her that genuinely saw motherly love as tantamount to personal sacrifices.

London, 2022

The next time Ma visited London was with her eldest daughter. The bustling street was teeming with all sorts of people from different backgrounds – some were immigrants, some local English people, some tourists like Ma and her daughter. The hustle and bustle of the metropolitan city brought Ma back to a time some twenty years ago when the love she shared with her husband shone with a radiance she had now lost all access to.

"Ma, why did you and Pa move back to Singapore?" Her daughter asked with curiosity as they ambled past crowded shops on their way back to their hotel.

"It was for the better," she responded bluntly. "Would you have wanted to be raised here? Where you're of a minority race with no roots to your real identity? You all wouldn't have existed if we'd stayed put here." She made it sound as if any vestiges of her own special memories in this place didn't matter anymore – as if motherhood overrode any personal history. Yet somewhere deep in her, she felt something stir.

Ma had once experienced the unfettered bliss of her twenties, but as usual, she could not associate that feeling with any recollection of her husband's face or body. Nor could she really remember the sights she'd espied or the paths they'd treaded. Perhaps his place in those key moments of her twenties had dissipated, and so had 1990s London. London Bridge still stood in its gleaming beauty, but her promising youth was gone. In her quest for a perfect motherhood, bliss only remained as a long-lost emotion devoid of any tangible truth.

"Were the streets also crowded during Christmas back then?" her daughter asked quizzically.

"I don't remember."

"Don't you regret having us? Five kids made you forget everything, didn't it? Maybe we shouldn't have been born!" her daughter joked.

"Come on ... I tolerated so much to raise you all!" Ma rolled her eyes, but deep down she couldn't help but feel a crippling guilt gnawing at her conscience, for she knew her daughter's words had self-depreciating undertones to them.

"Me personally ... I would never want to leave a place like this." Her daughter would never understand. Her eyes wandered around, as if lost in a haze of absorbing the same surroundings her mother had once found a semblance of heartfelt belonging in.

"When you have kids you'll understand." was all Ma answered drily.

"Nah, I won't have kids." Her daughter's response was immediate and curt. "I'd rather have my own independence."

That night, Ma contemplated her decisions for the first time. Was it a mistake after all? She could not arrive at any solidified conclusion. She did realise, however, that all those years of raising the children had now passed her by and she was left with the restless glimmer of an engulfing nostalgia she could no longer ignore. Especially not when she now walked along the very same streets her twenty-something year old self once strode jauntily on.

Later, when they had returned from their trip, Ma sat at her desk filling in the earthy shades of 1999s London Bridge. As she painted, she realised she could no longer imprison the feelings associated with this foreign yet sentimental realm. Random snippets came floating back, and this time, she let them. Remembering was no longer a threat but rather an acknowledgement of who she used to be. Of the young love she once encountered with her husband. Of the world they got to explore beyond home. It was true that she had been a more whole being before the children came into the picture, she couldn't deny that. Maybe motherhood had rendered her individuality dry. It had stripped her of independence, of passion. Either way, she couldn't deny that she had gotten what she wanted: the chance to be a mother. The chance to love her own kin. Perhaps motherhood was never meant to be perfect. She had spent her whole life chasing a self-imposed idea of perfection, only to realise life's inherent fluidity was entwined with the decisions she made and the concept of perfection need not be moulded in the rigidity she thought she needed.

To remember was to feel the ache of memories that gnawed at the fibres of her being. To remember was to acknowledge that her existence was once wholly unrestrained, and no amount of "perfection" could ever release the heaviness of what had been lost. Someday she'd forgive herself. In the meantime, she knew she had to allow herself to love without the confinements of a superficially projected perfection. To love, after all, was to accept the unbridled nature of every emotion. Somewhere along the way of life's journey, Ma's canvas had stopped being empty. Instead, her paintbrush bore an evocative power, detailing the co-existence of joy, grief and all the imperfect moments in between.

Reflections

Cherie Baird

My reflection flashes past me
in a train that doesn't stop.
A friend looks with horror at eyelashes falling
like petals to my painted cheeks.

I want to tell you about my favourite day, and how I wish –
I wish – I could have guessed it then.
It wasn't when we left our books
and ran headlong, joyous, hardly feeling a thing,
into the inlet that put ice in our veins.
Not when we stood on the wharf looking up
seeing stars explode into smoke and colour;
nor when we stood breaths from greatness, numb arms
outstretched, absently capturing a feeling I try to relive
over and over through unfocused videos –
when the crowd screamed,
we screamed with it, and I was weightless in ways
I have never felt again.
No, this was better: this was more.

It wasn't the day you said you loved me or when you
defended my fragile honour. It wasn't
when you forgave me, or held me, or tried
to puzzle my dissonant, crumpled components back together.
My favourite day was when we sat
on the overcast deck, drank
our tea, kissing cups with chipped rims
and watched the sky
and barely said a word.

I watch time break me down into my sundry parts, indifferent
to my fruitless attempts at collecting them.
I clutch at bundles of geraniums
even as they escape my arms –
to fall, to desiccate
and be lost, held in nought
but the frail and nebulous boundaries
of a memory.

An Angel with Me

Angela Fossi

Nanna's yellow dress blazed in the sun,
kissing me on my forehead,
as it blew gently in the breeze.
I danced barefoot in the garden,
trying to catch those kisses,
the way you might try catching a butterfly.

Nanna loved to grow hydrangeas;
clustered, dainty petals,
pastel blues and purples along the gate –
a sweet fragrance floating in the air.
She mothered them the same way
she mothered me.

Nanna moved with grace,
emanating a glowing aura,
and paused, resting her navy blue eyes
on me, smiling so tenderly.

"Nanna, I wish I had your blue eyes."
"I wish I had brown like yours."

Maybe she was the stars in the sky,
and I, the bedrocks in the earth,
but we were the same blood.
Her aura surrounds me now,
as I plant seeds in my garden,
waiting for her hydrangeas to bloom.

Worm

Emily Jean

I am ten and I am in the backyard of my TeeTee's home. The air is dry for a Jersey summer. My little sister is somewhere around here looking for me.

My TeeTee's garden is small compared to those of the neighbours, so I'm not sure if you can even call it a garden. There are two dying tomato plants, a cactus that I once dared my sister to hug, and the blackberry bush – my blackberry bush.

The opening under the bush is smaller than the last time I was here. I am sure it is smaller. I almost wonder if I won't fit this time. I lie down on my back and wiggle along the ground until my upper body is as far back inside the bush as it can go. I fit just fine.

My legs are too long, so they stick out. Without the shade of the blackberry bush, the sun will take full advantage of this; my legs will be sunburnt, again. If my TeeTee sees me, she will laugh and ask if the bush has dragged me back in again. Maybe it has.

This is my quiet little place. I don't know when I crawled in here the first time, but I do know I have been here many times over the years. It is just small enough so that the bush grows directly above my face, and there is little space for my shoulders.

From inside the bush, I can barely see the sky; leaves and branches tuck most of the light away. There are dried-up blackberries. I have eaten all the ripe ones. The ground beneath me is warm. I press my hands into the earth until I am sure that I am part of it. I wonder if this is how worms feel. In school, we learned that worms are decomposers; they break down dead things. At the time, it sounded gross. But now, it does not seem so bad. Worms get to sleep in the dirt forever. I think that maybe I am a worm.

It is quiet here. I close my eyes. My quiet little place smells like heat and the colour brown. Something crawls across my hand. I do not move. I am sure the bug is just happy to have company.

The bugs fall asleep around me. I let them rest.

Someone grabs my foot and shakes me awake.

My little sister has found me.

The blackberry bush lets me go and I wiggle out. My sister tries to brush the dirt off me, but I reach out to stop her. I tell her that I am a worm. She nods. She gets it. She says she is a princess. I don't think she gets it.

My TeeTee is outside on the porch. When she sees me, she points to my legs. I look down. From my bony knee and below, my skin is pink. I wonder how long I was under there.

I look up at my TeeTee. And she is laughing.

* * *

I am twenty and I am in the backyard of my aunt's home. Although not really. My aunt isn't here anymore. She isn't anywhere. Except in the ground.

My sister is in the car. She's waiting for me.

The blackberry bush is not here. Its absence is more obvious than its presence ever was.

It takes me a moment to find where the bush used to be, but then, I am sure. This is where the bush used to be.

I get down close to the earth and I lay on my back. I close my eyes.

I am a worm. And I am laughing.

A Window to You

Angela Fossi

Memories of my youth are all around as I walk these streets,
a quaint haven tucked away in modern times.
In the centre of the village, the fountain still beats,
in the distance the church bell chimes.

Pigeons peck around, seeking whatever they can find,
locals sit on the nearby benches, for a moment of peace.
Cafés and restaurants line the streets where I once dined;
so many things have changed, yet my memories do not cease.

I take a seat on the train, it pulls out from my hometown,
I remember the lace sleeves you wore, like a romantic poet
from times gone by; when I feel I could drown
I hold you close to my chest, as I would a locket.

The train glides along the tracks, taking me towards the city,
the steeple of the old church is still in view.
Whenever I walk by, I always think her so pretty,
some Sundays, I go inside, in pious prayer, seated in a pew.

As the train etches on the journey farther out,
my heart is left on a pillar of wild thorns.
In times when I doubt, I am not so devout,
I am often called back by a heart that mourns.

My faith takes me soaring like an angel,
I take a journey that needs no train.
Do your memories of me exist only as a fable?
Or do you harvest them as you would grain?

I remember the days we strolled through the park,
and no matter the season, we could always laugh,
and even on days we cried, we still found a spark,
because when we were together, we were each other's staff.

You had the finest strands of hair, threaded like silk,
your eyes held the spectrum of blue,
and your smile was soothing warm milk,
but our lives took different paths; to a distant land you flew.

The First Bite

Shania Daphne Andrea OBrien

You loved me like a storm that starts and circles where it ends –
It broke the trees but spared the root, then doubled back again.
I loved you like a painting cracked beneath a glass too thin –
Each touch reframed the damage, but I kept the canvas in.

We never touched at equal points, nor met with even weight –
One always ran, one always knelt, one came a breath too late.
Your heart was made of orbiting – of leavings and return
Mine, a quiet furnace that mistook the cold for burn.

I called you ouroboros, the end that eats the start –
You smiled like that explained it, then devoured my heart.
I gave you all my angles, let you mould me into round –
But circles don't have corners, love, they only spin and drown.

You said we had forever, like a curse disguised as grace –
But time repeats its sentence in a closed and airless place.
You wrote me into cycles, swore we'd never come undone –
Then left me in the silence where the ending had begun.

I learned to trace your patterns, every exit, every turn –
Mistook your vanishing for depth, your absence for concern.
You licked the wound, then named it love; I offered you the knife –
But hunger isn't healing, and consumption isn't life.

So let the serpent coil again and dream its ancient lie –
That something endless cannot end, that gods forget to die.
I'll love you in the shape you gave, unlearning how to bend –
A mouth that meets its maker, and a wound that calls it friend.

Twenty Years Love

Chloe Isabelle Pryce

It's been a year since I last saw you, last heard your voice on the phone. A year since we giggled over boys, as we've done since we were children.

When I think of you, you are wearing a confection of blush pink frills.

You are telling me how much I deserve from men, how much you like your new one. In my memory, the last call I made to you was as I walked the bay, gravel crunching underfoot, the heady mangrove smell.

There was no announcement. The hope leaked from me in tiny gasps.

> good luck this week! you're going to kill it
> *(I love you)*
>
> this is such a cute photo of you two <3 let's catch up soon! *(I love you)*
>
> merry christmas! thinking of you, hope you're having a restful break *(I love you)*

The words had no echo. You were living and breathing and drinking mocktails in pink dresses and not texting me.

I couldn't bring myself to ask why. To ask would be to acknowledge how wide the chasm had grown, how deep the hurt. How long and hard the fall to solid ground.

I spent six months spiralling. I had done nothing, but had I done something? Had I made the worst possible mistake, and forgotten, never realised? I must be such a bad friend, to hurt you so much and so thoughtlessly.

I should reach out. I had reached out. Should I have been more direct? More gentle? Had you been offended? Were you depressed, secretly, or controlled? But there was no reason to rediscover, no matter how many times I peeled back the scab from the crimson-coral wound.

There was no sense to it. The friend I had loved for two decades wouldn't ghost me on a whim. The friend I loved would tell me if something was wrong.

My apartment, still, is littered with remnants of our friendship. There are beautiful glasses and childhood pictures and a crochet pot plant that dangles in the window. It has been eleven months and six days since I moved here, to an apartment you have never seen. There are photographs of me that you wouldn't recognise, dresses that I would have worn on our summer escapades. I fell in love here, almost, with a man whose name you couldn't know.

My life, too, is littered with you. Half my stories, half my jokes, half my thoughts seem to run back to you. Your name on my lips before I've figured out how to use it. "My friend" seems wrong. Anything else is unthinkable.

The bite of it has faded now, but the fact of your abandonment can still wind me, any moment of the day. A quiet anxiety of mine, I have worried all my life that I could say the wrong thing, imperceptibly and unintentionally, and my loved ones would leave me.

I called it paranoia.

It is ruinous – to your peace, to your self-worth, to your being – to realise you are disposable. To finally see this irrational, intrusive thought come to pass utterly shattered me. Shatters.

Your birthday passed in silence, as mine had. When flowers came, impossibly, I thought they were from you. I thought of you all week, and I cried.

You texted me, finally, before my grandmother's funeral. She had loved you, too, when she could still remember. The message was like one you'd send to someone you'd lost contact with from school, who you think of fondly, occasionally.

And maybe that's how it was, for you. Maybe that was all you had to give me.

When I wrote to you, that last time, I wanted you to feel how far the ground had opened up between us. Not to cause you pain, but to show you mine. The ache is simply a function of loving you, so deeply and so well, for more than half my life.

> Grandma thought you were so funny and clever *(I love you)*
>
> I've been so confused *(I love you)*
>
> I hope you're well, and your partner, the family *(I love you)*

It is too far now, I think, to jump. But at my feet, still, stacked and scattershot –

The makings of a bridge.

Day One

Alessio Maugeri

Twenty-five-page document. $2,500 spent with a psychologist. A cute little biography about me from my psychologist's observations. **Level 1 Autism Spectrum Disorder** in bold text right beside my written name. A bunch of statistics to positively support the judgement too. You don't just "develop" autism, do you? It's been here from the very start. How come now, just a touch over twenty-one years into my life, I find all this out for certain? The signs must've been obvious from the very start, no? Perhaps it was all just boiled down to some kind of "chronic shyness" or something. I must've just been nothing more than a weird kid who'd grow out of it all and break their shell someday, or at least until they had no choice to. Surely somewhere, in every little memory and curious story from my past, there's an explanation or a clear history to all of this, right? How has this manifested throughout my whole life? How does it explain the years of confusion and oddities, the hardships and the struggles, the desperation and selfishness that was really just an unmet need?

Well, let's see here, shall we? The DSM-V. My psychologist's bible that decreed me to be what I am. Section A.1 in the diagnostic criteria, "deficits in social-emotional reciprocity." I remember as a kid, and even now, just saying hello wasn't so simple. I'd skip it completely, immediately ask if they liked

Super Mario or Pokémon, just like me. When the other kids said no, which they often did, I never knew what to do. Sometimes I'd skip trying to find our overlap and try to pull them into my world, show them something I found really cool and cared about and not even bother to pause and ask if they even cared. Usually I kept going until it was very bluntly stated I was annoying them. And in the rare instances where we did overlap, I'd always forget to ask their name. Hell, I still do!

Section A.2, "deficits in non-verbal communication." Haha, my mother knows about this one well, I know! She'd always ask me why I couldn't smile while I was growing up. I never knew what she meant. I'd always press my cheeks and try to show my teeth, but my lips just pulled back instead of raising themselves upward. A girl in primary school too, one day, out of the blue, just asked me what was wrong. I was so confused and said I was fine, and she just said "oh, ok. You just always look so sad is all" and she kept walking. Oh, and how eyes completely terrified me! Whenever people looked at me, and our eyes met, it was like they were staring right through me, exposing me for everything I was, everything they hated, and I hated looking back. I'd stare at their neck or their chest just to feel safe. Then I got older and looking at people's chests became rude, so I didn't know where to look anymore and instead just started drifting into the background. That only proved to be ruder though. I ended up settling on looking at their mouths.

Section A.3, "deficits in maintaining relationships." God, when hasn't this been a problem, really? I remember strolling in the school playground like some kind of disgruntled nomad or a dishonoured ronin, face down towards the ground talking to myself, imagining a brighter world far from this one. When life shifted into new domains, into high school and university, faced with the challenge of making new friends, I never stuck my feet the right way making headway on those goals. I didn't make my first high school friend until the end of my third term in Year 7, my first university friend not until second semester. None of the attendees at my eighteenth birthday were the same as my twenty-first either. All these people, coming and going, slipping through the seams of my fingers no matter how hard I held onto them fondly, never knowing how to get them to like me or if I even was something likeable in the first place.

Now, section B.1, "repetitive motor movements and speech." Haha, I remember as a kid I loved how fun it was sucking on my bottom lip! You can sometimes find old photos of me with a pinkish mark below my bottom lip from how hard I was sucking. I was a chronic biter as a child as well, though fortunately not in an aggressive sense. Anything I put near my mouth, you'd often find bite marks shortly after. Straws for drinks or even my stylus for my Nintendo DS. Often I did it without even knowing what I was doing or why. I just liked biting or chewing whatever was in my mouth. I used to even bite the fleshy parts of my arm gently just because it helped relieve my anxiety and anger a bit, and I really liked the little marks it left in my arm afterwards. I've been prone to recycling the same phrases just to get by in conversation. How easy it is to just say "fair enough" or "oh, nice!" to any little story someone tells you about their lives, and how it's salvation from the dilemma of uncertainty!

Section B.2, "insistence on sameness and routine." My diet was so limited as a child. I loved eating fast food fried chicken and my mum's cooking, which included whatever she packed in my lunchbox. I was on a baby bottle through all through primary school too because I couldn't handle changing to a proper breakfast. Whenever my family had a change of plans to what I was told as well, like no longer going out on Sunday or leaving half an hour later than we said we would, I'd get so frustrated and start shouting at them about when we'd leave or what we'd do. "You gave me a time and place, so follow it!" was all I could really think of then. Growing up as well, there's always been consistent dates/times for certain behaviours too. Lunch around 1:00 p.m. Dinner towards 7:30 p.m. Journal about the week every Sunday night before bed. Shave my face twice a week. Shower every morning. Any fracture or delay to any of these will lead to a burning frustration sizzling through the back of my mind.

Section B.3, "highly restricted, fixated interests." That was my whole thing growing up! I was better remembered by the one thing I always talked about more than my name. As a kid, it was always Pokémon. There was one time my sister was messaging a friend on her computer, in the glory days of 2010 Facebook, and I asked if I could send a message to her friend. Oblivious, she said yes, and all I wrote was "Pokémon." I just wanted anyone to hear about it. I'd even try to find creative ways to squeak it into my classwork just because it was the only thing I wanted to think about. When school ended and I made it home, I always ran straight for my DS, sometimes even before eating afternoon tea or changing out of my uniform. Then in high school, I kept talking about The Beatles. I managed to pull a few friends into my obsession and we went to Comic-Con cosplaying as Sgt Pepper's Lonely Hearts Club Band together. My Beatles t-shirt was my favourite one to wear in high school. I always saved it for my dates with my first girlfriend because it brightened my mood even further when I was wearing it. In Year 9 Drama class, I wrote the script for a play we had to make for an assessment, and since there were four characters, I named them after The Beatles with some liberations to fit the context of the story. Paul, John, Richard and Georgina. It even came down to my appearance too. Everybody compared my look to John Lennon, and they were right to make that observation, because I grew out my hair to be just like his, even wearing round sunglasses to complete the look. I always told people I liked music, but up until the last few years, I really meant that I like The Beatles and a few other bands adjacent to them. My fixations never leave; they just evolve alongside me.

Finally, B.4, "hyper- or hyporeactivity to sensory input." I suppose that combines well with my repetitive behaviour to touch my face. For the last few years, I've never smooth-shaved my face and have always left a little bit of facial hair. I think it's just because there's something so nice about caressing the small little points of hair sticking out of my face. It eases my tension in the same way petting a cat does. And I've always hated tight crowds of people, not just because of difficulty around people either. I hate how constricting on all my senses it is. The noise of it all, and how small it makes me feel, being surrounded by everybody with such little space. Sometimes I walk in the opposite direction I need to go just to take the bus at an earlier, quieter stop, avoiding all the pressure and getting a seat I can sit comfortably in. I always fight for a seat because my sense of balance is terrible too. When the bus takes a hard stop or turn, my feet just give in and I have to cling onto the railing for dear life. I've often depended deeply on my headphones as well. They're my only escape when the world gets overwhelming, a place in which the oppression of noise may vanish, and I may find peace within myself. They're my safety item, and without them, I am at odds with reality. I remember, when I was a kid, my dad always tried to make me wear a singlet during the winter, to the point where he'd go grab one from my drawer before he'd help me get dressed. I kept throwing it back in my drawer because I hated how it felt. The whole thing just felt awful to me, from the tag scratching along my neck to how tight it made my body feel. I always avoided wearing jumpers in school too. I hated how much they made my arms itch, and I always just stuck to the jackets or blazers. And I despised wearing ties because it meant I had to do up my top button, which felt like I was being choked all day. In high school, I had to do my tie extra tight just so the teachers wouldn't be able to spot that the top button wasn't done up. If my future job requires wearing a tie, I'm hoping this old strategy continues to be effective!

Well, that's all the criteria for diagnosis. I'm a textbook definition! So the signs were all there all along, throughout every year of my development and life, and continuing in new and persistent ways even now. Nobody had the courage to tell me until I was out of high school though. How much pain and confusion, misery and anxiety could've been avoided if just one person created a safe space to just talk about it. It's funny though, really. It's honestly cute looking back at these memories, regardless of how funny, painful, or difficult they are for me to reminisce upon. These little stories are like those dots towards the large X on a treasure map, a collection of little fragments that have all been building up to this exact moment, sitting here with my diagnosis finally in my hands. There's no shame, not now, and not anymore for any of those memories. I used to dread some of those things about myself, hide them as much as I could, or look back on them and appraise them as irreparable flaws within myself. There's a sense of freedom and liberation from that now. They're just memories where my true self leaked out, a real me who, even when rejected by the world around them, remained proudly themself.

Night-child

Chloe Isabelle Pryce

I have never been a dreamer
I wake each day as though from death
or coma; enchanted, hundred-year sleep

so to see your daughter: flaxen hair,
mischievous grin – your daughter,
who I have only known in pictures –
screaming and laughing in vivid definition,
seems like a god-wink, from you

in fullest dark we played in dappled light
I shielded her, I clasped her little hand
and I woke almost feeling
the tiny warm weight of her wriggling form

it is easy, today, to understand the ancients
whose visions were both mystery and portent
who sent her? for what reason?
it is strange to miss a girl I've never met

your daughter has a smile like sunlight –
or at least this night-child does –
and she runs in my mind's eye
as in a home movie, flickering joy

in the day's first reaches,
her image dissolves like spun sugar, and
I sit and I ponder the significance of dreams

Invitations

Saraa Purba

The acidic smoke of you, it's burnt umber scent on cheap lace. The concoction competing with warm and sharp cedar perfume – it is electric, ripping the charade of the present into a time before.

Do *you* miss *me*?

* * *

We often confused obedience for loyalty; this murkiness poisoned us all with a fierce hunger:

a) of guilt

b) of control.

And on the eve of our young adulthood, we pledged allegiance to either party. No pure support really existed – but we soothed ourselves with the binary. I was in business with God from birth; I didn't exactly understand the precarious nature of the contact my parents had signed till later. My sister and I found that God was in our cabinets, wardrobes, bathrooms, classrooms, and minds. We hadn't exactly invited the company, but our preferences weren't particularly pertinent to the tradition. I recited surahs that I didn't know the meaning of, memorising the sounds of language like music without questioning. Even after my departure from such "singing", I still hadn't taken to decoding them all – I had lost care for justification via quotation. This expectation of reason neatly bullet-pointed out why I left religion by those that remained loyal to God. I resented how they looked at me: deviant I was.

In a stroke of naivety, I had assumed some sort of liberation from piercing whispers … this was not the case. As I made my way through my undergraduate degree I noticed the exactness by which each of our stories had to be shared. With caveats of playful shame for dancing in darkness or desiring the touch of another woman. What loomed over our stories – in fact haunted the details – was the unsaid understanding we would one day stop and repent. I was lucky to be given the grace of tasting the ways of the white and free, but this was not to be made a habit of.

The diet must remain clean.

Unfortunately, such a healthy lifestyle came to sabotage the friendships I made in university. I spent first year constantly anxious of trains. The timetable tattooed itself into my consciousness. Each event became a task of mathematics, where the duration of the event was weighed against my parents' patience for my return home. At dinners with such friends I would begin to panic around 8:30. I would imagine that each second I didn't check the TripView screen another delay could derail my return home – track work, cancelled train, malfunctioning timetable, strikes! I was absent at parties I attended. Preoccupied by the pounding thump in my chest as I devised my way home. My friends would register the distress as a quirk.

In the clearing of one of these bitter smoky and sweet liquor-lit parties I met you. I had walked over from Newtown station to my friend's place – the distance between them was always savoured; I took pictures of the same moon, the same doorways, the same smothered-in-red brick resting in dawn's light. In the limbo of place, I licked at the delicious anticipation:

Who would I meet?

Would I fall in love?

What stories were to come?

But then there was always the acrid taste of *when do I go home?*

I entered such spaces with the feeling of performance: the curtains opened as I stepped forward past the doorway; the act of belonging was a demanding one. I adored my new friends – I never said yes to things I didn't want – but even things I wanted didn't feel entirely natural. An omnipresence of TROUBLE shadowed my movement on stage. I sat in lounge rooms laughing, but imagining that any second the police would smash through the walls and cuff me with spit forward screams asking, "Who the fuck do you think you are?" The crime of inauthenticity loomed large.

I was confident. Talking came to me naturally – talking distracted one from silence. We wrote love letters to our favourite films and dedicated tight five sets to memories of the past; we discovered one another outside the bounds of university. I mentioned that I had obsessively watched what I liked to call "the coming of age of adulthood films" – nobody was in high school, but everyone was lost all the same. These protagonists – people bordering on thirty and beyond – deeply cut into me. In a world that welcomed cemented identities and straight tracked futures past twenty-five, they were liquid. Julie comforted me while scenes from *The Worst Person in the World* played in my head like a perpetual reel. How the world remained still as she lived in motion with her messiness and her tender and stupid decisions was utterly surreal. Julie made mistakes over and over again, not because she was particularly cruel, but because youthful hearts are supposed to embrace impulsivity; and youthful exuberance is untethered from age. There were consequences, it was no utopia – but she chose where her heart took her. I longed for that liberation, but my fear of TROUBLE had struck me with Medusa's eyes. Julie's indecision electrified me – she was a medical student, then a psychology one; she became a photographer, and a writer. Julie was given the space to evolve – fluid she was.

She ended up a photographer taking stills during film production, right? Millie asked once.

Yes, yes – she had something to herself, it was perfect, I replied. It ended with her sitting in a room of her own.

But she lost the love of her life?

Yeah, well – yes. It's really devastating, but I think that is the point. Perhaps she did lose someone she could have loved endlessly, but now she knows how to do the same for herself.

And this is of comfort to you?

Millie reddened with mischief as she spoke. I loved that she reminded me of characters from comedy dramas, with deeply funny and deeply tragic pasts. Our words danced in a sort of sword fight as we talked; I was very lucky to know her. As if we were in a French salon of our own, she pushed deeper into the philosophical enquiry of comfort on her living room floor. She had posed that things that comforted her tended to annoy her all the same. That the returning itch of something was just as soothing as the cooling cream. Lara, Su, Rianon, Jess agreed vehemently, yes, yes – pain, annoyance whatever you call it was a part of it! I knew where this was going. Millie called out to the room, what was the biggest comfort? Lara claimed it had to be her mother.

The cultural symbol of MOTHER pierced me each time I found myself here. The point of the party where we would as ask B I G questions: love, fear, death; the clichés of stepping into *we're all just on this floating rock* was not lost on me. But it always crawled back to the origin point. The embryonic love I was unfamiliar with cradled conversations amongst young women. And yes! There was complication, perhaps one wanted to tear the hair out of the other, but there was always a love that underscored the violence. Lara looked up between her dyed blonde hair, she spoke about the endless breakdowns of young adulthood that made her reach for mother's teat. And by teat, the beloved phone call was meant by all conversing. That every minor inconvenience was met with a "what's wrong honey?" at the other end of the line. Perhaps – no, often – her mother made things slightly worse, they almost multiplied one another's distress; nonetheless, a distress was shared.

I mean, listen, I spent about thirty minutes on the phone crying trying to find my car, and she kept saying "what are you going to do without me?", but I don't know, I can't help it. She's my best friend.

Millie chimed in with her salon skills. "Babe, you're telling me. That's the universal experience. I almost flew home early when I went to go visit. Now I miss her."

The impulse to call my mother had never occurred to me.

Introducing the new and improved: MOTHER, she comes with an okay husband and possibly other children. MOTHER is your confidant. MOTHER holds you while you sob and shares your joy as her own. MOTHER is not your competition.

Since the age of fourteen such realisations had broken me. It was particularly embarrassing to watch the world choose one another and not be chosen. It wasn't jealousy, no. I didn't have an air of schadenfreude when my friends divulged the nuances of their softness, but I did feel acutely other. And this otherness stuck to me like black tar on my skin. I was marked by a guilt of resenting forgiveness. How deep can someone stick the knife into you before the damage is irreparable?

But there was you. I went out front to evade impending class participation. Through the doorway lingered the cool air of an August night; its subtle intensity pronounced the warmth on my cheeks, and I was suddenly re-awoken to being alive. I checked the train timetable. It was fucked, cancelled,

cancelled,

cancelled,

delayed.

I frantically called my mother: I'm going to be late and there is nothing I can do about it. I'm sorry – yes, I know, I'm doing too much. I just wanted to see my friends.

My mother screamed so obnoxiously I was almost relieved that by the time I got home she would have tired herself out. Maybe satisfied by her performance, we could move on. You tapped my shoulder and asked what was going on. I put myself on mute – she's a little crazy.

I'll drop you. I'm not drinking anyways.

Don't worry about it, I live far away enough that one of my friend's joke if I'm enjoying my time in the Big Smokes!

You laughed and said you liked driving in the night. Your deep brown hair fluttered in the wind and turned a little brighter under the lights Millie had draped outside. Its short ends flicked across your raised cheeks, Ivy. You presented your kindness like it was no big act, dangling the keys in front of me. I would have called you instead forever if you had let me.

Years later the same tinge of metal and sweet woody perfume remains on my top. I haven't worn it in ages, but I wonder if something would change in you if you saw it now. What a garish act that would be. You wrapped in a white gown that preserves every bit of you to imagination, the guests in embroidered jewel-tone cloth ... and me, in the lace top we first met in. When I was younger Mother had a real anxiety about such events; invitations remained at the centre of the fridge as the months went by. She would take out dusty suitcases filled with glittering lehengas and call tailors back in Bangladesh to account for recent puberty-related changes. Now, as I unpack what is left of these makeshift luggage-wardrobes I realise many of these will never be worn again. With Mother gone there is no one left to take care of them.

Back in June when I received your card, I hoped for a moment it was a joke. Unfortunately, promising your life to a man has remained ever possible. So I sent you a congratulatory message soaked in grief – on what I assumed was still your number, and you hearted it a week later. The strings that previously tied us together were thick and resilient; thousands of once empty spaces on my skin were connected to every bit of yours. Like baby sprouts through the crust of cement, we grew quietly and unexpectedly. How odd then, to see such vines dry and snap off. All that remains of us is one weak string – and through it you have sent me your wedding invitation.

* * *

A lingering wash of petrichor in the humid summer air, the wilting tomatoes in our sandwiches and our berry-centred treats left open without a care.

Will you choose to forget?

* * *

This morning, I awoke to the bruised sky; its throbbing purple bled into the highway as I made my way home. And in the dew of dawn in December I rolled down the windows and let the flickering droplets kiss my skin. You would always say this was an invitation for the sky to come with us. As I arrived back home, I wondered if you still let the sky into your car, or if I was the only one to enjoy such company.

Mother's closet felt heavy, each piece struck me as almost sweet and then quickly soured. They were laced with such a distinct scent of coconut oil and stale cotton. A plum sari was embedded deep in a pile of clothes I had to donate before the house went up for inspection. I would wear it tonight to see you.

During the summer you would pick me up on the birth of the sunrise just like the one outside Mother's window. The pulsing dawn became our close acquaintance. We would drive back to your place in the inner city (your parents seemed to always be away) and conspire in these secret moments together before meeting everyone at noon. Each day with our friends was double-edged in this way. There was the group, and insatiably, greedily, savagely, there was us. Jess' birthday would be a glorious picnic at the Botanic Gardens at around twelve. We had about five hours to ourselves before the rush of making sloppy tomato focaccia sandwiches became the primary mission.

In your bed I felt as if gravity melted off me, the weight of my existence became nothing at all. But within the silences, the moments between each breath, I remembered I would eventually go home. As we weaved into each other's limbs I began to mourn what had not died yet. Perhaps I was right to.

Where do your parents go?

You looked at me, surprised by my interest, um they work a lot. They like taking business trips together. But last week they left for Umrah. Should be back later in the night.

Oh, I just assumed since you're always out they weren't … I don't know, particularly practising.

They're selective, I guess. Enough about me though. When are you going to move out? I'm serious, this can't be something you deal with forever.

I jumped on top of you. NEXT YEAR! I swear it's happening. Su, Rianon and I are thinking of it doing it together.

You smirked at this little progress. It's a step forward, you said. At the time I wondered if I could ever be as fierce as you. Ivy, for me you had invited belief. I would slowly practise, worship your ways, pray to stop praying about guilt. You populated a magical island far out to sea with freedom; I wanted to meet you there. We got out of bed, made the sandwiches and drove to the gardens.

Jess lifted me with her familiar elation. I would never meet someone so kind – I promised myself to remember that as she held me in the sun. We handed her the tray of sandwiches, and she beamed like always. Millie had brought a blanket that asserted our little piece of the garden, Su baked raspberry tarts dusted with powdered sugar, Rianon and Lara presented a near masterpiece of a cheese board, and we ate and laughed like we were the first to. As the initial hunger faded Rianon finally debuted the story of her date from the week before (she had sent an ominous text, and like all good stories we had to wait to meet in person to hear it). It started with her getting ready at 5 for her ride at 8. He had alluded to picking her up and she liked to imagine he would do so. At around 7:45 her phone pinged and from that moment onward, Rianon claimed, it was truly and utterly fucked. We believed her.

He texts me – get this – when am I getting over to the bar? Are you actually kidding me? Chivalry has died! What happened to planning? The labour of a plan – that is what I want! Rianon laughed with fake despair, she had expected nothing less from a guy wearing a footy scarf to the club where she had met him weeks before. I looked over and briefly caught your eye in gratitude.

Finishing the last bite of her tart Su chimed in, so I picked this one up and went out to eat. Obviously, I would not let my fair lady leave without luxury – the feast at Oporto was a given.

Rianon's face began to flush with such intensity she defied the usual poker face of our complexion. Why are you turning red – oh my god, whatever happened you must tell us or I might kill you! I saw a rosiness in her that many brown women like myself seemed to catch later in our lives. See, in childhood we would all claim it as strength: our unfeeling skin would not expose us. Funny then, after we stopped running on playgrounds – our faces became so revealing, we grew vulnerable.

Listen, I know you're going to be "I told you so" more than anyone. We all leaned in, I was pretty sure of what she would say. Rianon whispered to mask her embarrassment: I met this girl at Bar Planet, and I think I'm going out with her tomorrow.

We erupted like wild animals; I had run a long campaign for the last three years to convince Rianon that she was bisexual. She had vehemently disagreed, but I was on a personal odyssey to convince everyone I knew that they were a little gay. We fought over her phone, and begged for photos of the mystery woman. She eventually provided us with the *documents* we needed to completely spearhead her one-way track to lesbianism. Rianon warned us not to hold our breaths over tight-top knot buns and a backyard wedding, but we couldn't help but a fantasise a little.

Millie began the planning process, listen it's going to be very clean and whimsical. But ALSO totally colourful, tasteful too. I just need to make a Pinterest board about this, and the vision will be clear.

Lara and I decided to take the playlist and auditory ambiance responsibility and began listing the must-haves in unison. Five string serenades obviously, we laughed at our musical togetherness.

What was the song you showed me a while ago? The green eyes ... the most romantic thing, you're going to love it Ri, it's really going to tie the event together. Lara was referring to *Green Eyes Siena*. I had by now so strongly attached it to you I hoped even in this fantasy the song would remain ours. I *chose* to forget with Lara, and we continued listing songs.

As time began unwinding, I'd be yours alone. Sometimes when we lay together, I could die and make my peace.

We drove home with the sky in your car and the song swirling around us. In a selfish way I began to wonder what our wedding would look like. Who would be there? Millie, Su, Jess, Rianon and her new beau. What of our family? You parked the car and jumped with panic as the shape of your mother walked by the window. You needed to drop me off immediately. In fact, you precisely said, you're not coming in. Whatever assumption of liberation I had constructed about your life shattered quickly after those words. With some of my clothes still splayed out across your bedroom, we parted ways with your driveway. You promised to return everything. Why did I think you were any different? The Persian deserts and Bangali banks were all the same, filled with a rotting shame that slowly ate at its landscape, its atmosphere, its people. Perhaps you were given the allowance to dance in the dark, but what became palpable that day was that your desire was monitored.

Longing was banned from the diet.

Even now, your promise punctures the fabric of my safety. Ivy, I didn't want you to return anything. I had stupidly hoped that shirt, those socks, my bra could linger in your bedroom forever. Recklessness is a temporary state; it either dies quickly or is forced to change. We drove back in gnawing moisture, the air between us thick with a tension that was slowly closing the gap in my throat.

I – I am sorry. That was just a lot. I'll see you tomorrow. You said it with such pleading eyes.

Maybe.

With the purple plum sari wrapped around my waist, and a bag of Mother's clothes I'll eventually donate, I smear blush on my cheeks for the last time in this house and drive to your wedding.

* * *

Sickly rose water sweets and fresh white lilies tussle for attention. The metallic smoke of your cigarette argues with a new deep vanilla and cardamom scent. The smell of you has mutated.

Is this our *farewell*, my beloved Ivy?

* * *

Millie walks into the reception hall with a face of awe that I have reserved for when weddings included fireworks. The bar for South Asian weddings has subdued the lust for long satin draped across the ceiling, the chandeliers, and hundreds of people you have met in life's passing. This is expected. And yet, as we sit down – all your supposed friends – a shock paralyses me watching you walk down the hall in heavy white. Your hair washes across your back in a waving motion, so quickly you move. He holds your hand as you make it to the stage, so quickly you move. You scan the audience for all those you have met in life's passing, including me, so quickly you move.

Far by the back of the hall, the group's table arrangement offers space to whisper incessantly without the heat of getting caught. Lara professes she assumed your husband would have been a little more striking – and not be rude, at least a bit taller. This comment I know is Lara's way of pledging her allegiance to me. Years after our tangled mornings, I confessed. The itch of you began to drive me crazy, and such strenuous memory was no longer bearable alone. The group had taken this to mean you were a MONSTER, RUDE, UNFEELING and closeted. I pretended to concur. Tonight we are out for material to dissect for the next five years. Each detail is a hunting ground for psychoanalysis:

1. The dress you wear.
2. Who else you invited.

3. The Bride of Honour's clearly fabricated speech.
4. The disappointing stature of your husband.
5. If you seem to love him even a little.

I know my beloved friends will reach the same results regardless of the data; the bias of my existence cements their opinions. Not because they enjoy the opportunity to be vicious, but because they love me viciously. Rianon's girlfriend, Mel, suggests we all take an edible before we are neck deep in the best man's beige speech. This certainly colours things and soon I am hiding the deep ache within me. Jess, like always, has been secretly monitoring if I am okay. She suggests we go outside for a moment – I could cry right here at the table with every eye on me like a not-so-fun entertainment quarter of the evening. She takes me outside into the warm night.

You know, love, this is sort of closure, right? Jess says. You can finally let go. I want you to be happy and being tied to this – whatever mindfuck she's kept you in for seven years is not worth it.

I just wish she'd said something before leaving, I reply. That stupid job in London, the lifestyle of *busy* that excused her seeing us – she forgot us.

And yet, we're at this wedding, aren't we? Maybe it's because she misses us, maybe it's because she thinks her 5'7 husband is something to brag about. Jess squeezes her arms around me and lifted my body to the streetlight like it is the sun.

I sit outside for a while by myself, and Jess ensures she will be back with food as the applause signals Mr Best Man has finally finished. Although I haven't ever been a smoker, the moment seems to call for a tool that evokes the macabre.

By performing this scene of catharsis perhaps I can convince myself of it.

FADE IN:

EXT. ROZELLE BAY – EIGHT IN THE NIGHT.

The venue rattles with conversation as the wedding party begin to eat. Outside, the protagonist sits by a curb staring at the stars. She must end the endless mourning; she lights a cigarette and smiles a little to herself as she speaks.

Protagonist

I'm going to be okay. Things that ache will soon be memories.

And then the unexpected.

Ivy

Hi you.

I look at you now unsure if I have completely lost my mind. To touch you was to know you were real. That is no longer an option. All I have now are my eyes. I invite you to sit down next to me and you do. Lighting a cigarette, you are careful not to get the ashes on your dress. For a while we say not much at all. Just the huff of weighted giggles wrapped around us. I finally the tear the skin open.

It's a really nice event. It must have taken a while to plan right?

Yeah, I mean Malik knows a planner, so it was actually a lot easier. How have you been?

Why are you outside? They'll come looking for you soon.

I watch as your brows crinkle, held together with a dignified and heartbreaking smile. You know it's my wedding, right? It's the ME show, I think I should be allowed to do what I want.

I pressed a little. You look different, it's a new look.

People change; I've looked like this for a while now. You've changed too.

I feel an insidious urge to say that I am actually stronger, that I have left home, that my mother is dead. Instead, I say: I was in love with you.

You hold my hand to your heart. This will change, you say.

A tear manages to escape your restraint; I chase after it with my finger. Goodbye Ivy.

And you say goodbye back.

* * *

It was easy to speak about freedom, of agency like it was a cloud we would never touch. We found comfort in its conceptual status; what was much more tightening was to speak about God. God invaded us like inescapable fog. God lurked in the cavities of our lives. He was unsaid and He was everywhere. So I created something else to pray for. In the car with Millie, Lara, Su, Rianon and Mel, I was *saved*. Perhaps we were all changing – you were right about that – but we chose to change together.

* * *

In truth, the traitors of God reeked of desperation, of love, of loneliness – this was our condition.

Purloin

Prue Foster

A row of plush cottontails as innocent as baby bunnies
compliant as the regulation grey, concrete shelter raised
up by knees and down with heads in shared screens.
.... Tik Tok, thought took
We slide beneath, no stealth needed, no intent but to ride
out the constrains of orderly days and a congested bus
heading darkly to another narrowing funnel entrance.
.... grid lock, grist clock
All eyes out, caught first by the umbrella of felt schoolgirl
hats, leaning down to lean thighs, leading down to expose
seams no different than the join of arm and sleeve, but still.
.... quick look, quiet shock
Pulling back, the pane reveals my own eyes to me,
while the males gaze past, out of magic windows to thrill
at taking a ride for free, heads turning still.

……….. eyes lock, sights hook
A mother's pull to warn and censure those that don't
know and those that know better to take the blame for
who,
for what, for sooner or for later the turn of yearning will
follow.
……….. moral shook, mind block
But the time bypasses all transportation,
descends into its burrow, gives right of way
and thoughts loop back around to the grind,
the dark oily slip left trailing behind.

The Art of Gift Giving

Urvi Agarwal

Let's talk about gifts, the historical act of giving something to strengthen social relationships. There are three distinct types of gifts, regardless of the occasion. First, there are ones that we give merely as an outcome of societal obligation. Similarly, there are ones that are reciprocal, given simply as a part of an ongoing gift cycle with someone. Both are a function of gift-giving slowly being morphed into a pawn of modern-day capitalism and expenditure.

But, transcending capitalism, ultimately there are gifts that stem from an innate desire to give, without expectation of reciprocation, an item or gesture of personal value to someone important to us. This could be given to evoke an immediate grand reaction from the recipient or to remind the recipient that we are thinking of them. And sometimes, we hope to make a mark with a gift so intimate to a relationship with someone that no one else could've given this to them.

You scoff. It's not every day that you find yourself reading an elaborate article on giving gifts. In fact, you're not even sure why you're doing this. This isn't one of your regular magazine mediums, like *Buzzfeed* or *The Guardian*. It's an anonymous article from some shady-looking site called *thirtysix*, some article you found open in your phone tabs that you must've checked last night.

Besides, it's not like she's expecting a gift from you. Neither will she feel hurt if she doesn't receive something from you … will she? You skim past the flowery shit and get to the crux – a step-by-step question guide that is supposed to help you with the choice.

You've stumbled here in your search of a gift that sends a message. Fear not, we have a distinguished set of questions, designed to aid your ideation. Keeping your recipient in mind, join us on the journey of self-discovery to guide you towards the best choice.

What is your gift budget?

Straightforward question, you think, makes sense. If all options for a gift need to be confined by any boundary, it should be a dollar budget.

Three months ago

All you can see is light. Refracting and reflecting and bending across surfaces everywhere. The sources of the glimmer are two primary things. Glass and stones. Rows and rows of stones embedded on rings, shelved inside glass panels to be examined by peering, hopeful people, each hoping to take home with them a token for their lover. And that's precisely why you're there, bathing in this light.

"Hey love," you look up to the kind face of the clerk behind the counter. "What can I help you with?"

You smile and scratch your head. "I ... well, I'm looking to buy a ring."

"That's nice," says the clerk with a smile, "and who is it for?"

Just then, your phone lights up with an incoming message. You see a spam text about buying windshield wipers, but that quickly flies by your notice because what you're really looking at is your lock screen. Frozen still in time, you see a picture of yourself standing in front of a fountain, your face contorted into weird shapes because you're laughing hard. You're bent like the Hunchback of Notre Dame, bent by the labour of carrying the most beautiful girl in the world.

"Her," you say, lifting your phone up.

"She's gorgeous," says the clerk, eyes twinkling, as though seeing what you see. You appreciate this even though you know it's not possible, because who can see the layers of love and beauty you see all at once?

"How long have you two been together?"

"Just a week short of two years," you say.

"And tell me, what's your budget, love?"

You shrug because you don't even know how to put a price on what you're about to do; you were hoping to figure that out here.

The clerk scans you for a second and nods. "I think I know what you need." Out comes a ring that is split three-way, simple, but with a little heart dangling between the second and third layer. The clerk quotes you a price that makes your heart jump a little. You do some quick math in your head and create at least five plans in which you can make it work.

Ten minutes later, you walk away with this ring, one that isn't like the others at all, and that's fine because she isn't like the others at all.

What is your recipient's love language? Think about their preferred receiving language as you shape your idea.

Twenty-five months ago

You can feel almost each blade of grass underneath your back, prickly and slightly damp. Your arm is across your face, shielding you from the brightness of the sun that's embracing you and the world around you.

In the greens of Camperdown Park, you are secluded from the loud noises of the vehicles of Sydney. Rather, you are surrounded by some chatter here and there. The sun is casting its warmth but there is a slight breeze in the air so it's also cool. In all, the setting is perfect. And the best part is that when you lower your arm and turn your head even slightly to the left, you see her there. She's gleaming and picturesque, as if she was the model child of the sun itself, sculpted to perfection, and intricately placed at this exact point in time next to you.

She turns sheepishly and looks at you. Your cheeks burn a little because you realise you've been caught looking, but she doesn't seem bothered because she soon returns to her position of basking with her eyes shut.

"You know what love languages are, right?" she asks.

"Yeah, of course I do," you say, "the five things and all that." Just two months into dating her, you are driven by a need to impress her.

"What are your love languages then?" she asks.

"Umm," you pause to think.

You're not sure, really, because who has even asked you that before? Who has ever specifically cared to know what your ways of loving are? Consequently, you haven't examined yourself to know the melodies of your own heart.

You're about to utter sounds to delay your answer when thankfully, she speaks. "I took the test yesterday," she says. "They say that my 'giving' language is physical touch and quality time. My 'receiving' language is words of affirmation and acts of service."

You consider that.

"They're probably right," she adds, "but I am pretty sure 'receiving gifts' should be on there. Not gift cards of course, but I enjoy cute trinkets."

You don't say anything. Your mind feels blank, like an empty echo chamber. You have nothing to say, because really, you're just in awe about how self-aware she is.

By the time you decide to tell her that you guess your love language is probably something along the lines of words of affirmation, even though you haven't taken the test, because words are all you've ever known, you realize that she's fallen asleep.

What was the first gift you ever gave the recipient?

You think hard and try to remember. The first thing you ever gave her was a small stuffed Baymax, the white balloon-y robot from *Big Hero 6*, her favourite animated film. She had been delighted and kept it atop her dresser and later added a little handmade paper crown to it. She insisted you two to watch the movie again that night and you could feel the joy radiating from her, it was contagious.

Though it was merely three months into dating her, it might have been the first time you knew you wanted to be around her forever. You loved her energy, you loved her glee and you wanted to be flushed by it over and over again.

You glance at stuffed Baymax sitting in the corner of your room, bum facing up. You roll your eyes at it.

When was the first time you had a conflict with the recipient?

You are a little surprised by the bluntness of the question. You decide to ignore it and let your mind carry you into the early days of your relationship

Twenty months ago

You see your reflection move as you approach her and she cranes her neck to blow a kiss at you. You look at her in the mirror first, then move around to stand in between her and the mirror so you can see her in real space.

She looks stunning. Wearing a long floral skirt and a black tube top, she looks like the kind of girl that turns every head in the movies. Her hair is braided to the side, and she wears blue earrings in the shape of jellyfish that dangle from her ears. You stare into her eyes in awe. Lipstick in one hand, she looks back at you and blushes.

"What?" she asks, which is really a rhetorical question because she is smiling, her face aglow with a blush, as she asks it.

"Nothing at all," you say, and you kiss her because you can't help it.

"Great," she says, rolling her eyes and feigning a pout. "I have to redo my lipstick."

"Worth it for me," you say, shrugging. She playfully nudges you away from her so she can look at her mirror. You simply sit at the edge of her bed and let her get ready.

A few hours later, hand in hand, the two of you walk into a small, cozy and dimly lit room. There is light chatter around, people with wine glasses and some instrumental music playing from some corner. Though both of you only know the host, she easily situates herself in the crowd. You admire her ability to do that, to float in a space and simply attract attention, but you're not surprised because you recognize her magnetic force.

She refers to you as her partner and you blush because you are humbled and honoured to be a duo with her. You mostly just listen to her while the others converse, contributing with a "yes" or a shy nod occasionally – you are not much of a talker, you're not sure what you would say. However, you enjoy listening to her, so you don't mind.

Soon she gets pulled away by someone introducing her to someone else, and then she is here and there, and you are standing in the same place, unsure what to do. You tune into the music and try to sync into the notes when you hear her laughter above the music, drowning out the melody of the piano with a melody of its own. Suddenly you feel so alone. You wish that she was taking you with her wherever she was being pulled towards.

You try to join a group chatting near you, who are talking about the weird absence of the mention of COVID-19 in movies made after 2020, and you realise that this is truly her type of party and her type of crowd. At some point they look at you and you offer a smile and politely excuse yourself; any possible insights or words caught in your throat.

You go to the kitchen island and get yourself a glass of red wine in the hope of liquid courage. But as it sinks into your body, you feel drowsier. With every moment, the chatter feels deafening and you want to get out of there.

You spot her near the speakers and walk towards her. You call out but you're not loud enough and the sound doesn't really reach her. So, you tap her shoulder, and she turns to look at you.

"Are you okay to leave?" you ask softly.

"Umm," she says and glances back at the group she is talking to, "you wanna leave already?"

"I feel ... like I want some silence."

"Okay," she nods slowly. "Do you want to step out with me for a bit?"

"Uh, okay, yeah, that works," you say. She excuses herself from the group and you both step out onto the balcony.

She crosses her arms and rests them on the railing and looks out into the stars. After a moment, she turns and looks at you.

"All okay?" she asks.

"Yeah," you say. "Just needed a moment."

"I get it," she says. "It can be intimidating in there. We can step back in after a bit."

You laugh a little because you doubt that she is intimidated by this. She is fierce and smart and attractive. Everyone wants to talk to her. You look through the glass panel into the room. The thought of going back in there makes you exhausted.

"I don't really want to go back in there," you say. "I don't know. I feel lost. I don't know anyone."

"You should've just come around with me," she says. "I'm meeting them for the first time too."

"I don't think it's me people are trying to take around for introductions and striking conversations," you say.

"Come on," she says, "just move about with me. It's pretty obvious we're a package deal, people probably assumed you'd come along anyways."

You can feel that it's not true. How can the two of you be a package when no one notices your absence?

"No, it's okay," you say, "you're having a lot of fun without me anyways. I don't want to hold you back."

She furrows her brows. "How can you hold me back?"

"It's fine," you say, not wanting her to see you as a broken puppy who needs rescuing. "You don't have to do all that. Like take me along and all. I think I'll go home anyways." You offer a smile to indicate that it's fine.

"Hey," she says, annoyance creeping in her voice. "I know I don't have to. I want to. You need to trust that I don't do things out of obligation."

You feel embarrassed because you know it's not true and now you just feel like a burden. "Whatever, it's fine, really. I am leaving."

"You know I can't let you leave alone," she says, "it's late at night. Just come in for a little bit, let's enjoy for some time and we can leave together."

"I don't know," you say. Then you breathe out. "I'll wait out on the balcony, just let me know when you're done."

"Just join me inside? It's stranger for me to be inside and leave you alone on the balcony."

"You didn't mind leaving me alone earlier," you sound accusatory without meaning to. It's the late night and exhaustion talking.

"I wasn't *leaving you alone*," she says defensively. "It's a party. You were with people." She sighs. "I don't know what to say."

Sharing the sentiment, you stare at the ground. She huffs.

"Whatever," she says, defeated. "Okay fine, let's leave." The annoyance in her voice is evident.

Suddenly, you feel bad, but before you can say anything, she walks inside, says a few words to the host, grabs her jacket and looks at you expectantly. You follow quietly, and neither of you say anything for the rest of the night, except for a murmured "bye" when you get out of the Uber at your place.

You apologise the next day for being grumpy. She apologises too and says that perhaps you both should be more cognizant of social situations next time.

You feel guilty but you don't know how to explain that it's different for you. People don't just gravitate towards you. You are not the type people are eager to have around. You're just you, and without her by your side, sometimes you might just be nothing.

Is the recipient a beach person or a mountain person?

What a random question. You begin to question the integrity of the article.

Whatever. Mountain person. You know for a fact that whenever she needed an escape from her thoughts, her world, and very rarely, you, she would run to the mountains.

This is why three months ago, you rented out a cabin in the Blue Mountains, to celebrate a special two-year anniversary. Funnily enough, this is also why, the next morning, she asked you to leave her there and go back to the city on your own.

Weird question, you think. Weird article.

Think about a time they were vulnerable with you.

Seven months ago

You're standing frozen. Your body is tense. You try to feel, think, but the thoughts inside your brain are like rainfall and trying to think is like an attempt to catch a single raindrop. Impossible. So, you close your eyes and decide you won't catch a single drop, you will just accept whatever lands on you.

Five senses, you remember. Time to use them.

You can feel your brows knitted so tightly together that they could snap. But you're frozen, so you can't undo them. Slowly you notice the chill of the cold marble floor beneath your feet. There must be magic at play because as soon as you realise this, the chill spreads up your body like a current. Electrocuted, you can now move. You wiggle your toes and unknit your brows.

Your mouth tastes like bile and it's dry but also gross with the saliva that has been sitting there since you last moved, last swallowed, possibly five minutes ago. You need to drink water.

You never end up trying to smell because suddenly and simultaneously you're hyper aware of what you're seeing – her, crouched in the opposite corner of the bathroom across you – and what you're hearing – sobs, mostly coming from her and sniffles mixed from you.

"I'm sorry," she is saying, "I'm sorry and I'm sorry and I don't know what else to say because I have to go."

You hate this. You hate the fact that three minutes ago, she told you that she had booked a one-way trip to Mumbai, leaving in nine days. And all you said was "what," because all you could think about was your upcoming anniversary, your search for a dog to adopt and the fact you recently turned down the renewal of your lease.

Furthermore, you hate the fact that two minutes thirty seconds ago, you received the worst news of *her* life. "Babe," she'd said, her voice slowly breaking, "my mum called at work today … my nanu just passed away."

She explained to you for fifty-seven seconds after that she wasn't able to call you right away, because she was consoling her mum and figuring out her flight to Mumbai. Because she is the only child, and she has to be there for her mum. Her words for those fifty-seven seconds were not words, but rather chilliest of the winds (–10°C), traveling straight to you from the arctic circle. The wind reminded you of the time your own grandad passed and how you crumbled with pain at that time. It made you realise that this moment, right now, is the pivotal point of the most meaningful relationship you've ever had. The girl you love will leave. And life will never be the same again. So thus, the arctic wind blew over with a fierce rage and subsequently you froze.

But now, it's nearly three minutes later. You're newly unfrozen and shame rushes over you because she's there and she's crying and nothing else should matter. You run to her and hug her because you don't matter.

"No," you say, "You have nothing to be sorry about. I'm here for you now. I'm sorry. We're in this together."

You sit against the wall and pull her towards you. You hold her tight and squeeze her. She puts her head on your shoulder and cries silently. You sniff her hair, it smells like eucalyptus, which is coincidentally exactly the smell you want to envelope her pain with, so it goes away. You kiss her forehead and hold her hand.

And just like that, both of you sit still, together, for many moments. Her breathing slows and her sobs are replaced by sniffles.

"Tell me, my love," you begin to ask, "what are you thinking about at this moment?"

She says nothing for a moment. Then she takes a deep breath.

"Kachoris," she says. "My nanu used to love Kachoris. He used to believe they're stuffed with the same molecular matter that someone's sleeping nightmares are made of."

"Huh?" you ask. "Kachoris don't taste like nightmares."

"No," she agrees and lets out a small, sad, laugh. "Because they're spiced and fried to be made delicious. So that once someone eats them, they're happy, and their nightmares are likely to go away."

"Ah," you say, "he was quite the master of conspiracy theories. I respect it."

This induces another laugh from her that quickly turns into more tears. You close your eyes and let tears flow down your face too.

Aptly, it rains that night and you drive out and bring her some Kachoris. She sobs a lot, and there is a lot more hugging and forehead kisses. Amidst the pain of the tragedy, something shifts between the two of you that night and you feel closer than you've ever been.

What do you admire most about the recipient?

Her eyes. They're a little glassy and every time you look at them, straight, it almost forces your reflection back at you.

How smart she is. Whenever you're in a quandary, she finds the simplest solutions, like the obvious ones you might miss. She always beats you at Scrabble and whenever you play Mafia, she is alarmingly great at being the Mafia.

The fact that she can create designs that move so many people. Whenever you look at her bent over her iPad, pencil in hand, putting together her work, you can tell that she is hardworking and that all her successes are well-deserving.

Her ability to make you feel like you are special simply because you exist in her life. There are so many people in awe of her, yet when she chose you, it felt like receiving a gold star in kindergarten.

Her thoughts. She has the most unique viewpoints on the movies she watches. She was the one who showed you the fountain from *The Matrix* at Martin Place. She loves rom-coms but she will be the first to tell you how ridiculously unrealistic some of the story lines are – how do people find love, undergo career changes and move cities all at the same time? Impossible, she thinks.

Her laughter. Her beauty. Not just that of her physical appearance but her soul. Her love. When she gives you love – when she suddenly hugs you from the back, tells you that you matter, tells you that she loves you – all the troubles of the past melt away and none of the pain of your past relationships or friendships matter. She fills all those voids with a love that's liquid – it takes the shape of the container it's put in – a mix of the blue that makes up the sky and the golden that is painted over the sky when the sun is at its brightest.

When this love is taken away, your life is drained of colour, and it's all black and white.

What is a life without them in it?

You grunt. It's almost as if this article was designed to push your buttons.

Four-and-a-half months ago

Life is a funny little cauldron of irony. You are standing across the love of your life. Love is in the air. Not in the warm, cute, romantic sense. But rather the sense in which love becomes passion, which becomes fire, which becomes rage.

People tend to forget that often this rage, which is the underlying tone of endless fights, has its own underlying emotion which is love.

In this moment you are struggling to keep afloat this love as it channels itself into the smallest of fights. You are exhausted.

"Say something," she says, coming closer to you. Ever since she came back from Mumbai two weeks ago, she has been restless and angry. She has felt displaced because she thought she was going to move back home forever, for her mum. She stuck by her mum and they both lifted each other up. But eventually, her mum, stronger than ever, sent her back, knowing her daughter's life and dreams and work were all here.

As for you, you absolutely hated your two months without her. Everything that made your days worth waking up for was gone. So, when the love of your life returned, you felt hope, like the rug was back beneath your feet. You, being the only one left with an active lease, brought her into your home, excited to pick up where you left off. To turn your home of one into a home of two.

But the version of her that returned from Mumbai was a changed one. She was burdened by the grief, pain and exhaustion over losing her grandfather. You, the pit of darkness that you've always been, were so relieved to have your (now flickering) light back, but you didn't know how to be the light for her.

So, you worked on yourself to slowly become her light. You journaled, you worked out, you did everything you could. You tried to be the pillar for both of you.

But here you both are, having the same arguments. Because for her, life feels like a restart. She feels like something is missing, she is not happy. You are already operating at maximum capacity; you don't know what you can be anymore of to make this better.

When was the last time you decided to choose a gift for them without a special occasion?

Three months and one week ago

You look at her, curled up at your sofa. Her face is expressionless as her thumb swipes across her phone screen. You sit across her on the sofa and nudge her gently.

She looks up at you and puts her phone down. "Hey," she says. You see that her lock screen is a picture of her with her nanu.

"Hey," you reply, you smile at her. She gives you half a smile back.

As you have felt over the past month, you once again sense her slowly slipping out of your reach. Like she is somewhere in some void where no one can get to her. She's been quiet lately – you haven't fought for two weeks which is a relief to you because you hate fighting with her.

You want to take her mind off things, but you don't know how. You think of the things she loves talking about. You spot the Architectural Digest sitting on the side table and pick it up.

Quickly, you flip it open and see the picture of a small house, cottage style, with luxury interiors on the inside.

You beckon the magazine towards her. "Okay tell me, what do you think of this house?" It's a familiar game you both have played many times before. Looking at luxury properties around the city.

She examines the page. "It's a little small ... but honestly, that's ideal. Less cleaning. The inside is beautiful though." She runs her hand over the page.

You gather all your chirpiness. "I think so too. In fact, it's perfect for two people and a ... dog, don't you think?"

"Yeah," she laughs a little. Then adds, "depends on what type of dog."

Seeing her laugh lightens your own chest.

"A Bichon Frisé, of course." You put on your most serious face to refer to her favourite dog.

"Perfect," she says. She smiles. She shuts the book, closes her eyes and lies on the sofa. Though small, your heart is warmed hearing her talk about a possible future.

You decide then that you want to lock in this future. Maybe not with this house – located in Rose Bay, one of the most expensive suburbs of Sydney, it is a little out of your (or anyone's) budget. But still, you want to take a step forward, together, with her.

And so, you plan to find a ring the next week. You want her in your life forever and she's finally smiling. You want to be the one being able to make her smile forever.

What has been a pivotal point in your relationship with them?

Two months and three weeks ago

The air is chilly and your hands shiver. You are cold but she must be colder because altitude-wise, she is a half a foot above you.

You're on one knee and holding out a box with a three-layered ring, with a dangling heart. She is smiling and this should make you happy, but it doesn't. It's the type of smile she puts out when someone tells her to smile for a photo.

It's a smile that's slowly dropping.

"I ... no ... I ..."

Your heart is contracting, and you are extremely confused right now.

"I am sorry I can't do this", she says.

"I thought you wanted this," you say. You fall to the floor, and she kneels to sit next to you.

"I thought I did," she says, and you can sense the guilt building exponentially in her voice. You look at her questioningly.

"I didn't realise you were going to do this now," she says, "I'm sorry. I'm not ... happy. I've not been since nanu passed. Especially since I came back from Mumbai.

"But I don't understand," you say, "you said you were happier, you picked up on work again. Just a few days ago we spoke about our forever. With the house and the dog."

You try to meet her eyes but she looks away. She runs her hand over her hair and a feeling of betrayal creeps over you.

"We have been so good this past month," you urge on. "We haven't even fought."

"Isn't that the problem?" she asks, looking down at her hands. "I looked at the mountains yesterday, looked at the vastness and realised how I have been in limbo. I realised ...

that I have stopped fighting with you. With myself. With life. I'm not alive anymore; I'm just on autopilot."

You know this feeling. You know it all too well. That's the feeling you have spent your whole life working on. You take a step and think. You need to fix this. "We can work on this," you say. "That's alright, we can take our time."

She looks up at you and there are tears in her eyes. "I don't think we can ..."

The next morning you leave and now, you're the one on autopilot again. She extends the cabin stay because she needs time for herself. She can't be with anyone right now, she says. Her life has changed in an indescribable manner, and she needs to do this for herself. All you know is that she is extremely sorry. She is unhappy and no one can make her happy right now and vice versa, etc. etc.

So, once again, pain becomes a tenant in your heart – the pain of not belonging and not being enough – as you walk away from the love of your life.

Reflect on all these questions. What are you feeling right now?

Pain. Annoyance. Disbelief of the strength it required to build yourself up these past three months without her in your life. Trying to forget her and be unfazed. Until your calendar, so kindly, reminded you of her birthday.

Close your eyes and form a picture of your recipient in your mind. What is their essence? Capture the essence in the form of a gift. Now, imagine a bridge between yourself and your recipient. Let the gift sit on the centre of the bridge and see if it collapses. Hopefully, this should give you your answer.

A bridge? How corny. How do people come up with this stuff?

Anyway, your first thought is to send her the ring. The ring you have not returned, with the heart still dangling the way your own heart is. Well, you have no use of the ring now. And maybe that can be the souvenir of your relationship for her.

You shake off that intrusive thought. That's silly and petty. Still, you wonder what to give her because you seem to have zero ideas.

What is a gift if not a symbol of a relationship? How do you symbolise something that's broken?

The art of gifts is that it can mean and convey anything one would like. Be truthful to your heart and your recipient's heart. Some relationships cannot be captured in a token and that's okay.

There is nothing you can be that will be enough for her. You couldn't be three months ago, maybe it's best to not try to be right now. You have come a long way since then and you can decidedly put your heart to rest. You don't have to be all cute and personal anymore. It's fine, big companies gave people like you an easy way out for this exact reason. No need to dig deep. Just get this over with.

The next morning, you leave her gift on her doorstep and quickly turn away. It's time to close this chapter.

What have you decided then? We are sure this guide only helped you pick out the most apt gift. Happy gift giving.

You toss your phone away and imagine her seeing the gift.

Happy birthday!! Have a blast xx

A note with a Kmart Gift Card sitting over a box of Kachoris.
You snicker. So much for preachy gift-giving guides.
Such a weird article ...

Homecoming

Purny Ahmed

When I was little, my ammu would teach me how to pluck fruit out of the sky.

In my front yard, there is a pyaara tree. I have known it my entire life. It grows firmly in the soil, so immovable amongst the herbs, vegetables and flowers that root and unearth themselves cyclically. The tree sits at the edge of the yard by our neighbour's brick wall, its wide leaves swaying in the wind, its branches reaching towards the clouds. I know that long after I am not here – when the land is demolished over, the house is in ruin and dirt shrouds this family – the roots of that tree will remain stubbornly earthed beneath the soil. Like all memory, the pyaara tree will disappear one day, but it existed.

My ammu would climb up onto our orange brick wall, leveraging her foot on the pearly curves of our white fence, her colourful kameez tucked between her legs and her orna tied at her hip. Her hair would run down her back in soft, wet curls, soaking the cotton with coconut oil.

With the sun glaring in my eyes, I would stand at the base of the tree in my hot-pink singlet, catching the fruit as she threw them down. She would smile down at me, so proud of the ripeness of the fruit, its firmness in her palm, the green of its flesh. She would glow in the spring air.

Soon after, I was climbing the wall on those warm Sunday mornings. I would pluck the fruit off the tree with a tight twist and pull, feeling the branches shake with each tug and loss. Leaves would flutter to the concrete footpath, laying beside my ammu's feet as she'd direct my next target, urging me to manoeuvre deeper and deeper into the tree. I would pull the branches closer to me, finding my target, reaching in further for the fruit dangling a few inches from my fingertips; grasp, twist, tug. I would throw down the fruit, ripe and green, and she would catch it. When I looked down, my ammu seemed far away; the tree was taller then.

Those were the days when my ammu seemed larger than life. She and the pyaara tree had that in common: they were both meant to be immovable objects, unchanging and constant.

In the early afternoon, around when the sun had perched itself over our orange-brick home, my ammu and I would climb up the cold marble steps laughing, our arms heavy with bags upon bags of fruits. I remember that the steps were unworn by time then. My sisters would be stirring awake, with my abbu already in the kitchen, reheating his mug of tea. I remember the doors were not broken; the glass had no cracks; but memory is often misleading. I followed the sunbeams from the hallway into the kitchen.

My ammu would find the plate, the one with the ornate design around the rim. I would find the salt and the chilli powder. When my ammu would slice the pyaara into wedges and plate it with the salt and chilli and pass it to me, that was pyaar in its purest form, wasn't it? We spent our mornings doused in laughter, sharing a bed with my sisters as we gossiped over the plate of fruit. Salt blended into chilli blended into salt – flavours coming alive as they melted on our tongues. The seeds of the pyaara glistened with its juices.

I still remember the sun from those days. I see it so clearly still, the way the golden rays danced with the dust. No part of the home was left untouched by the light. The sun's warmth doesn't reach past the gates of the front yard anymore; I have not seen a sunny day in this home in years.

I left home, sometime between then and now. I disappeared into a starless night with nothing but a bag full of memories in hand. You don't realise which memories you want to keep until you're stuffing them into a tote, frantically searching around your room to find them before time runs out. I didn't steal a glance at my childhood as I left. I just turned the corner and it was over. Has it been months or years since I've been back home?

Upon my homecoming, I saw that the branches of my pyaara tree had been slaughtered and left bare of any leaves or fruit. Only yellowed, overripe pyaara remained disregarded on the grass, waiting to waste away. All the profoundness I had attached to the memories of the tree haunted me. It was as if my own arm had been cut off – I could no longer reach for the fruit that no longer hung on its branches. I was left wounded and wanting; a dog gnawing at its own tail. The space the tree used to once occupy was instead a gaping emptiness; I could see the sky through the branches.

My palms sweated as I wiped them against the denim of my jeans. The tree trunk remained, its roots firmly in the soil. The fruit didn't taste as sweet and would rot quicker than anyone could pluck them. There were no longer enough mouths to feed. The tree's branches were breaking past the bounds of the home and soon the neighbours would begin to complain. It was necessary to cut the branches so the fruit could grow back riper and so the tree could grow to become larger than life again.

When I walked through the old wooden door of my childhood home, I already knew that the pyaara tree wasn't the only thing to have changed. Perhaps it was the uglier truth that nothing had ever really changed at all and I was only now accepting the cracks beneath the surface of my home. As I climbed the steps, the broken slab of marble on the cold steps cut into the heel of my foot. Dust had collected in the curves of the railing, turning the pearly white into a duller, dirtier shade. The crevices were thick with black dust. The home was silent and slow; I was a lost bird returning to an empty nest. Grief had taken everything that used to once stand so tall and made it small. The tree was no longer tall and life had made my ammu curl into herself.

I found her in her room, alone. She sat on her bed, below the window; a crack ran deep through the glass. This room used to glow once, but was now a dull grey. She sat in the same spot she used to when we were all together, where she would roll and squeeze curried rice between her fingers and feed us. The absence of laughter had drawn tight wrinkles between her brows on her young face. Her cotton orna was drawn lazily over her head to cover her loose curls. A blanket was tucked around her waist as she rested on thin, unsupportive pillows.

When she saw me peering in through the door, she shuffled over, making room for me to sit, tucked at her hip. I set my bag down to curl up against her. Her scent settled deep in me; the same spices and the same earth. She whispered to me as she stroked my hair, as if swapping secrets about everything that had changed, all the things I now needed to know; she began with the pyaara tree and ended with my abbu.

I spent my hours rotting in my bed, feeling the springs of the mattress press into my flesh. The mattress sunk low; it had gotten used to the shape of my body, the way it curled in on itself. My curtains were open, tied at each end of the dirty window with mismatched ribbon, but only a clouded white light entered the room. A bird chirped outside the window, but within the house it was quiet. Ammu was at work, abbu was wandering the cold hallways like an uninvited ghost. I tossed over to face the white wall instead of the window, pulling the blanket over my head for a mere semblance of warmth. The springs pressed against fresh soft skin.

I woke up to the sound of the microwave whirring. I waited for it to stop. I was tucked under the darkness of the blanket, still. My warm breath made the suffocatingly small space damp with condensation as I exhaled. The microwave didn't stop. It kept beeping, echoing through the walls over and over.

The air stuck to the cold sweat of my skin and the tiles pricked at my bare feet as I walked down the grey hallway to the kitchen. My abbu's mug sat idle in the microwave, already starting to grow cold. The tea had poured over the already stained porcelain onto the turning glass in a brown pool. I lifted the mug out and set it by the sink. Tea dripped down the already marked paths in droplets, marked like the glimmer of tearstains against a cheek.

I stood in the cold hallway and watched my abbu in the living room. The television was on, playing Bangla songs that I never learned the lyrics to. The light from the television bounced around the room in bright colours; saree-clad actresses danced on the screen in fluorescent fields and mountains. Abbu sank into the maroon leather couch, unmoving, unaware of the way the world moved around him.

"Abbu?" I said to him.

“Ji, ma?” His eyes flickered up to me for a moment, but didn’t hold my gaze.

My abbu didn’t call out for me again as I walked back into the kitchen and plated some khichuri onto the nice plate – the one with the designs. In the lounge, the songs changed from Bangla to Urdu; my abbu’s childhood classics. I remembered these songs, although I didn’t know the language. I had memorised them simply from the tone of my abbu’s voice – the way his voice would rise and fall with each word. I rummaged the cupboards for a small vial. The microwave whirred, beeped and then fell silent.

The khichuri was fragrant with turmeric and chilli, watered down and soft with beef pieces falling apart at a touch. I twisted open the cap of the vial and the liquid medication came out in small drops over the yellow rice before disappearing like invisible ink; I counted ten drops. I carried the plate in one hand and his mug of tea in the other, setting it before him on the low coffee table, gently asking him to eat.

Abbu was diagnosed with frontotemporal dementia a couple of years ago, but he was more or less the same as he was before. The illness came upon us slowly but was no big shock. One day, abbu was there and then slowly, one day, he wasn’t anymore. I once joked with the doctors that we were not sure where dad stopped and the dementia started; impulsive, occasionally apathetic, often aggressive, banging against locked doors. No one laughed.

Yet there was something in this version of himself which was familiar; the most recognisable part of him from my childhood. It was soft. Confused. Slower. It made me gentler with him in a way I had not been in a long time. He remembered the time when the sun would enter the home, like I did. Amidst all his anger and all his loss, and as his symptoms worsened, my abbu's memory returned to when I was eight years old. He reminded me of a game we used to play – his eyes shining and phasing out like he was pulling at threads of the memory.

"Mone ase, ma?" He asked so softly, as though I was the one forgetting. He called me his circus monkey, after so many years.

I leaned against the wall to hold myself up with a gentle smile on my lips to not scare off the memory.

Pale yellow streams of light would filter in through the red curtains, pooling onto the ruby-red Persian carpet in golden patches of sun. Wherever your feet would touch would fire up your entire body with warmth. Abbu and I would steal the maroon square cushions from the couch and, one by one, create a pile in the middle of the carpet. I would spend the long hours of the afternoon running through the kitchen into the living room – my small feet against the cold tiles before they leapt above the pillow-pile and landed on the soft warmth of the carpet. My abbu would clap each time, despite the mundanity of it all, declaring me the best circus monkey in the event of pillow jumping. We would fall to the ground laughing, catching our breath by the balcony in the warmest pool of golden sunlight. He would set down his cup of tea to drink the imaginary cha I handed him.

Behind his thin black frames, his eyes used to be young and sharp. Now, thin gold frames perched on the curve of his nose; the glass was a thick wedge, magnifying the deep grooves of age in his deep brown skin. His eyes, big and scared, were always looking somewhere beyond your face, like he was never really there.

The pyaara, if given too much time to lay idle, would ripen beyond limits before rotting. They would rot on our dining table, in the fistfuls of bags that we had packed but couldn't manage to give away or eat ourselves. My abbu would always say he would eat them all himself lest they go to waste, taking a knife and slicing the mushed fruit between his fingers. There were just too many to get through. The smell was pungent. I used to wish they had just cut the damn tree and been done with it.

Dementia develops from a similar idleness, and my home reeked of it. My abbu would rot at that dining table with the yellow fruit, eating his dinners alone in the dark, in the cold. The table stretched out in front of him with its torn leather dining chairs and empty placemats. The straw weaving of the mats had slowly come undone over the years; tea had stained its frayed edges. It must've been cold in that kitchen with no company, no laughter, no light. I feel it now. All but one room of the house was shrouded in his darkness; the clouds settled over the sun. I wonder if he ever stood at the crack of golden light which leaked out of the door of our bedroom; if he ever pressed his ear to the broken wood to hear us laugh, again.

Abbu used to wake us up in the early mornings with the sound of his teaspoon clinking against the inside of his tea-stained mug. Tring-Tring-Tring. My sisters and I were all sharing one bed then, our legs tangled with the heavy blankets and each other's limbs by the morning; our arms sprawled across the closest body we could find in our sleep. Nothing could have woken us up except for that sound of the stirring teaspoon in the early morning. We covered our faces with pillows to shut out the noise before the shoving would begin as we woke.

Ammu would serve breakfast on the dining table; beef curry, paratha and a side of fresh, home-grown pyaara. We would eat together. Steam would rise from the hot pot of curry in long ribbons of grey, carrying the scent with it. Spices, yes; chilli, turmeric, garlic, cumin – but something sweeter, too. Our hands would burn from tearing into the fresh paratha too quickly. We would throw the soft bread down onto our plates, blowing onto our fingers to soothe them. There was always something to talk about, some new gossip, some new chatter, something to laugh about. No matter how tired we were, there was always laughter.

The oils in the curry glistened in the sun, like glitter, golden and bright. There was always something playing on the television, although none of us really watched it. My abbu paced in the open space between the living room and the kitchen, mug in hand, singing along with whichever song was playing. If I had known how to pack up a memory and take it with me – to keep it close forever, to never forget – I might have taken that one: Sunday mornings, laughter and sunlight. The sound of my abbu's teaspoon clinking against his mug; I would have carried it in the creases of my palms if I could.

I returned home, thinking I would find the sun perched over the pyaara tree, my ammu and I amongst its branches, but nostalgia failed me, like it always will. The sun exists and it glistens and dances and sets the world ablaze somewhere else. But I exist here, in the cold and the dark, within the walls of my family home, where the echoes of laughter haunt me in the night and the memory of my parents haunt me in the day.

The pyaara tree will become stronger and healthier and larger than life again, without me, without any of us. The tree goes unnoticed as we slowly begin to forget it but continues to grow in our front yard; it does not suffer from the loss of our memory. But people aren't trees. They do not become stronger, healthier or larger than life each time their limbs are cut off. They age and sink into their skin and into their couch and they rot. And then, they forget. I suffer from memory. I lay alone in my grey room, shrinking into myself. I have entrenched myself in the soil of this home, intertwined myself with the dirt and the roots of the pyaara tree, so stubbornly earthed where I cannot grow.

My Last Day

Komal Gupta

It is my last day sitting here with you.
It is my last day to lounge under your tree.

The last to receive the warmth of a solar blanket as I finish a chapter from my book.

To hear birds above me, high up in the canopy, exchange their sweet chirps.

I will miss ...
The sound of leaves falling swiftly to the ground.
The howling wind reminding me it is here.
The roaring rain softening into
a soft pitter-patter.
The strong smell of petrichor.
Leaves unfurling into dark green emeralds.

It is my last day sitting here with you.
Just the thought of it pierces me inside.

My Last Day

It has been a pleasure to sit by you these past four years.

I stutter just thinking how to say goodbye,
But then you sweep up your leaves as a final goodbye.

Well then, that is it. I leave with your leaves.
Each leaf will remind me of a moment
when I sat under your canopy and turned over the leaves.

Liver Spots

Zara Hussain

to love is to know how to care/ for your loved ones/ when they cannot/ to care for those who have cared for you/ before/ I sit on the cold marble floor/ my grandmother's foot outstretched/ soft weight pressed against my thigh/ toes spread wide/ for me to attack the gnarled grey lacquer/ of nails/ it is 10:50/ I move to my grandfather next/ white shirt a deflated ghost/ cast over the back of a lonely chair/ his back laid bare/ shoulders protruding/ delicate and inquisitive/ as the starling's beak/ peeking out of its cage/ I sit/ massage out the winter snap/ settling into porous old bones/ vapours of pungent red balm curling into watering eyes/ I blink and return/ to the white scars on my grandmother's stomach/ cut open/ thrice for daughters/ once for a tumour/ all nourished by the self–same body/ down the hall again/ I picture the stent in his heart/ left there last year/ aspirin/ a lifetime prescription/ a break a breath and I return again/ her feet like overrisen dough/ water retention fought with red pills/ in pastel pillboxes/ pale and soft/ light seeping in/ soft/ like the marrow/ of her left clavicle/ it's just life – it's *still* life/ blink twice/ a lost heartbeat/ the time – ripe midnight/ I fall at my mother's feet next/ the trapdoor to heaven/ creaking under me/ my shadow falling on the wall/ of my childhood home/ the paint pencilled over with my height/ dated 2015/ in my grandfather's cursive/ sit at your mother's feet/ pray for a tender old age/ full of love/ health wealth prosperity/ *mobility*/ pray for your dead/ count them off on your fingers/ till you run out of hands/ twice over/ bleeding soft grief/ into your hands/ warmed by this lingering love/ that ran out of time.

About the Authors

Urvi Agarwal

I am a recent graduate of the University of Sydney, where I completed my Master of Creative Writing to pursue my childhood dream of writing and telling my own stories. I'm an avid reader and a film enthusiast. I co-wrote and was in the amazing crew of short film last year for which we won the *USU Create awards*, I occasionally contribute to *PULP Magazine* as well. I am currently working on my children's chapter book.

Arani Ahmed

I'm a Bengali Australian writer living on unceded Gadigal land. I was a recipient of Varuna's 2025 Trans and Gender Diverse Fellowship, and my work was published in *Between Two Worlds: SBS Emerging Writers Anthology.*

Purny Ahmed

I'm a Bengali Australian writer, artist and avid lover of prose, metaphors and the rule of threes. I am currently studying a

Bachelor of Visual Arts/Bachelor of Advanced Studies at the University of Sydney, where I have also had the privilege of editing *Honi Soit* in 2025. My article, Pulling out the roots, was awarded "Best Feature" at the 2024 *Honi Soit* awards night. When I'm not writing or working, you'll find me annotating Oxford commas into my favourite published novels.

Sarah Ayoub

I am a freelance journalist, bestselling author and academic based in Sydney, Australia. My bylines have appeared in *The Guardian*, *The Sydney Morning Herald*, *The Australian*, *Marie-Claire*, *ELLE*, *Sydney Review of Books*, *Meanjin* and more, and I regularly appear at many of Australia's major literary festivals. I am the author of three teen novels, including the Inky-longlisted *The Yearbook Committee*, and five children's picture books, including *The Love That Grew* and *How to Be a Friend*. My work has been translated and published internationally, and my advocacy for Australian writers and writing has seen me consult on policies and approaches for government and industry bodies. I hold a PhD in ethnic teen literature; I am a sessional academic at the University of Sydney; and I sit on the board of the Australian Society of Authors.

Cherie Baird

I work in book publishing as an editor and production executive. I'm a University of Sydney alum, having graduated with a Bachelor of Arts in English and Philosophy in 2019 and a Master of Publishing in 2021. I was one of the recipients of the inaugural Ultimo Prize for my poem "Passer-By", which was published in *Everything, All At Once* (2021). I had three poems published in the 2022 USYD anthology, *Networks*. My poems "Let's Pretend I Exist" and "Celestial" appeared in *The Wild Goose Literary e-Journal* in 2019 and my poem "Filing Cabinets" received a high commendation in the Dorothea Mackellar Poetry Awards.

Rory Blue

I'm a second-year USYD student studying English, Ancient History and French. I've been reading and writing for as long as I can remember, and I'm especially passionate about modernist, queer and metafictional works. In my spare time, I enjoy making zines and working towards my grade eight piano certificate. My favourite authors are Virginia Woolf and Margaret Atwood, and my favourite book is *Nightwood* by Djuna Barnes.

Yenfay Camp

I've been writing creatively since I could hold a pen. After graduating from the University of Sydney with Honours in English and being published twice, I've come to see creative writing as a lifelong companion. Without it, the world would feel empty.

Annis Chan

I'm an undergraduate student and writer who finds poetry in memory, in mundane moments, and in the quiet rituals of living. My work often explores nostalgia, time, and the way emotions root themselves in sensory details and simple acts of remembrance and longing. For me, poems are places where forgotten selves come to speak, and writing is a way of listening closely.

Rosanna Chim

Taking inspiration from Michelle Zauner's *Crying in H Mart*, my work explores memory, grief, and cultural inheritance through experimental and fragmentary forms. In my prose, I reflect on bittersweet memories of my late father, blending myth, story, and personal recollection as a way of navigating loss. I'm interested in how migrant parents act as anchors to heritage and identity – in my case, my Hong Kong roots – and how their death can sever that connection. I'm currently completing a postgraduate degree in Creative Writing at the University of Sydney and work as a lit editor for *PULP Magazine*.

Jensen Chou

I'm an emerging writer whose work explores trauma and identity. I'm currently studying at the University of Sydney.

Mona Elhassan

I'm a Lebanese writer based on Bidjigal and Gadigal land and I'm currently completing a PhD in English Literature/Creative Writing at the University of Sydney.

Angela Fossi

I'm an Australian-Italian living in Sydney and currently studying for my Master of Creative Writing at the University of Sydney. My poem "Belonging" was published in the University of Sydney Anthology: *Nothing Rhymes with Orange*. First inspired by Emily Dickinson, I write from the heart, aiming to bring messages of hope and healing.

Prue Foster

I'm old enough to know better, but I've recently returned to university almost three decades after finishing a BA in Communications to undertake my Master of Creative Writing. In the years between, I found ways to turn almost every job I had into a writing job, whether it was meant to be or not. I now work in publishing and as a freelance copywriter.

Lachlan Griffiths

I'm a third-year English student fond of poetry, sunsets and sitting on lawns reading as an afternoon breeze glides gently into evening.

Komal Gupta

I have recently graduated from my Bachelor of Arts, majoring in English and Music at the University of Sydney. As an editorial assistant, I have read and reviewed pieces, helping authors move from submissions to final pieces and have been through this stage myself when getting my piece "My Last Day" finalised. "My Last Day" is a reflective poem dedicated to my time spent at the Royal Botanic Gardens before and after class at the Conservatorium of Music, whether that was reading a book or writing prose/poetry. This place means a lot to me and I hope you are able to understand my love for it through my poetry. My poem "Looking Up" has been published by the University of Sydney Poetry Society and Vellichor Literary through their collaboration called The Remix. My poem "Pages of Time" was published in the 2023 University of Sydney Anthology, *Living Twice*. I also have an Instagram account that I use to share the literary events I go to and, of course, my writing.

Raghad Hilles

I'm an undergraduate student of Politics and International Relations. Through my writings, I try to bridge the personal and the political, reflecting on belonging, loss, and how people resist and survive under conditions not of their choosing.

Zara Hussain

I'm an English major who reads a lot and writes less often than I should.

Saraa Islam

I'm an Australia-born South Asian writer who hunts for the tender and pulsing in the ordinary passing of life through literary fiction.

Emily Jean

I'm a postgraduate student at the University of Sydney, passionate about storytelling in all its forms. I host *Founders in Jeans*, a podcast featuring conversations with founders and creators from around the world. In 2023, I was named "Student Writer of the Year" at my previous university in recognition of my contribution to student writing and creative expression. Outside of my studies, I share short writings and poetry on TikTok, where my work has reached nearly half a million viewers and received over seventy thousand likes. Through my studies, podcast, and creative projects, I'm committed to exploring the power of words to connect, inspire, and make meaning.

Kuyili Karthik

I'm a student of Comparative Literature at the University of Sydney. I'm a Tamil woman raised in Chennai who now lives on Gadigal land. I'm particularly interested in the aporias of migration and the philosophies of monism.

Aishmita Kumar

I'm an English major with a deep interest in writing. I'm drawn to liminality, elusiveness, and the voices that don't shout but whisper. As the daughter of immigrants, I explore the complex navigation of identity and belonging, and how capitalist systems contribute to feelings of isolation and alienation within diasporic communities.

Jacob Lucas

I'm a writer and journalist based in Sydney's Inner West. I recently completed a Master of Creative Writing at the University of Sydney, where my work explored queer identity, Mormonism, and the quiet apocalypse of daily life. I have strong opinions about amateur theatre and once cried during a live recording of Mariah Carey. Right now, I'm working on my debut novel and hoarding Pokémon cards – pretending it's research.

Joseph Parker Lucas

I'm an emerging writer working and living on Gadigal land. I'm interested in queer stories that cover anything from nightclubs to whales to Addison Rae. In 2022, I completed a Bachelor in Media Arts and Production at UTS, and I'm now studying a Master of Creative Writing at USYD.

Alessio Maugeri

Ciao, ragazzi! Sono Alessio! I'm a philosophy and psychology student who writes for all the sentimentalists in the world, inspired by the heartbroken romantics of noir film and jazz. Whether the bittersweet or the beautiful, I try to pull at the hearts and minds of my readers and place them in a world that helps them reflect on and recall their own humanity fondly. As you read my work, I invite you to approach it with an open mind and savour every emotion you feel. Really embrace your humanity and relish it – it's a beautiful commodity to be human these days.

Sagar Nair

My work has been published in *SmokeLong Quarterly*, *X-R-A-Y Literary Magazine*, *Vol. 1 Brooklyn*, *100 Word Story*, *The Shore Poetry*, *The Suburban Review*, *Voiceworks* and elsewhere. I won the Editors' Choice Award for the 2025 *Honi Soit* Writing Competition and was shortlisted for the 2025 USU Creative Awards.

Ujjwal Nandal

I'm a Doctor of Medicine student at the University of Sydney who finds comfort in storytelling – particularly the kind that lingers in the quiet spaces between grief and grace. I enjoy writing narrative and personal pieces that explore memory, loss, and what it means to endure, often blending abstract structure with more traditional realism. My work is driven by a love of language and a belief that sometimes the softest truths hit hardest. I'm still figuring the rest out, one sentence (and coffee) at a time.

Shania Daphne Andrea OBrien

I am a journalist and editor who holds a Master of Creative Writing from the Universiry of Sydney. My work has been published in several mainstream and independent newspapers and journals in Australia, India, and the United Kingdom. When I'm not writing, I enjoy painting with gouache, baking London fog cakes, and reading bildungsroman.

Chloe Isabelle Pryce

I'm a Gadigal-based writer who graduated from Sydney in 2016 and returned to work here in 2021. I consider myself a full-time nostalgist, melancholic and lovergirl.

Jennifer Scarini

I completed my Masters in Special and Inclusive Education at the University of Sydney, and I currently teach students with diverse learning needs in Sydney's Southwest. I've always been interested in storytelling and the arts in general. I enjoy the challenge of writing to a prompt – in this case, nostalgia – and I hope others can find something in my perspective on life and what it's like to be human in my skin.

Amalia Stone

I'm a writer, a lawyer, a mother, a wife, and a greyhound owner. I hold a BSc (Hons) and LLB from the University of Sydney, and a Master of Arts in Creative Writing from UTS. My stories have appeared in *Overland, Speculate* and the 2024 University of Sydney Anthology, and I've had stories longlisted for the Emerging Writer's Speculate Prize and the Peter Carey Short Story Competition. I write on Gadigal land.

Clara Tan

I'm a Sydney-based writer from Singapore. Since I was young, I've loved writing and illustrating, as I believe these are evocative ways to express myself. You can find more of my work in *Honi Soit*!

Ananya Thirumalai

I'm a writer and editor studying Digital Cultures and Business Law at the University of Sydney. My work spans journalism, cultural commentary, and creative nonfiction, with bylines in *Indian Link*, *Honi Soit*, and several youth publications. I'm passionate about storytelling that preserves memory, reclaims voice, and explores what it means to belong. With experience across editorial, communications, and media roles, I'm particularly drawn to the intersections of literature, identity, and digital culture. Raised in Jakarta and now based in Sydney, I bring a unique lens to everything I write – whether it's an article, essay, or something in between.

Lakai Tungafasi

I'm a writer, video editor, filmmaker and painter based in Sydney. I'm currently completing a Bachelor of Arts at the University of Sydney, majoring in English and International Comparative Literary Studies. My creative work often draws on themes of memory, nostalgia and emotional dissonance, shaped by my multidisciplinary background to create stories that are both visually rich and emotionally resonant. Across different media, I aim to reflect a critical and imaginative engagement with the quiet complexities of human experience.

Vanessa Yenson

I'm an emerging author who graduated with a Master of Creative Writing from the University of Technology Sydney (UTS) in 2025. My memoir essays have appeared in a range of anthologies, including "Proprioception" and "In the Depths of Winter" in the 2024 Sydney University Anthology; "More Than", "Life Lessons with Mr Whale" and "Ladybird" in the UTS Writers' Anthologies (2023–2025); "Mah Jong Instructions for Life in the *SBS Emerging Writers' Competition Anthology* (2023); and "Mother's Day" and "Hidden Grief" in the *Grieve Anthologies* (Hunter Writers Centre, 2015, 2017). Although I mostly write memoir, my short fiction has also been published, including "Deliria!" in the *Lane Cove Literary Awards Anthology* (2023) and "The Wilting Narcissus" in *Blood & Bone*: *UTS Writers' Anthology* (2024). I served on the Editorial Committee of the 2024 UTS Writers' Anthology and am currently working on my first novel and a braided memoir that interweaves my essays.

About the Editors

Michelle Agnelli

I am an Italian-born writer and editor in my final year of my Bachelor of Arts in English at the University of Sydney, where I've found a home in the worlds built by literature. My work as an editor for a literary magazine, a bookstore and the University of Sydney Anthology has deepened my fascination with how language preserves memory and shapes identity, strengthening my belief in editing as an act of care that bridges voices, cultures, and generations. Growing up between languages has made me attentive to the rhythms and textures of words, and to the ways stories preserve fragments of belonging and identity. I'm drawn to translated fiction and writing that blurs the boundaries between history and imagination, and I continue to explore the spaces where scholarship and storytelling meet.

Urvi Agrawal

Over the past two years, I have been a member of the University of Sydney Anthology editorial team, where my responsibilities have included typesetting and maintaining the publication's blog. I also spearheaded our first audiobook project, converting last year's anthology into audio format. Happy reading!

Rosanna Chim

As a proud Chinese Australian writer and editor, I focus on cultural connection and platforming voices in our diaspora community. I'm currently working on a book and film with Soul of Chinatown, uncovering the rich history of Sydney's Chinatown through stories told by its incredibly resilient people. In my free time, I like to indulge in Hong Kong culture through the familiar comforts of mahjong, and I'll always say yes to yum cha!

Annabelle Dwyer

I'm an undergraduate student studying English, and Media and Communications at the University of Sydney. I've always loved reading and creative writing in both English and Japanese, and I'm passionate about stories which explore mixed identities like my own. Aside from books, I am also interested in other storytelling mediums such as film and podcasting. I hope to one day study creative writing in both England and Japan.

Holly Ford

As a child, I loved immersing myself in the fantastical worlds of books, from Hogwarts to Camp Half-Blood to Middle Earth. At that time, I didn't realise how this passion would greatly impact my life. Fast forward to now and I have just finished a Master of Publishing at the University of Sydney and am working as a Sales and Marketing Assistant at NewSouth Books. This is the third University of Sydney Anthology that I have worked on, and it has once again been a pleasure.

Tao Gower-Jones

An avid reader and supporter of indie fiction, I'm fascinated by the global reach of books. I'm finishing a Master of Publishing at the University of Sydney and work as a Rights and Contracts Coordinator at HarperCollins.

Komal Gupta

I am a recent graduate of the University of Sydney with a Bachelor of Arts, majoring in English and Music. I have nearly two years of experience working as an editor for the University of Sydney Anthology and the Australian Society of Authors. Additionally, I have experience in beta-reading and proofreading works by my fellow authors. I hope to continue my passion for writing and copyediting through careers in publishing and/or media industries.

Hanna Holford

I am a lifelong reader who has always had a fascination for words and storytelling. I completed a Graduate Certificate of Publishing in 2024 and now manage a secondhand bookstore and do editing for a small publisher. I have been part of the

University of Sydney Anthology team for three years, and have done the typesetting for the three books we have produced during that time.

Shaan Lloyd

Advocacy, empathy and relationships have always been at the heart of what I do. It has been a joy and privilege to collaborate with the authors and editors of the University of Sydney Anthology again, especially as I complete my Master of Publishing degree. A former English teacher and lifelong reader, I now work in publicity and book marketing. I am passionate about improving our reading rates, championing Australia's outstanding authors and their stories, supporting our local booksellers and fostering a joy of reading.

Sumi Mahendran

I spent years perfecting corporate copy before realising I'd rather polish prose that means something, so I've swapped editing technical documents and business jargon for literature. My true love is language, and I'm obsessed with all things literary.

Nikita McEwen

I am a Master of Publishing student at the University of Sydney with a background in creative writing and professional experience in bookselling. When I'm not working with books, I'm usually found reading them, browsing independent bookstores, or on my couch with a coffee in one hand, a crochet hook in the other and *Gilmore Girls* on the TV.

Helena Parker

A lover of the written word and language, I am passionate about uniting books and readers. I am currently undertaking my Masters in Publishing at the University of Sydney, while working as the International Agencies Team Coordinator at Allen and Unwin. I have a background in poetry, theatre production and writing, and I love supporting writers' voices through the process of editing.

Charo Palenzuela

I am a Sydney-born writer and editor currently undertaking a Master of Publishing at the University of Sydney. I hold a degree in Communications from the University of Queensland and a graduate certificate from New York University's Summer Publishing Institute, where I cemented my desire for a career in books. I am currently seeking representation for my latest novel – an epic adult fantasy with roots in Filipino folklore and mythology.

Olivia Russell

I am a final-year Master of Publishing student at the University of Sydney. I love character-driven stories, stories which find the absurd in the ordinary, and anything that will make me cry. In my free time, I am on a constant hunt for the best lemon sorbet in Sydney.

Nilab Siddiqi

I am a burgeoning publishing professional currently working in marketing and interested in everything! My academic background is varied, covering psychology, literature, creative writing and publishing, but one thing has been consistent over all these degrees: my love of reading! I've been a reader, reviewer, editor, seller, and now marketer and I'm very keen to see where life takes me next.

Zara Stewart

I am a Sydney-based writer and editor in my final semester at the University of Sydney. I am a lover of all things literature, with a particular fascination with translated, cross-cultural and multi-medium texts. My favourite writers/artists are Sophie Calle and Lauren Child, but I am no stranger to Joan Didion and Annie Ernaux. At the moment, I work at a publishing house and a bookstore, whilst also writing and editing for local and commercial magazines.

Ray Zhou

I completed my PhD and now teach English and Writing at the University of Sydney. In my previous life, I was a literary translator and editor. In my current life, I am a non-fiction writer, working on a book-length memoir.

www.ingramcontent.com/pod-product-compliance
Lightning Source LLC
LaVergne TN
LVHW010602100826
845148LV00014B/2815

* 9 7 8 1 7 4 2 1 0 5 8 7 1 *